Darkest at Dusk

EVE SILVER

BOOK DESCRIPTION
DARKEST AT DUSK

ISABELLA BARRETT SEES GHOSTS. BUT THE
DEAD AREN'T THE ONLY ONES WATCHING
HER.

Left penniless and alone after her father's sudden death,
Isabella accepts a position at Harrowgate Manor, an
isolated estate shrouded in secrets and sorrow. Whispers
stalk the halls. Icy fingers graze her skin. And shadowed
figures watch her from the dark. The spirits want something from her—and their intentions are growing darker.

Her new employer, the enigmatic Rhys Caradoc, is a man
forged of silence and secrets. He claims to need her help
cataloguing his rare book collection, but Isabella soon
realizes he knows far more about her gift—and her past
—than he should.

As the line between the living and the dead begins to blur,
and Harrowgate's buried horrors claw their way to the

surface, Isabella must decide if Rhys is her protector... or something far more dangerous.

For readers who crave haunted manors, brooding heroes, slow-burn desire, and chilling ghostly mysteries, this standalone historical gothic romance will leave you breathless.

PRAISE FOR EVE SILVER'S GOTHIC ROMANCES

"Silver expertly matches a brooding sense of atmosphere with a generous measure of suspense..."—*The Chicago Tribune*

"A dark and delicious gothic. I gobbled it up in a single sitting. Oh, how I have missed books like this!"—*New York Times* **bestselling author Linda Lael Miller**

"Riveting! A dark, steamy and twisted tale!"—*New York Times* **bestselling author Lisa Jackson**

"With her ability to create the perfect chilling atmosphere, a dark, tormented hero and an intrepid heroine, Silver rises to the ranks of Victoria Holt and Daphne du Maurier..."—*RT Book Reviews*

"...an outstanding tale about two wounded souls with so much feeling and emotion that there were times my eyes became a little misty...Eve Silver deserves praise for this complicated and moving story."—*Fresh Fiction*

DARKEST AT DUSK

eISBN: 978-1-988674-37-7

paperback ISBN: 978-1-988674-39-1

hardcover ISBN: 978-1-988674-38-4

www.EveSilver.net

ALSO BY EVE SILVER

BOOKS FOR ADULTS:

HISTORICAL GOTHIC MYSTERY ROMANCE:

REVENANT ROSES SERIES

(Books in this series can be read in any order)

Darkest at Dusk

DARK GOTHIC SERIES

(Books in this series can be read in any order)

Dark Desires

His Dark Kiss

Dark Prince

His Wicked Sins

Seduced by a Stranger

Dark Embrace

DARK MAFIA ROMANCE:

BOOKS WRITTEN AS BECCA KANE

The Vegas Vicious Series

Twisted Fate

Ruthless Vow

Dark Promise

BOOKS FOR TEENS:

THE GAME SERIES

RUSH

PUSH

CRASH

Join Eve's VIP Reader Group for the latest info about contests, new releases and more! www.EveSilver.net

Follow Eve on Bookbub!

PROLOGUE

The asylum crouched behind a high wall slick with moss. Rain slid down the iron spikes and gathered in the grooves of the gate like tears. Metal bars blocked the windows. Inside, the corridor smelled of limewash and soap, of scrubbed stone and stagnant water. Edging closer to Papa, close enough that the wet wool of his coat scratched her cheek, Isabella Barrett made herself smaller. Smaller still.

He patted her hand.

"Only a consultation," he had said that morning, his voice gentle and frayed, his gloved hand closing around hers as the carriage wheels struck puddles and dirty water fanned against the windows. She had nodded and lied with her eyes as she always did when he asked if she was afraid. She had practiced that lie in the looking glass, widening her eyes, keeping her chin steady. It was not that Papa would be disappointed or angry. It was that he would feel guilt that he had allowed fear to touch her. And that, she could not abide.

When she had been very small, the translucent people

had been interesting, even pretty. Imaginary playmates, Papa had called them, when there were no real children to be had. But the years had taught them persistence, and the whispers had grown more insistent, braiding through her days and nights. New people found her when she left the house. They reached for her, touched her, pleaded with her. And she pleaded in return—for peace.

By the time she was eleven, Papa had no longer smiled or patted her head.

He had begun taking her to doctors and she had been poked and pinched and prodded. They had given her tonics. They had prescribed hot baths. Cold baths. Open windows. Closed windows. Stoke the fire. Bank the fire. She had been bled and purged and dosed with all manner of vile potions. Nothing quieted the voices or stilled the visions. Only pretending helped, and even then, just a little.

Now Dr. Hargreaves, the third doctor she had seen in as many weeks, met them in the corridor of St. Jude's. He was a narrow man with a narrow mouth and a smile that was all teeth and no warmth. "Mr. Barrett." A pump of Papa's hand. "Miss Barrett." His glance landed and lingered, his expression cold and hard.

Matron joined them, a stout woman with wide shoulders and a thick neck, rings of keys at her waist, her mouth pinched prim with importance.

Papa settled Isabella's hand in the crook of his arm as they were shown along a row of doors, each with a small square of glass webbed with wire. Isabella gasped as a face suddenly appeared in one, nose scrunched against the pane, eyes wide and unblinking. The pane fogged with the man's breath and cleared again, fogged and cleared, and still he pressed against the glass.

When a woman drifted along the corridor beside them, a pale seam of cold moving with her, Isabella took care not to glance her way.

A palm slapped a wired window. A howl carried through a door, answered by another that came from deep in the bowels of the building. Isabella's pulse jumped.

From within the wall came a tapping, slow and deliberate. *Tap...tap...tap.* The sound threaded up her spine on icy fingers. She began to count her breaths to drown it out —one...two...three...four—then lost count and started again.

"We prescribe hydrotherapy," Dr. Hargreaves said to Papa. "Music. Fresh air. Gentle work. We are not practitioners of the former age's cruelties." He smiled his all-teeth smile.

Keeping her eyes directed straight ahead, Isabella stepped past a little boy sitting cross-legged in a square of light on the tiles, a boy Matron walked straight through. The hum that began at the edge of hearing rose, a thin, needling chorus she had learned to bear over the years. Usually, it was accompanied by a drift of cold and a feeling of being watched. But today, it was muted, soft, even sad. Hopeless. The feeling wormed through her bones like a January storm. It was this place, she thought, that made even the wraiths sad.

Dr. Hargreaves brought them to his office, a small white room with a clean desk and two hard chairs. Matron crossed her arms and positioned herself at the door. When Papa moved to sit with Isabella, Dr. Hargreaves shook his head. "I will see her alone, if you please."

"I do not please," Papa said, and positioned himself

behind Isabella's chair. "You will see my daughter with me in the room."

The doctor frowned, then smoothed it away and looked to Isabella. "Tell me about the things you see. The things you hear. Be precise."

She had practiced sounding precise while being *imprecise*. And so, she said, "Sometimes, I dream badly and wake with a start. Sometimes, the house creaks and I mistake it for footsteps." She lifted one shoulder. "When I was younger, I heard a woman humming in the afternoons. I told Papa I could hear Mama."

He wrote something, nib scratching, his cold gaze flicking to Isabella then away.

"Hallucinations following bereavement are quite common," he said.

"My wife died when Isabella was born. She never knew her mother," Papa said.

The nib paused, then resumed. "A sensitive disposition, then. Perhaps, you have indulged a fancy, Mr. Barrett. Grief is a family ailment. It can be transmitted. I am certain that with care, your daughter can recover in time." He rose. "I suggest we further tour our facility. To reassure. To make plain that we are a house of science, not a gaol."

Isabella looked back at Papa. She wanted to ask him if they could leave, to say that she did not wish to tour this place.

Papa's jaw tensed, then he nodded at the doctor.

They passed the women's ward, all whitewashed arches and iron beds. A girl stared at the ceiling and twisted her face in unnatural ways. In the corner, a woman sat on a rumpled bed, hugging herself and rocking to and fro. Both the woman and the girl were quite real.

They turned down a narrower corridor. More doors with wired panes.

Tap...tap...tap.

"Quiet rooms," Matron said.

"To calm agitation," Dr. Hargreaves added.

Papa said nothing.

On they walked until they reached a door with no window. With a flourish, Matron drew a key and unlocked it. Dr. Hargreaves opened the door, soundless on well-oiled hinges. Isabella glanced inside. The walls were bare. No furniture adorned the space, only a straw mat upon the floor. There was no window, no air, no light but what crawled under the door.

"A seclusion cell," Dr. Hargreaves said. "A period of solitude can work wonders on an excitable disposition." He offered an oily smile. "Step in." When Isabella hesitated, he added, "Unless you see something inside... Is that it? A spirit? A ghost? Oh, I know what you said in my office earlier, a whitewashed tale of hearing footsteps when the house creaks. But I have consulted with the doctors you saw before me and am well versed in your case. I know what you've claimed before. Hearing voices. Seeing people who are not there. You can be honest here. I cannot help you if you are not honest, my dear."

Isabella glanced at Papa. He was frowning, his jaw set.

"There is no need to be afraid," Dr. Hargreaves murmured and gave the smallest nudge.

She stepped over the threshold just as Papa said, "No."

The door slammed. The sound clanged like a bell. Iron

was cold against her palm as she seized the handle. It did not yield.

"Papa," she said, her voice high and thin. *Do not leave me here. Do not lock me away. Papa!*

"Open it," Papa said, voice carrying through the door, calm and flat.

"Just a moment," Matron replied. Keys chimed.

Dizzy with fear, Isabella turned a slow circle. Nowhere to go. No seam to pry. Only barren walls and ceiling and floor that she could barely make out in the paltry glow that eked under the door. She pressed her palm against the wall, smooth and cool beneath her touch.

Tap...tap...tap said the wall, delighted.

The air at her back tightened, colder, heavier, bringing the chill of cellar stone and the smell of old damp leaves. Something touched her ear, something like breath or the weight of being not-alone. She could not see in the dark, but she knew the presence of a wraith as well as she knew her own fear.

"Open. The. Door," Papa said, each word its own blade. "Now."

A key grated. The latch lifted. A slice of light cut the dark, burning her eyes. Then she saw Matron's scowl, the doctor's thin patience, and Papa, pale and unyielding. Heart pounding so hard she thought she might retch, Isabella stepped out as if she were not fleeing.

"That will do," Papa said. "We are finished."

"We should admit her—"

"We should not," Papa cut in, clean as a knife.

He settled Isabella's hand in the crook of his arm and walked her through the corridors, past the wired windows and the faces behind them, out into the rain. The sky was a flat sheet of pewter, water stinging the air.

In the carriage, Papa cradled her cheeks in his palms. "Isa," he said, fear humming through her name. "You see nothing. You hear nothing. Never say it. Never show it. Never. One day I will be gone. I will not be here to protect you. If you speak then of voices and visions, they will lock you away. Do you understand?"

The words scored deep. "I understand," she whispered.

It was no lie. She *did* understand. If she heard the voices, saw the wraiths, felt the icy touch of their fingers, then she was not of sound mind. Those not of sound mind were sent to an asylum with iron bars on the windows, cold stone walls, the sounds of distant screams. A place like St. Jude's that would cage not only her body but her mind, until the whispers were the only company left to her.

Leaning her forehead against the glass, she watched St. Jude's recede into a smear of stone and water. She did not look at the wraith who sat in the opposite corner of the carriage, eyes like hollow pits, watching her. She fixed her gaze on the rain instead, and told herself, *you see nothing, you hear nothing*. Because she could not afford to look at it or others like it ever again.

CHAPTER ONE

Isabella Barrett woke to the sound of male voices, one low and calm, the other raised in anger.

"You...you blackguard... Get out!"

She jerked to a sitting position and swung her legs over the side of her bed, pulse flicking like a trapped bird. The angry voice belonged to her father, and that was nigh impossible. Malcolm Barrett was by nature calm and reserved; any display of strong emotion was limited to untrammeled joy when he discovered a rare manuscript or book or engaged in conversation about rare manuscripts or books. Only once, in the icy hallway of St. Jude's when he had coldly ordered that a door be unlocked, had she witnessed him step outside his norm.

Somewhere below, more words were exchanged, Papa's voice and that of another man, the content of their discourse muted by the plaster walls and ceiling. But her father's tone was unmistakable, and his voice, though lower now, still shook with the force of his wrath.

Then he shouted, "Get out. Leave this house and do not return. Do you hear me, you wretch?"

Never had she heard such insults cross Papa's lips, not even in jest.

Fingers fumbling at the tie, Isabella pulled her wrapper around her, cinching the quilted flannel tight at her waist. Her bare toes peeked from beneath the hem, pale against the threadbare carpet, cold prickling up through the nap, a draft nipping at her feet and ankles. She was by no means ready to be seen by a visitor, but etiquette lost value beneath the weight of her concern. She opened the door and inched out onto the landing as footsteps pounded across the floor below. The front door creaked open, then slammed.

Papa muttered under his breath. Then he fell silent, the sudden lack of sound more jarring than his tirade had been. As Isabella set her bare foot on the top stair, her father yanked the door open once more and stormed out. The door slammed behind him, rattling in its frame.

Intent on following him outside, Isabella rushed back to her room, grabbed her boot and tried to force it onto her bare foot, heel skidding along the lining.

Then Papa's voice came again, this time carrying from the street below her window, loud and rough. Kicking free of the half-donned boot, she then ran to the window and pulled aside the heavy gold brocade drapes. The glass was cold against her fingertips, a stark contrast to the firestorm of her father's fury.

Papa stood on the front walkway, hatless, coatless, his chest heaving with his rapid breaths. His right arm was extended, index finger pointing at a man Isabella did not recognize.

The stranger was tall, the fine fabric of his well-tailored black coat accenting the broad, powerful set of his shoulders. His legs were encased in fawn-colored trousers, his shiny black boots planted firmly apart, a stance that suggested a refusal to yield. He stood like someone accustomed to wielding control, someone to be viewed with caution. Even the morning mist curled near but did not touch, as though it too was wary of his presence.

But Papa showed no such hesitancy.

"Begone!" he cried, his outstretched arm shaking with rage, head jutting forward, shoulders hunched with a fury never meant to be felt by a man of his normally mild disposition.

A pulse of fear throbbed in Isabella's breast. Papa was not well. His heart was fragile, his breathing often ragged. She had never seen him so enraged. A whisper of dread coiled through her, and she gripped the window frame so hard that her nails ached. What if this fury was the thing that ended him?

She undid the latch and opened the window just as her father snapped, "You are a trickster, a would-be thief. I will not part with—"

Papa cut himself off, his face twisting with something more than anger.

Fear.

But the stranger did not move, did not speak. He simply existed, tall and solid, his stillness unnerving.

Papa's hand went to his chest, fingers splaying wide. Isabella's own heart lurched with concern.

"You do not understand what you are asking," Papa rasped, the words wrenched from him, harsh and discordant. "It is not safe. You would open a gate that can never be closed. One that might well swallow her whole."

"You speak of safety," the stranger said, low and

smooth. "But leaving her in ignorance is a danger of a different order."

Isabella stiffened. *Her.*

Were they speaking of *her?*

The moment stretched, tight and brittle.

The man lifted his head and turned toward her window. From this angle, the brim of his hat concealed the upper part of his face. Though she could not see his eyes, she felt his gaze search her out, piercing through the crack in the curtains.

The breath left her lungs in a sharp exhale.

His attention was neither the polite glance of a gentleman nor the flickering assessment of a stranger. It was something deep and heavy and knowing, stripping away her layers, searching for something beneath her skin.

A slow, suffocating sensation unfurled inside her, a certainty that he could see past her carefully constructed composure. Past her mask. Past the lie of normalcy she maintained.

She did not know this man. And yet, she felt as though his gaze had plundered her secrets, laid her bare. As though he knew her, and all she fought so hard to hide.

Her heart kicked hard against her ribs. She should look away. She should break the moment before it consumed her whole. But as the seconds ticked past, she did not move.

Then Papa twisted to look up at her, his skin gray as ash, slick with sweat.

She forced herself to step back, letting the drapery fall...but not all the way. A thin sliver of space remained, just wide enough for her to see the stranger below. He stood motionless in the street, tall and unwavering, his presence like a jagged rock just waiting to gouge the hull of any ship that drifted too close.

The tilt of his head revealed the hard angle of his jaw, the hollows beneath his cheekbones, the line of his mouth. His hat cast a shadow over his forehead and eyes but did little to obscure the severe handsomeness of his face, all sharp planes and unyielding strength.

There was no softness in him. Only calculated precision. Deliberate stillness.

She swallowed, disconcerted, his attention unfamiliar, unwanted. Unbearable.

And yet, she could not look away.

A thread of something flickered at the edge of her thoughts. A strange, inexplicable *connection,* like a memory or dream she could not quite grasp. It slipped away, vanishing, a reflection swallowed by rippling water.

Then a whisper came from behind her, soft and indistinct. Cold unrolled over the back of her neck, then pressed, pushing through cloth and skin.

The scent of damp earth and icy metal curled into her nostrils. She went rigid as the air around her grew heavy and dense, pressing against her lungs.

Words swirled through her thoughts, tangled and fragmented.

See me...I am here...

Not *her* words. Not *her* thoughts.

She clenched her jaw, ignoring it all, ignoring the way the air changed, the room changed, the way the very fabric of reality quivered around her. She refused to look, refused to let her mask slip.

The stranger still looked up at her window. He had not moved. Not an inch.

Chest heaving, Papa puffed himself up, squared his shoulders and took a step forward.

"Please, go," she called down to the man through the open window, her voice just loud enough to carry.

"Isa!" Papa cried. His right hand clutched at his chest, knuckles white. His face was flushed, rivulets of sweat streaking his temple and brow. "Close...that...window," he said through heavy, gasping breaths.

Isabella's heartbeat turned sharp and frantic with worry.

"Please go," she repeated, her tone tight and strained. "Leave now, sir."

The stranger glanced at Papa then turned his gaze back up to her. He dipped his chin in the barest nod.

"As you wish."

He offered a shallow bow and murmured something low, meant only for Papa's ears. Whatever he said made Papa's eyes narrow and his jaw tighten. The stranger turned and walked away, his measured gait marked by the almost imperceptible favoring of his left leg.

Pausing at the end of the street, he turned and looked up at her window once more. He was too far away for her to decipher his expression, but she *knew* he turned back for her.

Her stomach clenched. Her hands trembled. Deep inside, a feeling of apprehension and inevitability unfurled...a foreboding certainty.

She had not seen the last of him.

And when he returned, he would not be so easily sent away.

Rhys Caradoc did not look back until he reached the corner, and even then, he let himself have only a glimpse of the scene: the gold drape framing brown hair tumbling in dishevelled waves around a pale, oval face; a breath of fog; Barrett, bareheaded before the house, one hand to his chest as if to pin his heart in place.

It had not been his intent to stir the man so.

Isabella.

He had hunted her, and now he had found her.

The hum that lived at the edges of the world, the thin, maddening chorus of unquiet, had settled the moment she had opened the window. Not silent. Never silent now. But even with him standing in the street and her a storey higher, the noise had ebbed as if the wind had changed direction and taken the keening with it. A too-brief respite. A mercy that had allowed him to almost remember the sound of silence.

Madness, he had been told. And for a time, locked away behind a thick door with a wired window, he had believed it.

But what he had learned from the written notes of a dead man had suggested a different answer.

He had come today to buy what could be bought and to measure what could not, to make offers and cajole acquiescence. He had not come to frighten a scholar into apoplexy in his own street.

With a clarity that came too late, he thought of the way the man had said, "*swallow her whole.*" Not *break.* Not *harm. Swallow.* A word with a throat and entirely different implications. He filed it away with the others.

His plan redrew itself: offer of employment again, but sweeter...wages paid in advance, the restoration of a library long starved of attention. If Barrett still refused, there were other avenues to consider: debts, habits, collectors. He would not use force. He would only invite necessity to do its work. Villainy wore many names, and of them, collector of rents was one the world forgave. He would make immediate inquiries of the owner of the house that Barrett rented, discover what price he must offer to purchase it outright.

He ought to leave London now and let things cool. He ought to think only of locks and shut doors, of the ash-stink that crawled from the north wing at night.

He ought *not* to think of dark hair and dark eyes, the precise tilt of a chin at the window, the way the curtain had allowed a slivered glimpse and no more.

The air to his left went a degree colder; he did not turn. He had learned long ago not to acknowledge their presence.

Setting off once more, he favored his left leg as little as pride allowed. The ache sang along the old burn scars, a useful hurt, keeping a tally. He would have both the woman and the other half of the book, one way or another. He would empty his house of the thing that had brought so much death to his door, had made a pyre of his father and called it kinship. If the only key to that lock was a living one, if Isabella Barrett was the mechanism by which his goals could be achieved, then he would arrange it. Gently, if he could. Otherwise—not.

"Who was he?" Isabella asked as she joined her father at the breakfast table. He was already seated, a steaming cup of black coffee clutched between trembling hands, his breakfast of shirred eggs, ham, and toast barely touched.

As he lifted the cup to his mouth, his fingers shook so badly that the liquid sloshed over the rim and onto the tablecloth, a dark blotch marring the pristine white.

She took a sip of her tea, forcing her tone to remain soft and even as she prodded him. "Papa?"

His gaze remained on his plate rather than lifting to meet her own.

"No one." The words came too quickly. "He is no one."

She set her cup down with exaggerated care. That was not an answer, it was an erasure.

"He is not *no one*," she said, the sharpness of her growing concern leaking into her tone. "You were in the street shouting like a fishmonger at *someone*."

He exhaled on a ragged sigh then pushed his plate farther away, the silverware clattering. Isabella narrowed her eyes.

An icy hand settled on her shoulder, sending a chill spreading through her like frost spidering across a windowpane.

The hand was not real.

And yet, it pressed cold through flesh and bone.

Breath, damp and frigid, touched the curve of her ear. The hem of a translucent, colorless skirt wavered at the edge of her vision. She glanced up into a face that was the color of lead then back down to her plate.

Too slow. Papa caught it.

"What are you looking at?" His voice was sharp, frayed at the edges.

"I was not looking *at* anything," Isabella said, her fingers tightening around her fork. "I was looking *away* from you in exasperation."

He did not smile. He knew the shape of the lie. Suspicion hovered, but he let it pass. Isabella lowered her gaze to the tangible things on the table...bread, tea, the gleam of cutlery.

The clang of a door slamming shut. Cold iron on her palm.
Tap...tap...tap.
Never say it. Never show it.

Lessons learned in a whitewashed corridor with a door that locked from the outside. She had trained herself not to look when the ghosts glided into her line of sight, not to flinch when their fingers, frigid and clawed, brushed against her skin, leaving trails of icy dread.

But sometimes, when she was not wholly focused on *not* looking, she *did* look as she had just now.

Isabella sighed and took another sip of tea, then reached across the table and pushed her father's plate back toward him. With a soft exhalation, he resumed his meal. The woman floated to the corner and stayed there.

Only when her father was done, the last morsel swallowed, did Isabella say, "Who is he, Papa? Why were you so angry?"

"He is a scoundrel."

Isabella arched a brow. "So you indicated with a variety of fascinating words. Why was he here?"

Papa hesitated. "He wanted something I am not willing to give him," Papa said, his voice rough, his mouth turning down, his shoulders slumping forward.

"One of your books?" That was the only possibility that made any sense at all. Papa was ferociously protective of his collection.

"The books are not—" His gaze flicked to hers, then away. He clutched the edge of the table as if to anchor himself. "Something more precious than that."

The words sent a sharp, uneasy pang through her chest.

Papa grabbed Isabella's hand. "If you see him again, do not speak to him, do not acknowledge him." His grip grew uncomfortably tight. "Do you understand, Isabella?"

He sounded desperate and old and afraid.

Widening her eyes, she made her voice sincere. "I will not speak to that man. If I see him, if he approaches me, I will not engage. There, is that better?"

Even as she said the words, she knew them for the lies they were. If the stranger were before her now, she would not only speak to him, but she would demand answers.

Papa let go of her hand and stared at her in silence.

"What is it, Papa?" she asked gently. "What has distressed you so?"

He made a strangled sound and buried his fingers in the wiry, white hair that surrounded his head like a coronet, leaving the top of his scalp bare and shiny.

"Was it a mistake?" he whispered, his voice raw. "Did I make a mistake? I thought I did right. But now, I do not know. I do not know."

Alarmed, Isabella jumped to her feet. She moved to stand at her father's back, resting both hands on his shoulders.

"Papa, tell me what this is about."

He turned his head and looked up at her over his shoulder. She was horrified to see there were tears in his eyes.

"The books...the secrets—" He cut himself off and shook his head. "You're a good girl, Isa. Always a good girl," he said, patting her hand. He held her gaze for a long moment. "But what if I was wrong?"

"Wrong about what?" Isabella asked with a flash of both fear and confusion. And then, recalling the moment when both Papa and the man had seemed to be talking about her, she whispered, "Wrong about me?"

Papa rose to his feet and enveloped her in a hug, the action so unexpected that she fell silent.

He smelled of tobacco and coffee and the tonic he used in a failed attempt to smooth the remaining strands of his unruly hair. She closed her eyes and hugged him back. His ribs beneath her hands were sharper than they had been a month ago. The weight of him, too little now, made her throat close.

After a moment, he released her and stepped away, offering a strained, exhausted smile.

"I love you, my girl. You know that. And if I made a mistake or two over the years, you know it came from a place of love, from my need to keep you safe?"

His voice cracked, brittle as old parchment, before dissolving into silence.

"Papa," Isabella whispered. "Why are you saying these things? You are frightening me. Are you unwell? Shall I summon the doctor?" She rested the back of her hand against his forehead but found no indication of fever.

"No, no." He shook his head, caught both her hands in his and gave them a light shake. "Not necessary. Just an old man being foolish." He glanced at her abandoned toast then forced a smile. "Sit. Finish your breakfast, my dear. I insist."

Befuddled, Isabella stood watching as her father left the room, muttering under his breath, snatches of his words carrying to her. "She was meant to be safe...It was never supposed to come to this... Maybe I should let her read them... I cannot... no, I must not..."

The sound of his footsteps grew softer, fading down

the hall. And then a pause. She heard him draw a single, ragged breath before he whispered, "Forgive me," so faint she thought she imagined it.

Almost did she chase after him, demand an explanation for his odd words and behavior. Almost. But he had already made it clear that he would not give her the answers she sought.

And so, she let him go, listening to his footsteps on the stairs then the sound of the door to his bedchamber closing.

She turned away from the doorway to find the woman in the corner watching her with hollow, burning eyes, fathomless dark pits in her translucent gray face. Those eyes conveyed both hunger and expectation.

A different sort of chill crept in slowly now, curling through Isabella's limbs, crawling up her spine like icy fingers. The cold pressed in, claiming her space, her breath. A silence, absolute and unfamiliar, roared in her ears. The wraith's smile widened.

And then, she vanished. The place where she had stood darker now, as if she had left behind a shadow that swallowed all it touched.

CHAPTER TWO

"Papa?" Isabella called as she tried the door to his study. Locked again.

She paused, one hand poised to knock, the other tightening around the tray she carried, laden with tea and toast and the soft-boiled egg he'd requested over an hour ago, now cooling in its cup. A thin trail of steam rose from the teapot, the scent earthy and smoky with a hint of sweetness.

She pressed her ear against the panel. At first, she heard nothing, then a rustle, a whisper, the flutter of pages turning.

"Papa?" she called again.

There came the scrape of feet shuffling closer, then the unmistakable groan of something being dragged across the floor. In recent days, he had taken to wedging the back of a chair under the handle of the door, determined that no one disturb his work. Was he dragging it into place again now, or away? She could not tell.

"Papa, you must not lift heavy things. You must not exert yourself. We have discussed this," she called through the door. She waited as a moment oozed past, then another, slow as pitch. When he gave no answer, she said, "May I come in? I've brought—"

"No!" The word cracked like a whip. "Not now, Isabella. Leave it there."

"But—"

"I said leave it." The words were impatient, cold, angry. They struck like a slap. Never in all her life had he spoken to her in such a tone. For a heartbeat, she could not breathe.

Something was wrong. Had been wrong since the visit from the stranger, a man wrapped in shadow and threat.

Each day since, Papa had increasingly withdrawn into himself. He shut himself away for hours at a time, emerging pale and trembling, his shirt damp with sweat. His hands, once steady and meticulous, now fumbled at the smallest task. He jumped at soft sounds. He whispered to himself and cast wary glances over his shoulder. Once or twice, she had caught snatches of words not meant for her to hear. "Two halves...the circle...hinge and key...not without a vow."

Two nights ago, she had found him kneeling before the brass-bound trunk in his bedchamber, the key trembling in his grasp. But he had not opened it. He had rested his brow to the lid and whispered, "Choice. She must choose. Free will. But at what cost?"

She had remained frozen in the dark, aching to go to him, knowing she would be rebuffed.

Now, she stood at his study door, worry dragging through her, slow and suffocating.

"You haven't eaten today," she called through the panel. "Come now, Papa. Let me in."

When he made no reply, she hesitated, then lowered

the tray to the floor, porcelain clinking. As she turned away, she caught a flicker of movement at the far end of the hall. A pale figure stood silent and still in the shadows...the woman, her gown translucent, her face blurred as though viewed through breath-fogged glass.

"Not now," Isabella whispered. "Please."

The figure did not move. Habit snapped its leash and Isabella fixed her gaze on the safe middle, spine straight, hands quiet.

A torrent of fractured words and sounds slammed through her thoughts, sudden and sharp. And then the woman vanished, leaving only a dark, empty space behind. Relief came thin and weak. The quiet never lasted.

Before dawn the next morning, Isabella roused from uneasy sleep to the faint clink of metal against wood.

She rose, pulled her wrapper tight across her chest, and stepped barefoot into the corridor. The floorboards beneath her feet were cold and uneven, their surfaces warped with age, the grain darkened by time.

The door to her father's chamber stood ajar, a flickering candle casting elongated shadows across the paneled walls.

"Papa?" she called softly.

He was hunched before the brass-bound trunk at the foot of his bed, his hands braced on either side as though to steady himself, his back bent beneath the invisible burden he bore. The room smelled of spent tallow and old paper, mingling with a sharp, metallic tang that made her nostrils sting. Something within her balked at that scent, her mouth filling with the taste of a bitten coin.

Books lay scattered across the worn rug, their spines cracked, their pages yellowed and curling at the edges. They formed no discernible pattern, yet they surrounded the trunk like a guard.

One folio had fallen open, its vellum margins marked in ink. Isabella caught an image, two semicircles nested together, like a broken ring reaching to be made whole. Before she could draw breath, Papa's hand darted out, his palm flattening over the image. His eyes when they lifted to hers shone with a warning sharper than words.

"What are you doing? You should be sleeping. You need your rest," she said, her voice scarcely more than breath.

He straightened abruptly, his features drawn and gray, the pouches beneath his eyes dark as bruises. Sweat clung to his brow, glinting in the candlelight. A fine tremor passed through his limbs.

"You ought not to be here," he said, his voice hoarse. "It is not safe."

"Safe from what?" Her tone was careful but the concern beneath it was not.

"He has stirred what should have been left to rest. I should never have replied to his letter. Never opened the door. But he spoke with knowledge no man should possess. He made promises I was too weak to resist."

"You mean the stranger who came to the house? The one who made you so angry?" she asked. "What did he want?"

"Not a book," he said, turning his gaze to the floor. "Not truly. Though he would have been happy for that, too. No, he came seeking something else. Someone else."

She took a step backward. The words chilled her, though she could not say why.

"Who was he?" she asked.

Papa gave no answer. Instead, his gaze returned to the trunk. His hand rose to the chain around his neck, drawing forth the iron key he always wore, the one that belonged to the brass bound trunk before him. He pressed the key to his lips, as though it were a crucifix and he a man condemned.

"I thought I could protect you," he murmured. "But I was mistaken."

"Protect me from what?" Isabella asked, her thoughts spinning to the visions, the voices, the wraiths. Did the stranger somehow know of her madness? Almost did she ask, but fear stilled her tongue. Papa believed she no longer saw them, heard them... If she spoke of it, she would betray the truth and tear down all her carefully constructed lies.

Papa leaned forward and began to whisper to the trunk itself, a low chant that seemed to vibrate within the very bones of the room.

The candle flame flared tall and thin, its light no longer golden but tinged with blue at the edges. The pages of one of the open books lifted and rustled, stirred by no breeze. The air in the room grew heavy, close, clinging to her skin like damp wool. A shiver crawled through her.

From the doorway behind her, a new sound arose. Soft at first, like the rustle of silk across stone. Then a whisper, faint and urgent, brushing the edge of her thoughts. She did not turn to look.

Instead, she fixed her eyes on her father, his gaunt face, his hunched form, on the key still clutched in his clenched fist as though it alone might hold the darkness at bay. He shuddered, the candlelight illuminating the trembling curve of his mouth.

"Go now, Isa," he said without looking at her. "Leave me."

Distress suffused her at his distant, resolute tone. Her thoughts spun through events of recent days, back to the morning it had begun.

And suddenly, he was there, the stranger, not in flesh but in memory, the man who had stood unmoved while her father's fury buffeted him. His presence had filled the street. His gaze had pierced the glass, finding her, pinning her, seeing too much. It was not merely a fanciful notion. She had felt it that morning, silent, precise, inescapable, like a dagger sliding beneath her skin.

"Papa, let me—"

"Please, Isa," Papa cut her off. "Go."

She hesitated, her breath coming shallow and fast. Papa's voice had always been her anchor, her compass. Now it was foreign, distant, devoid of warmth. Devoid of hope.

The candle flame flared high and blue. The pages of the open books strewn across the floor lifted and danced in the still air. The whispers flew at her, curling around her like choking vines. She could not breathe. She could not think. There was something dark here, something evil.

"Go," Papa ordered.

With a gasp, she turned and fled.

And the whispers followed, eager as hungry dogs.

The house was silent save for the rain that fell in slanting sheets and the wind rattling the shutters. Water spilled from the gutters in thick, silvery ropes. The study door stood ajar. Isabella froze, wariness snaking through her. For weeks now, Papa had taken to locking himself in whichever room he occupied, barricading the door with chairs, chests, or stacks of books.

But now, at the end of a long and silent day during which she had neither seen nor heard him, Papa had left the study door not only unbarred, but open.

A fly buzzed at her ear. She brushed it away and stepped inside.

When she saw him slumped in the worn, burgundy brocade chair he favored, eyes closed, chin resting on his chest, she forced a bright tone and said, "Papa, pray do not sleep here. You'll have a crick in your neck come morning. You always do."

The air felt thick and stale. Darkness dripped down the walls and pooled on the floor at her father's feet. Light from the dying fire painted one side of his face, leaving the other in shadow. One arm lay across his chest, fist curled at the base of his throat; the other dangled loosely, fingers slack. An open book lay on the floor.

Isabella frowned.

"You missed supper," she said as she crossed the room and retrieved his book from the floor. She set it down with unwarranted care, unease coiling through her as she stared at it.

Because a part of her knew.

A part of her had known from the second she crossed the threshold.

Still, she asked softly, "Are you hungry?" Her voice

trembled as she turned back toward her father and stepped closer. "Papa?"

His lids did not flutter. His chest did not rise.

A cold, crushing weight settled over her, pressing inward, slow and merciless. It found the soft places beneath her ribs and burrowed deep.

With a gasp, she fell to her knees at his side and cupped both his cheeks. His skin was too cold.

Her breath hitched in her throat. Her voice broke as she whispered, "Papa..." The word came out small, her voice that of a child.

She pressed her ear to his chest. Listened. Waited. Willed his heart to beat. Wishing so hard. Wishing in vain. The silence roared.

A sob broke loose, raw and helpless, as she rested her cheek against the worn fabric of his sleeve. The shadows crowded closer, silent witnesses to her grief. A whisper slithered through the hush, curling into her ears, through her veins.

The wraith by the fireplace drifted forward, one arm outstretched, fingers curled like talons. The ever-present whispers became a storm, growing frantic, clamoring to be heard. *Gone...Lost...Darkness...Alone...So alone...Do you see me...Can you see me...See me...See me...Hear me...I am here...I am here...Let me in...Let me touch...Let me...*

Grief loosened the knots she tied in herself, rushing in through every gap. It was ever this way when she was unable to maintain the barrier that kept the wraiths at bay, when fatigue or strong emotions chipped away at her carefully constructed wall and the voices carried through the ethereal place that was not quite of this world.

Cold sweat beaded on Isabella's brow. Her chest tightened, bound by invisible cords, the whispers cinching tighter with every breath.

He is dead...he is gone...gone...But we are here...we are here...

In her mind, she cried out, "Leave me alone. Go away. Go away!" But aloud she said nothing. She longed to slam her palms against her ears to block the voices, but she knew from experience it would not help.

She would still hear them.

And they would still know she could hear them.

But to admit by word or action that she heard them would be to admit she was mad.

Never say it. Never show it.

"Oh, Papa." Her throat was thick, her mouth dry. Grief flayed her, her heart left naked and shivering.

Limbs heavy, thoughts foggy, she pushed to her feet. The voices she pretended not to hear rose and fell, making her shiver, following her when she moved through the house, half-blinded by tears. She drew the curtains and stopped the clocks to mark the moment of her father's passing. She hung black veiling over the mirrors to prevent his soul from being trapped in the glass. Not that she believed his soul was at any such risk. His voice was absent from the cacophony that surrounded her, which meant he was gone, truly gone, his soul no longer here.

But she had no way to explain that to the servants, so she followed the rituals of death in order to mask the truth behind their familiar shape. She had learned to wear the pretense of sanity like a second skin—tight, fragile, always at risk of tearing away to reveal the madness beneath.

As she carried out her grim duties, she thought that she could summon the housekeeper and the maid and the cook. Perhaps she should. But she felt it was her place as Papa's daughter to see the things done with her own hands. So, she carried out the tasks alone save for the whispers that lifted the fine hairs at her nape.

At last, she settled on the floor at Papa's side and held his hand as the night crawled by, his still form draped in a blanket she had fetched. The shadows swelled and twisted at the edges of her vision, the whispers swelling with them. A pile of ash and a few glowing embers were all that remained of the fire when she roused herself hours later. By then, her tears were dry, and the whispers had faded to a rustle of dry leaves.

Her hands found the chain at his neck, lifted it over his head, and drew the iron key free. Its weight settled in her palm like a brand. She curled her fist around it, her grip tight, her resolve tightening with it. Papa had worn this key always; now, she would do the same. The legacy it locked away was hers, whether she wished it or not.

CHAPTER THREE

Days later, Isabella endured the procession to the graveyard. The first carriage held the minister and pallbearers—six decrepit old men, contemporaries of her father's. She half-feared they would all perish from overexertion in their effort to carry the casket to the grave.

The hearse came next, a black carriage with glass sides, its silver fittings dulled by the drizzle and grime. The undertaker had urged Isabella to choose one with four horses, a canopy of ostrich feathers, velvet coverings, and an elaborate cornucopia of flowers to flank the coffin. She had declined, settling instead on a hearse and mourning coach with one horse each, a modest floral arrangement, and a complete absence of feathers.

Papa had never been one for elaborate displays in life; she could not imagine he would want them in death. A good thing, that. Though she did not yet know the whole of it, she knew that Papa had left their finances in a less-than-ideal state. The figures she had not yet dared to total rustled at the edges of her thoughts like papers in a draft.

Isabella sat in the third carriage clutching a posy, accompanied by Mr. Christopher, her father's solicitor. He was a middle-aged man with plump, ruddy cheeks and kind eyes. She had hired mourners to walk before the hearse, but there was no one else to remain at her side for Isabella had no close relatives to weep with her on this day. She had been a late life baby, a child neither of her parents had expected, an only child born to only children. Her mother had exhaled her last breath as Isabella drew her first. It had always been just Isabella and Papa. And now, just Isabella.

A bluebottle droned inside the carriage, slow with cold, butting the glass with dull, stubborn taps. She fixed her gaze on her gloved hands and tried not to hear it knock.

This was the finality of death, not the cold body in the chair or the closing of Papa's eyes, but this endless, hollow procession. A line drawn across her life: before, and after.

Mr. Christopher stared out the side window and did not speak. That was for the best. There were words that needed to be said, but not yet. After the burial would be soon enough.

At length, the carriage rocked to a halt next to a tall hedge that surrounded the cemetery. Mr. Christopher helped her down and escorted her around the hedge, past the mausoleums that rose on either side of the main laneway, past row upon row of crosses, angels, and engraved stones. The grass was winter brown splotched with puddles of mud, the trees bare and stark. It was too late in the year for snow, and too early in the year for the trees to bud or flowers to push through the barren ground.

Rain dripped from the edges of the black umbrella Mr. Christopher held for them both. Droplets fell from the brim of Isabella's mourning bonnet, and despite the presence of the umbrella, the hem of her skirt was sodden. Cold crept up her calves and lodged behind her knees.

At the graveside stood several older men, more of her father's contemporaries—scholars, rare book aficionados, antiquarians—their umbrellas gleaming like black beetles huddled close.

Set apart from the mourners stood a younger man, shadowed beneath the brim of his hat. He was tall, broad-shouldered, and both the cut and cloth of his elegant black coat suggested the garment had come at some expense. He stood facing away from her, far enough that he could be visiting another grave and not be part of this service at all. But close enough that he could be.

At his back, a single wraith hovered, pewter mist edged in charcoal, its clawed hand resting on the man's shoulder. He did not twitch or shudder, but the way he inhaled, deep and slow, made her think he felt the frigid touch. Some people didn't. Some did. Those who did were wont to laugh nervously and say that someone was walking over their grave.

And then there was Isabella, who felt them, saw them, heard them.

For a fleeting second, she glimpsed high cheekbones, a straight nose, an angular, clean-shaven jaw. A tug of recognition stirred then vanished as he turned away.

Frowning, Isabella took her place as the minister began to speak in a slow, steady drone. The words held no comfort. Her heart was as leaden as the sky.

Before her was the open grave, the earthen sides giving way beneath the onslaught of the rain, oozing down in clumps and streams. Her father lay in the casket at the bottom of the hole. The life she had known was in there with him.

Water dripped from her bonnet onto her face, blending with her silent tears. Her eyes felt swollen, her lids heavy. She did not wail or sob. She did not fling herself upon the casket. She only stood by the grave and willed her spine to stay straight, her trembling legs to hold her, and the whispers to stay quiet.

They did not. Of course, they did not. She was in a graveyard, after all.

They came, faint and scattered, but she pretended not to hear them. She refused to let them shatter her composure here, in this moment, when all she had left was the dignity of her grief.

After the service, her father's friends filed from the grave murmuring condolences as they passed her. She nodded and murmured appropriate replies. One or two clasped her hand before they went. She had never felt so alone.

At length, Mr. Christopher urged her to return to the carriage.

"A moment, if you please," Isabella said. "I'd like a moment alone to say my goodbyes." She glanced at the posy clutched in her hand.

Mr. Christopher hesitated and looked up at the sky. The downpour had stilled for the moment. With a nod, he said, "I will wait there," and gestured to a large marble angel a few feet away.

Isabella shook her head. "Please. I want to be alone with him one last time." Though she knew it was unlikely, a tiny part of her hoped that Papa's spirit had stayed, that it would appear to say one last goodbye before leaving forever.

Mr. Christopher frowned and looked as though he meant to argue, so she whispered, "Please," once more.

"Very well. I will wait by the carriage." With a last wary look at the sky, he strode toward the tall hedge growing along the wall that separated the graveyard from the road. He rounded the far end and disappeared. In the distance, the gravediggers stood beneath the shelter of an ash tree, caps pulled low, shoulders hunched. They made no move to approach, waiting until she was done.

Isabella turned back to the grave. For long moments, she stood looking down, saying nothing, her heart a lump of coal in her breast. She heard them, the whispers of those who begged her to listen, but she refused their plea. She wanted to think only of her father.

Memories danced through her thoughts: Papa reading her stories, tucking her in, placing a cool cloth on her forehead when she was sick with fever. The pride in his voice when he complimented a job well done. His excitement when he acquired a rare and wonderful volume after a lengthy hunt. The twinkle in his eye when he brought home a box of her favorite sweets or a ribbon for her hair. His wheezing laughter that always ended in a cough. Never again would she hear it. Never again would she hear him humming to himself as he worked.

"Papa, I will miss you," she whispered. "I hope you are with Mama. I hope you are at peace." She smiled a little. "I hope there are shelves and shelves of wonderful books for you to read and catalogue." She brought the posy to her lips and placed a kiss on the petals, then she dropped the flowers in the grave. Cyclamen. The symbol of resignation and goodbye.

Choking on a sob, she spun away. Her foot slid on the wet earth. Arms flailing, she struggled to regain her balance, to no avail. She fell to the ground, cold mud seeping through her gloves as she landed on her hands and knees, the sodden hem of her gown pooling around her. She made to push herself up, but her boots slid uselessly beneath her, offering no purchase.

A gloved hand appeared before her. Expecting Mr. Christopher, she reached for it and looked up, only to snatch her own hand back in surprise.

The man towering over her was not Mr. Christopher.

The dark-haired stranger she had noticed earlier stood before her. A single wraith, grim and ominous, floated at his back.

She had thought he'd departed with the others.

His hand remained where it was, an offer of assistance.

Isabella hesitated. The tall hedge hid Mr. Christopher and the carriage from view. But surely he was close enough that he would hear her should she call out.

"Miss?" the stranger said.

"My gloves," she said, rocking back on her heels and holding up both hands to show the mud dripping down her fingers. She couldn't imagine he would want that smeared on his pristine glove.

She was wrong.

"Dirt of that sort can be washed away," he said. He reached down with both hands and closed his fingers around her wrists, then pulled her to her feet as though she weighed nothing at all.

For a breathless moment, they stood close...closer than propriety allowed, closer than strangers ought.

His irises were pale gray, rimmed in storm-dark charcoal, his lashes long and dark and curling, his eyes too pretty for a man. And yet they did not make his face pretty. His face was all masculine angles and hard edges. His mouth was unsmiling, his expression unreadable.

His presence struck her with a jolt. Something unfamiliar flared, cold beneath her ribs.

The whispers rose again, sharp and sudden, buffeting her. Instinctively, she made to pull her hands from his.

He released her immediately and stepped back, leaving several feet between them. He did not look directly at her, but rather past her, to a point beyond her left shoulder. For an instant, she wondered if he saw something there, if he saw the wraiths as she did. And then she pushed the thought aside. Of course he did not.

She frowned as a flicker of recognition stirred again, stronger now. But those eyes...no. Had she seen them before, she would remember.

Looking down, she took a second to steady herself on her feet and twitch her wet skirt, so it fell in some semblance of order. Almost did she try to brush away the mud, but stopped herself, suspecting she would only smear it and make things worse.

The voices dulled to a hush. Only then did she realize they had not sounded alarmed. They had sounded … expectant. Excited.

"My condolences, Miss Barrett."

"Thank you." She glanced at him.

"May I see you to your carriage?" he asked, offering his arm.

She gingerly accepted, grimacing as she left smears of mud on his coat. Together, they started toward the hedge.

"Did you know my father well?" she asked. Given that he knew her name, it seemed likely that he was here for Papa's funeral after all.

"Not well," he said, eyes forward. "We corresponded several times but met in person only once."

"I see." She did not see. It was odd that a man who had barely known her father should make time to attend his burial. "I'm sorry, I don't believe we've met. You are...?"

"Rhys Caradoc."

The name was not familiar to her. "You corresponded with Papa about books?"

He cut her a sidelong glance. "On occasion. But mostly about something else."

His answer struck her as both evasive and deliberate. What could it have been if not books? Her father's interests had been rather limited.

As they neared the carriage, he leaned in and said, "There are things I would discuss with you, Miss Barrett. But not today. Today is not the time."

She knew then that this meeting, however accidental it might seem, had been anticipated, perhaps even orchestrated. She opened her mouth to question him, but Mr. Christopher stepped forward, clearly dismayed as he took in her mud-splotched form.

"You've taken a tumble," he said. "Are you injured, Miss Barrett?"

"Not at all, Mr. Christopher," Isabella replied. "It is only my garments that are the worse for wear."

The solicitor offered a polite nod to the man at her side just as the clouds opened and the rain began once more. Mr. Caradoc handed her up into the waiting carriage and closed the door. Then he exchanged a brief word with Mr. Christopher, the content of their discourse drowned out by the patter of raindrops on the carriage roof. A moment later, Mr. Christopher joined her inside.

She looked out the side window, her gaze fixed on the man walking away. She hadn't noticed it when they had walked side by side, but now she saw that his gait was slightly off-kilter, favoring his left leg.

Her breath caught. She knew him.

He was the stranger who had met with her father, the one who had elicited Papa's uncharacteristic ire. She had not recognized him because she had seen him only from her window and his face had been obscured by the brim of his hat the morning Papa had chased him into the street.

And because she could not have imagined he would be so bold as to come to Papa's burial given the enmity between them.

"Wait," she called, shoving open the carriage door, ignoring the startled look the solicitor gave her. "Wait!"

She wanted to question him, to know what he had said to anger her father so. She wanted to know how he dared show his face here. His relationship with Papa had not been cordial.

But he did not wait.

He walked on, his long strides eating the ground, his limp barely a hindrance. Within seconds, he was too far away for her to catch.

And then, as if summoned by her distress, the whispers returned, not as a murmur or a breath, but as a ravenous chorus, howling through the rain.

Rhys cut behind an angel, past a row of stones worn by years of wind and weather, then stopped by the hedge. From here he could see the open grave, the raw edge slumping in the rain, the small splash of cyclamen on wet soil. He had learned through too many shapes of farewell that grief had a variety of sounds: the shudder of the coffin settling; the small, obscene thud of the first clod of earth tossed in the hole; the muted sob or gasp or sniffle.

He had not expected the silence.

When he had grasped Isabella Barrett's wrists, the ever-present hum that was his penance had dropped away. It had not disappeared completely; he was not granted such tender mercy. But it had quieted to a degree he had not experienced in years. The hush had struck like cool water on fevered skin. He had wanted, absurdly, to keep hold of her hands and let the world go still.

Which was precisely why he had let go. *Want* was not his compass; *duty* was.

Rain soaked the brim of his hat and found the burn scars on his leg. He reached into his pocket and withdrew the chemist's tin, clicking open the lid. He set a lemon drop on his tongue, tart and sweet. A habit he had built through loss after loss, telling himself citrus mellowed the taste of grief.

He reviewed what he had learned simply by observing. There had been no family to stand at her side. Her dress was mended twice at the cuff, her gloves worn thin. And then there were the things he had learned through inquiry. The house was rented, the landlord unforgiving. Enough leverage to move a life, if one were the sort to put a shoulder to it and push. He dismissed the notion of buying the freehold. There was no need of a cudgel when a hard landlord and a quiet word would tighten the vise. Finally, there was the ally he had made with little effort. "My condolences," he had said to the solicitor, and then added, low, the bait for the trap. There would be an offer for legitimate work, respectable lodging, an ample wage. "Mr. Barrett's books will be cared for," he had added, letting the man hear the reassurances his conscience required.

Rhys had deliberately let the solicitor see a benefactor, a persona the man had been eager to accept.

As he heard Isabella's carriage pull away, he did not track the hedge-line for a glimpse of her profile in the glass. He stood in the lee of the angel as an icy chill swallowed his left shoulder and the beautiful quiet frayed back into noise that tunneled beneath his skin. He tamped it down with the taste of sugar and lemon and the clean geometry of his plan.

He thought of how Isabella had looked up at him from the mud, the wet curve of her mouth, the refusal to let grief and sorrow make a spectacle of her. He had known too much of grief to do anything but admire her composure and the work it took to maintain it. What caught him as surely as a hook beneath the breastbone was the way that, even kneeling in mud, Isabella Barrett had more dignity than most men on their best day.

He smothered the thought that rose, unbidden and disloyal to the moment—the heat of her lips parting beneath his, the soft catch of breath if his thumb found the pulse at her throat.

He would bring her to Harrowgate. He would use her. He would keep her safe. He could live with the cost; he would have to.

With the dead dogging his every step, reaching clawed fingers to drag at his coat, clinging to his arms, hovering at his back, he strode through the rain and pushed open the cemetery gate on its rusted hinges, the sound shrill and discordant, too loud for the business of death.

CHAPTER FOUR

T wo days later, a note bearing Mr. Christopher's seal arrived late in the afternoon. Isabella slit it open and began to read.

My dear Miss Barrett,

A prospective employer, a gentleman of means, will call upon you tomorrow afternoon to discuss the possibility of engagement as a secretary and cataloguer of rare books.

The position includes lodging and a salary of one hundred and twenty pounds per annum.

You are under no obligation. I advised him you may not yet be ready to receive callers, but he was most insistent. I believe it is a genuine opportunity.

Yours respectfully,

G. Christopher, Solicitor

She stared at the words, hope warring with cynicism. A gentleman of means who wished to hire a young woman without credentials. A salary that was not merely generous but extravagant, almost to the point of absurdity. She was reluctant to trust such unlikely good fortune.

The following morning, she pinned her hair into a modest chignon. She was too thin and too pale, with shadows beneath her eyes. She dressed in her mourning black and left it at that, deciding to add no adornment. Papa's key lay against her breastbone under her collar.

Then she dusted the parlor and lit a fire there, the first in days, for since Papa's death, she had placed frugality above comfort.

There came two crisp knocks, then a pause. She allowed herself a moment to gather her thoughts and calm her mind and nerves.

Another knock. Then silence.

She went to the door, opened it, and gasped.

Mr. Caradoc stood on the stoop. His too-pretty gray eyes met hers, his gaze sharp and assessing.

She had not expected him, though now she saw that she ought to have known given the careful wording of Mr. Christopher's note.

"Mr. Caradoc," she said, her voice tight.

He offered a spare bow. "Miss Barrett. Please accept my condolences."

"You already offered them at the graveyard." Her fingers twitched as she contemplated simply closing the door in his face. She recalled her father's fury, his flushed face and shaking hands. *You are a trickster, a would-be thief.*

Papa had wanted her as far away from this man as possible.

And yet, beneath the dismay, beneath the sudden throb of wariness, something else stirred. A flicker of curiosity. A dangerous kind of interest. The morning that she had told Papa she would avoid this man, she had known her assurances were lies. She had wanted answers then. She wanted them now.

Mr. Caradoc took advantage of her hesitation and said, "After your father's reaction to my visit, I thought it prudent to request Mr. Christopher's endorsement before approaching you. You have every reason to reject out of hand an offer bearing my name, but I hope you will hear me out."

She studied him for a long moment and made her decision. "Well, since you are here, you might as well come in."

He stepped into the narrow, dim entryway, glancing around with cool detachment. The floorboards, warped and dull, were covered by a threadbare burgundy and gold runner. The walls were wainscoted in dark oak panels. His presence made the space feel even smaller.

She made no offer to take his coat. Let him keep it on. Better he be ready to leave rather than stay. He was neither friend nor guest and she had no obligation to make him welcome.

Turning, she led him to the parlor where the fire popped and hissed and the translucent woman stood in the corner, watching.

He looked around the room, his expression neutral. His gaze lingered in the corner for an instant then moved on. He stepped toward the hearth and, leaning his forearm against the mantel, stared into the flames.

"Do you know, I offered your father a position...lodging, salary, work cataloguing my collection," he said.

She had not known. One more thing that Papa had kept from her. She recalled her father's rage the morning Mr. Caradoc had come to call and his uncharacteristic behaviour every day that followed. "That cannot be the whole of it."

"I wrote to him several times." He glanced at her, then back to the fire. "Each time, he refused."

"Did he? And yet, despite his refusals, you came to our door uninvited that morning. You incited his rage. Why?"

He turned to face her once more. "I am not easily dissuaded."

The words settled between them. She almost dismissed them as arrogance, as the hallmark of a man who believed the world owed him its obedience. He was, by all appearances, a man of privilege and power. But there was no flippancy in his tone, no smirk curving his lips. She had the sense that if she barred the door, he would find another way in. Not through violence. Through...certainty.

"Your father said that your health was the reason he declined the position." His tone was measured and neutral.

Confusion swelled. "My health?"

"He claimed that removing his daughter from her home would be detrimental to her health. He spoke of her...delicate nature. *Your* delicate nature. Unless there is another daughter hidden in the attic..."

Isabella glared at him. "Papa would have said no such thing." But a whisper of uncertainty snaked through her. *Purges. Tonics. The clang of the door slamming at St. Jude's.* Had Papa thought her weak? A flush of heat washed through her, then receded, leaving her chilled to the bone.

"I have only your word that he did, with no way to verify your claim."

"Did you just call me a liar?" His laugh was low, edged with something sharp. "It is rare that I receive such an insult to my face."

"Do you prefer insults uttered behind your back?" she asked.

"I prefer not to be insulted at all." He stepped closer. She did not retreat. The space between them crackled like the air before a storm. "I was impressed with the most recent volume of the catalogue of your father's collection and notes that accompanied it, Miss Barrett."

"The catalogue...? How did you come to see it?" Had Papa shown him the catalogue when he had called here? That made no sense, given that Papa had chased him off like a crow. "The catalogue was not my father's work. It was—"

"Yours," he finished for her. "Which brings me to the reason for my visit. I make you the same offer I made your father...lodging, salary, work cataloguing my collection and repairing the state of my library. A state that is sorry, indeed. I believe Mr. Christopher outlined the terms of employment in his note. They are generous."

"They are, but that does not allay my concerns." Her thoughts spun. Papa had turned down this offer. He had warned her away from this man. She had no reason to trust him and every reason not to.

"I suspect it is not the work that unsettles you," he said, voice low. "It is me."

Her heart thudded. She made no reply, her silence answer enough.

"Accept the position," he said. Not a request. A declaration, softly spoken and inarguable.

A feeling of foreboding settled over her. His offer felt both sincere and forced, the situation contrived, though she could discern no reason for such subterfuge. But then, that would be his intent, would it not? To keep her oblivious and unaware of his purpose?

"I think it is time for you to leave, Mr. Caradoc."

The moment stretched as he watched her with those too-pretty eyes, and then he said, "As you wish, Miss Barrett."

She led him back to the entry and opened the door.

He paused. "Take this. It is a ticket for the train to Maidenhead. I will arrange for a post-chaise to convey you from there to The Crown in Marlow. My carriage will meet you in the square." He held out a train ticket. A single slip of paper, innocuous and yet...not. "The ticket is for four weeks from Monday. That gives you time to decide."

She looked down at the ticket, then back to his face. His expression was unreadable.

When he spoke again, his voice was low and measured, each syllable carefully placed. "You will be paid well to carry out a task you enjoy. You will spend your days with books."

The proposition felt too neat, too perfect. Books. Shelter. Safety. A quiet refuge where the voices might be softer, the wraiths less insistent. He dangled sanctuary. They both knew it.

The picture he painted ought to have felt harmless. Appealing. But it made something tight and cold prickle across her skin. Curiosity. Dread. *Apprehension*.

Intrigue.

She inhaled deeply. "You maneuver. You withhold.

You hide behind civility. I cannot trust a man who is not honest."

His mouth shaped a feral smile, white teeth and sharp danger.

"I make no claim to be kind or good...or even civil. But my offer is honest enough and exactly as outlined." He took a step toward her. The shadows lengthened across his face, leaving his eyes gleaming like shards of glass. "Come to Harrowgate Manor, Miss Barrett."

Neither of them moved. He held her gaze and she felt as if he looked deep inside her, seeing secrets she had no wish to share.

Her chest rose and fell with shallow breaths. His presence surrounded her, not with touch, but with some unseen current that hung in the air, sparking like a storm.

She did not trust him. But for reasons she was not ready to name, she did not refuse him outright. Her hand lifted of its own accord. She took the ticket, her fingers trembling as they brushed against his. The brief contact sent a jolt up her arm, a cold spark jumping under her skin.

"I make no promise that I will come," she said, her voice more composed than she felt. Something twisted in her belly...fear or anticipation, she could not tell.

"But you will consider it." His voice was a snare, rich and dark, curling around her like silk.

She stood in silence as he stepped out onto the stoop. And then she shut the door behind him, train ticket in hand, her heart pounding a harsh rhythm in her chest.

The following afternoon, Isabella answered the door to find Mr. Christopher standing on the stoop holding a large basket covered in a checkered cloth. She was expecting him as he had sent a note earlier to apprise her of his visit.

After they exchanged greetings, he held out the basket toward her. The end of a loaf of bread protruded from beneath the cloth.

"Thank you," she said, a wash of heat touching her cheeks. That he knew her larder was empty filled her with quiet humiliation. It felt like judgement, even if kindly delivered.

"Oh, do not thank me. I found it on the stoop when I arrived," he said.

"On the—" She leaned out and looked right then left but saw no one in the street.

Mr. Christopher cleared his throat and looked at her sadly. "I trust that this is not an inconvenient time. Perhaps we should wait until—"

Isabella set the basket on the narrow, claw-footed hall table.

"Waiting will not change my circumstances," she said, not wanting his pity. She had no illusions as to the state of her affairs, a situation he was here to clarify. Once she knew the whole of it, she would formulate a plan. "Please do come inside. We have unpleasant business to discuss. I see no reason to make it even more unpleasant by discussing it where all and sundry can hear."

And she saw no reason to delay the conversation. Waiting would not bring coins raining down from the sky.

With a sigh, he stepped inside.

She did not ring for a servant, for there were none about. She had dismissed the three women with excellent recommendations and an extra pittance she could ill afford. They had been grateful and kind, murmuring words of praise for her father and words of encouragement for her. She took his coat herself and draped it over the banister, then accepted his hat and placed it carefully atop the folded wool.

"This way." She led him down the hall. At the door to Papa's study, she paused, her heart constricting as she stared at her father's chair, empty now. Empty forever. Beside the chair, the hearth was cold.

Papa's worktable was piled high with projects: a fifteenth century leather-bound tome with blind tooling on the cover. Another from 1728 with a lovely Cambridge panel design on both front and back covers, the edges sprinkled in red, the spine decorated with gilt. Several works by Shakespeare, their covers ragged and worn. On the floor were more piles, the tops of which were level with the table. Sorrow wrapped her like a choking vine.

The wraith had done her a kindness and kept away.

She entered the room and turned away to pour a thimble of her father's whisky for herself and second more generous portion for Mr. Christopher.

"To my father," she said, then drank down the entire portion, ignoring Mr. Christopher's raised eyebrows. There were so many more words she could have spoken, words of love and loss, but those words were hers alone. They lived in her heart and in her memories. So, she let those three suffice.

Besides, the fit of coughing that took her after she downed her tiny glass of whisky precluded any attempt at further speech. She had never developed a taste for spirits.

When her eyes stopped watering and her throat

opened enough to let air pass once more, Mr. Christopher said, "To Malcolm Barrett," and drank down his glass as she had hers. He, however, was not taken by a fit of coughing.

Once they were seated, she on the horsehair settee, he in an overstuffed armchair, he said, "You were your father's secretary..."

"I was."

"You are so young and a...woman..."

"I am twenty-three." Not so young. Not a child. But to him, she was still a fragile thing, barely a shadow of competence.

She made no comment on his second observation as there was really no comment to be made. She knew where his thoughts wandered. She was a woman, alone in the world, and her sole training was as secretary to an antiquarian, a situation that would not stand her in good stead in a search for employment.

She met Mr. Christopher's gaze. "Tell me the whole of it," she said. "There is no point in putting it off."

"You have thirty a year," he said bluntly.

The number rang in her ears.

She did a mental calculation. The yearly rental for the house alone was twenty-five pounds. A year's coal was close to fifty.

"It will not be enough." Even if she lived frugally, hired no help, cleaned and cooked for herself, she could not continue to rent the house, not if she intended to eat. She should not have been surprised, but a tiny flicker of hope had clung to her, a traitorous ember now snuffed beneath the weight of truth.

Mr. Christopher did not pretend to be oblivious. "It is

something," he said, "but not enough to continue to rent this house, pay servants, sustain yourself." He paused. "What will you do? Have you had an offer..."

"An offer?" She wrinkled her brow. He knew that Mr. Caradoc had offered her employment. It was Mr. Christopher who had sent her the introductory note. She was about to point out exactly that when his meaning dawned. She could not hold back an incredulous laugh. "You mean an offer of *marriage*?"

"Well, you are a lady of... That is to say, you are attractive... I mean..." He cleared his throat and looked at the ceiling, then the floor, and finally at his fingertips as he pressed them together.

Isabella resisted the urge to roll her eyes. She knew what he meant. Her hair was dark and thick, her skin clear, her brown eyes framed by long, dark lashes. She was of medium height with a pleasant figure, and her voice was neither too quiet nor too shrill. She had thirty a year, and while that was no great fortune—not even a small fortune—it might be enough, coupled with her appearance, to capture a man.

But therein lay the rub. Even if there had been someone who showed interest, she did not want to marry. She wanted her books and her father and the lively conversations they had had, the visits with his contemporaries, the intellectual stimulation...she wanted her life back. A thing not on offer.

For an instant, she considered telling the solicitor exactly that, but the hopeful expression that wreathed his features made her hold her tongue. He would not understand. In his estimation, women had their place.

She had learned that very lesson when, at the age of

fourteen she had been sent to Mrs. Trevisham's School for Young Ladies. Papa had been concerned that there was no feminine influence in her life, and that as she came of age, the lack would do her a disservice. But she had quickly come to understand that she was not the sort of young lady Mrs. Trevisham's School preferred.

She had lasted five weeks.

Her return home had been accompanied by a lengthy letter from Mrs. Trevisham which had included observations such as: *Her needlework is appalling. She cannot play the pianoforte at all. She has no knowledge of watercolors. She does not interact well with the other young ladies. Too outspoken...not feminine...was caught reading a book of human anatomy...disruptive...cannot be tolerated...*

Papa had burned the letter and continued to educate her himself, encouraging her not only to finish that book on human anatomy, but read another should her interest lead her in such a direction. She had been glad to be home, even if she had missed some of the girls she had met at the school and had wished she had the chance to pursue those friendships. She had written and, in the beginning, they had written back. But the foundation of her association with them had been too brief and the passage of time had seen the letters grow infrequent and then stop altogether.

Which left a simple but unyielding truth: with Papa dead, she had nowhere to go, no one to rely upon. She was completely and utterly alone.

"I have had no offer of that sort," Isabella said.

"I see." Mr. Christopher continued to frown down at his fingertips. "Will you accept employment with Mr. Caradoc?"

She ought to say no and end the matter. She ought to remove that option completely.

Instead, she murmured, "It would mean leaving London," effectively ending that line of inquiry while avoiding a direct reply.

She looked around the room at the shelves upon shelves of her father's treasured books. How many times had Papa run his gloved fingers over these leather-bound spines, whispering their titles like prayers? How often had he told her that these books were his life's work, and hers by inheritance.

A hollow ache bloomed beneath her ribs. Each title felt like a farewell.

She squared her shoulders and lifted her chin. "I will sell my father's collection."

The wind rattled the windowpane as though in protest, a long, hollow sigh threading through the cracks. Isabella ignored it, steeling herself as she met Mr. Christopher's gaze. Somewhere deep in her chest, an ache formed, a premonition, perhaps, that this decision would lead her down a road from which there would be no return.

Mr. Christopher's eyes widened. For an instant, she thought he was merely surprised that she would part with these treasures. But then his frown deepened, and he said, "I'm afraid your father sold the collection in its entirety several months ago."

Shock and hurt rendered her speechless. She felt wounded that Papa would have done such a thing, sold the collection and said not a word. He had made no mention that their straits were so dire...

But as she thought back, she realized that while he

might not have said anything, there had been indications she had chosen to ignore.

The small gifts Papa had loved to bring her—a ribbon, a book, a bag of sweets—had grown infrequent and then absent. She had thought it was because he was ailing and left the house less often. They had not hired an upstairs maid to replace the one who left. She had told herself it was because they had no need of an upstairs maid in their small and comfortable household, that their maid of all work was adequate. Most telling, Papa had stopped purchasing rare books, even when she heard whispers of the availability of an original English translation of a Cornelius Agrippa text from 1670. He had explained away his uncharacteristic disinterest with a wave of his hand and the excuse that his shelves were full.

Isabella had known that they had grown ever more careful with their money, but she had not known— or was it that she had not acknowledged? —the whole of it. There had been coin to pay the bills. No creditors had knocked at the door. She had allowed herself to believe that was enough.

"If the books were sold, why are they still here?" she asked.

"Mr. Caradoc agreed to let your father keep them here until the collection was fully catalogued."

Isabella stared at him as the name registered. *Mr. Caradoc.*

After a moment, she gathered herself and said, "The collection *is* fully catalogued. I completed the work myself."

"Yes. And with your father's demise…" Mr. Christopher cleared his throat. "Mr. Caradoc has already contacted me to arrange for transfer of the collection."

Mr. Christopher waved a hand to encompass the shelves that lined the walls and the stacks of books on the floor.

Isabella's thoughts spun to the locked trunk in Papa's chamber. Not all his books had been catalogued; not all had been sold. Not the ones in that trunk.

They had titles like *Petit Albert*, *Dragon Rouge*, and *Grimorium Verum*. Some had no titles at all and were more journal than tome, diaries of spells and conjuration, written by souls long passed from this earth.

The key she had taken from Papa's closed fist the night he died hung around her neck. Cold and impossibly heavy, its presence was a dark whisper against her skin.

"Do you know Mr. Caradoc well?"

His gaze slid back, open and honest. "Well enough. He is a gentleman."

Not according to Papa.

"You invested the funds paid to my father for the collection," Isabella said.

"At your father's instructions. Without that, you would have nothing." Mr. Christopher paused. "What will you do, Miss Barrett?"

"I shall seek employment," she said.

"So you *will* accept the position Mr. Caradoc offers?"

Did he sound eager? She did not know him well enough to say for certain.

"Other employment," she said. "Here in London."

Mr. Christopher's lips drew in a tight line, and his expression was one she could not interpret. Then he sighed and said, "I can make some inquiries, see if someone is looking for a governess or companion."

She closed her eyes and pinched the bridge of her nose between her thumb and index finger. She knew nothing about children, nothing about being a governess, and even less about the activities and obligations of a companion. But she knew a great deal about being a secretary, cataloguing books, repairing them, restoring them. Unfortunately, women were not usually hired for such positions.

Unless the employer was Rhys Caradoc.

She opened her eyes, feeling defeated before she even began.

"Thank you," she said. "I would appreciate that. I will send letters to my father's colleagues, as well. Perhaps one of them will know of a position." And perhaps one of them knew how to fly and another knew how to breathe underwater.

There was nothing else to be said and Mr. Christopher soon took his leave.

After closing the door behind him, Isabella paused by the basket of food on the console table. She removed the checkered cloth that covered it and examined the contents: bread, a wheel of cheddar, a small clay pot of butter, dried figs, a handful of fresh eggs wrapped in straw, a piece of salted pork, some carrots and turnips, a twist of paper containing candied almonds, and an oval chemist's tin, japanned black, with a thin gilt rule circling the rim. She opened it to find a pleated rosette of waxed paper cupping pale yellow lemon drops dusted in sugar.

She stared at the basket, feeling no temptation to sample this bounty.

When had she eaten last? She could not recall. The hunger that gnawed at her was not for food. It was for answers, for certainty, for a clear path forward.

Absently, she tore a small chunk from the edge of the bread and nibbled at the crust. She tasted nothing, but she forced herself to chew. She swallowed then turned and walked along the dim hallway. From behind her came a soft sigh. Then a whisper, like sand sifting. She did not turn.

Her throat grew tight; her shoulders tensed. She hung her head and for an instant, just an instant, allowed herself to acknowledge her despair. Then she drew a breath, drew herself upright, and went to her father's desk to write letters.

CHAPTER FIVE

Papa's study felt small in the presence of the three large men who had come to crate his books. Isabella supervised their work, making certain they packed everything away with care, then watched from the window as they left, her throat tight, her eyes prickling. The cart creaked and groaned under its burden, its wooden wheels grinding against the cobblestones with an uneven, mournful rhythm as it proceeded down the fog-drenched street. The sight tore open wounds not yet healed, scraping her raw.

Another piece of her life gone, as if it had never been.

But was it *her* life? Or had it been her father's life, and she a mere piece on his game board, a pawn forever moved by a will other than her own? No, she had been something even less defined, an *accessory* to his life, bending and shaping herself to fit the contours of his wants and needs, his interests and fascinations. The recent days she had spent alone in this silent house had left her nothing but endless time to ruminate on every aspect of her life.

Oh, she had no doubt as to the depth of Papa's love. She had felt it every day in a thousand different ways. But her life had been a reflection of his own. Yes, she loved books, but what else? She'd never had the space to discover what might fill her own inner shelves, unchosen by another's hand. What titles would they bear, those unwritten spines? What would she choose if the pages were hers to write?

She had loved her father, loved the discourse with his contemporaries to which she was exposed, allowed to sit in the shadows and listen. He had never forced her to attend, she had gone willingly, soaking up knowledge. She had been content, or so she had told herself. But a part of her had always wished for...for *something*. Not *more*. Just something that was *hers*, a life that was hers. Her aspirations. Her choices.

The thoughts made her feel disloyal and small. She lifted her chin. Wanting was not betrayal.

Her hazy reflection stared back at her from the glass window, gaunt, pale, eyes hollowed by sleeplessness. A girl trapped in a house filled with shadows and whispers.

There had been times she had imagined how grand it would be to see Paris or Rome, to see the ocean, to walk in forests she had only read about, or sit in a tea shop with girls her own age and laugh and talk. To have a friend to share confidences and hopes and dreams.

But those were not things she *needed*, only things she *wanted*. She had trained herself to live on necessities, to believe that wants were luxury items, shelved high and out of reach.

She had been happy with her life...hadn't she? The answer slid from her grasp.

She turned and studied the empty shelves.

Papa's books were gone.

Nearly gone.

There were still his private books, the ones he kept locked away.

Isabella pulled on the chain that hung around her neck and drew forth the key her father had clutched against his chest even as he took his final breath. The metal was warm in her hand, warmed by her skin, but the key felt heavy. She let it drop against her bodice and went to her father's chamber, to the brass-clad wooden trunk in the corner. The wraith followed, drifting in her wake.

She knelt and traced her fingertips along the engravings. Scarabs with wings splayed open. Cobras with their hoods flared. The eye of Horus.

She lifted the key, her breath coming fast and shallow.

The whispers were there, always there. They skittered across her skin like icy fingertips, tangled in her hair, and sighed in her ears.

The wraith hovered, translucent and gray, her hollow eyes fixed on Papa's trunk.

Isabella turned the key, then hesitated. Papa had locked these secrets away for a reason. He had always been careful and calm. Yet the man he had been in his final weeks had spent more and more time with the contents of this trunk, and that man had been different than the Papa she had always known. Furtive. Secretive. Haunted by sorrow and regret, burdened by the weight of secrets he refused to divulge. The man he had been in his final days had carried a kind of madness. The contents of this trunk had changed him.

She wondered what might awaken in her should she delve into those tomes—not knowledge, but *inclination*. What if these books were not merely Papa's interest, but his affliction? And what if she had inherited the craving? After all, was she not already just a little bit mad?

Before she could talk herself out of it, she pushed open the lid.

The air stilled, the silence so profound it felt like it had a weight of its own.

She reached for a book, its cover charred, the edges of its pages curled and blackened. The scent of old smoke and something ancient and bitter rose to meet her. Or did she only imagine it? Her fingers hovered, a feeling of foreboding seeping through her.

She feared these were not merely books, but dormant things, coiled, waiting, watching, eager to awaken beneath a reader's gaze.

The memory of her father's voice filled her thoughts. *I will not tell you that these books are not for you, Isa. It is no person's right to tell another what they may or may not read. But I will offer a warning. If you open this chest, if you open these books, be certain that you wish to see what secrets lie within. Once known, they cannot be unknown.* His expression had been mournful, filled with regret.

Was this the mistake he had alluded to that morning at breakfast? Had he believed owning these books was a mistake? Or had he believed that keeping them locked away was the mistake? Or had he been referring to something else entirely? Questions nested inside questions.

The ever-present whispers became a roar. A deep dread threaded through her, and with it the certainty that the dead craved what was in this trunk, yearned for the knowledge in these pages to be set free.

She jerked back. The pressure of the air eased, the weight on her chest lifting enough to let her breathe. Her mouth tasted of ash and metal.

"I am not in the mood for secrets today, Papa. I have more practical matters to address," she whispered. Then she gave a sad laugh. "Or perhaps I am just a coward."

That was a small truth. She *was* afraid, not of these books, but of what they might awaken and of the part of herself that wanted to know regardless of cost.

After locking the trunk once more, she left the room. But even as she returned to her father's study, she could not shake the feeling that she had not permanently locked away the danger, merely delayed it.

In the days that followed, letters arrived, some in response to hers, others to the notice she had posted. Those from her father's colleagues offered condolences and regrets rather than employment, and while she appreciated the former, she was in dire need of the latter.

Each missive she read felt like peeling away another layer of possibility, only to find it hollow within.

Often did her gaze fall on the train ticket to Maidenhead sitting on the corner of the desk. To use it would not merely see her removed from London, it would deliver her into Rhys Caradoc's keeping, into the very hands of the man Papa had despised. And feared. She could not persuade herself that entering his employ was a choice she ought to make, yet neither could she convince herself to toss the ticket into the fire and foreclose the possibility altogether.

One letter contained a marriage proposal, suggesting she might care for a particular gentleman in his declining years in exchange for a roof over her head and food on her plate. She knew of the gentleman, a foul-tempered, foul-mouthed creature, not a friend of her father's but an acquaintance of an acquaintance. She replied at once, declining, polite and firm, offering no opportunity for rebuttal.

Another invited her to call and present her credentials for the position of governess, but when she did, the woman interviewing her had stated in rather blunt terms, "A plain woman would better suit."

Isabella was not a fool. She knew exactly why a plain woman might be preferred where there were the master of the house and his two strapping sons to consider. It would matter little if she reassured her interviewer that she had no interest in pursuing any of them. A woman's interest in such matters was not usually a consideration for a certain type of man.

The next day, she tried again, tipping her umbrella as she hurried along Holborn, skirts caught in the draught made by an omnibus shouldering past. The city was a tangle of movement and sound, iron rims biting stone, a newsboy's thin cry, the wet slap of hooves, each noise making a notch in her nerves. She had an interview off Red Lion Street in fifteen minutes and ink on the thumb of her glove that would not come off however she worried at it.

If this interview went like all those that had preceded it, she would be thanked for calling and shown a polite door.

A disturbance in the air touched her bare wrist where her glove had worn thin. Cold, quick, seeking. She knew the feel, like a draft from a cellar mouth, and set her face forward as if the street were all she could see.

An icy hand caught her arm, though no one was at her side.

Isabella did not turn. A person looking straight at nothing drew trouble.

Help me...See me... The voice was thin, barely a sound at all.

Habit rose, well-worn as prayer. See nothing. Hear nothing. Never say it. Never show it.

She stepped round a costermonger's barrow and almost collided with Mr. Caradoc. She stumbled back a step.

"Forgive me." He set a palm to the side of the barrow to steady it and, with his other hand, steadied her. The touch was light, proper, but the heat of it struck through glove and nerve. He wore his dark coat buttoned high. Rain jeweled the brim of his hat.

"Mr. Caradoc," she managed.

"Miss Barrett." He released her slowly, as if attentive to the possibility she might sway. His thumb lifted last, a fraction late, leaving a ghost of warmth behind. "You're in haste."

"I have an interview," she said, because that was true and safe to say. "At a—" She did not wish to name the shop in case she failed there too and had to walk past his knowledge of it later. "—a place that will be glad of me."

The corner of his mouth moved, not quite a smile, but not mockery either. "Any place would be." His gaze dropped to the ink on her glove and away again, a quick flicker that felt too intimate by half.

She told herself to step past him. She did not. Instead, she looked away.

Across the street, in the shadow of a print-seller's awning, a man stood where rain did not seem to fall on him. His cap was all wrong, too high on his head, and when a cart rolled through him, his edges trembled like heat above a lamp.

Mr. Caradoc's gaze followed hers.

"Do you see someone you know?" he asked, and the question landed like a thrown stone breaking water.

Isabella's gaze flashed to his. "No. I was only... thinking of the rain."

He did not look back across the street. He looked at her. "Have you given any thought to my offer?" he said.

"To catalogue Harrowgate's library," she said, wrapping the words in cool paper. "I have." She had spent too much thought there, like coins dropped in a well.

"And?"

"And I must make my own way, Mr. Caradoc." She heard the stiffness in her voice and wished she did not mind being stiff. "I will not be beholden to a stranger because he was kind."

He started as though the word pained him.

"I was not kind," he said, very low. "I was—" His gaze cut downward and away, brief and private, before it returned. "—selfish."

She could not decipher the meaning of that. She glanced away in confusion.

The man under the awning lifted his hand, rain stitching through his hat.

"Miss Barrett," Mr. Caradoc said softly, his gaze following hers once more. "What are you looking at?"

"Nothing," she said too quickly, then stepped back, as if by changing the angle of her seeing she might change the world.

A cry lifted three doors down, a woman scolding a dog, and an omnibus huffed to a stop, horses blowing, leather creaking. The driver flicked his whip and the lash whispered over the air where the wraith on the far side of the street stood. Isabella's throat closed. It was not the seeing that undid her. It was the wanting to acknowledge, to answer, to be useful to something that could no longer be helped.

Mr. Caradoc shifted half a pace, deliberately putting himself between her and the street, an easy motion that set his shoulder a little before hers so she would have to look through him to look beyond. The rain gathered and ran off the brim of his hat in one clear thread.

"I must go," she said.

"Come." He tipped his head toward the mouth of an alley—not a dark one, not a trap, only a passage running through to Red Lion Square. "It's a quicker way if you're bound east."

She hesitated. Then she nodded, because she had walked that labyrinth of lanes a hundred times and knew the shortcut was real. He fell in beside her, not close, not too far, matching his stride to hers as if it were second nature, his limp slight. Now and then, his arm brushed hers, a small contact that made her pulse misbehave.

The alley smelled of coal, cabbage, printer's ink, damp brick. A cat shot past and vanished into a stack of crates. Above, lines of washing sagged under the rain. She fixed her eyes on the black shine of the cobbles where the rain had smoothed them to glass.

"What will you say if they ask you for a reference you do not have?" he asked, not unkindly.

"The truth," she said. "That my father is dead and my skills are plain." She folded her gloved fingers around the damp handle of the umbrella. "That I can read a hand at a glance and keep an account and mend a book with paste and patience. That I do not trouble employers with *incon-venient feelings*."

At that, something like a wince flickered over his face and was gone. "Inconvenient feelings," he repeated, voice dry. "What a world we have made that would call them that."

As they came out on the square, a gust of wind capered round and plunged under her skirts, cold as a bucket from a well. At the same moment, a prickle rose at the base of her skull, the thin, bright tinnitus of wraiths drawing near.

A woman stood by the railings across the square, translucent gray, her hair hanging in ropes. She held a basket to her front with both hands, the posture of someone guarding a child. The wail of a babe tore at Isabella's thoughts. A babe no longer of this world.

Isabella went still. He noticed. His hand hovered, not touching but ready to offer assistance if needed. For an instant, she thought how easy it would be to accept, not only his arm here in the street but employment, safe and familiar.

"Miss Barrett?" Mr. Caradoc said.

She glanced toward the building where a gilt board swung: *MRS. ROCHE, Millinery & Mourning.* "This is my appointment."

He stopped beside the door. She had to pass very near him to reach it, and the closeness drew the air tight. She smelled the faintest trace of lemons, light and pleasant.

"My offer of employment stands," he said softly. His gaze made steady work of her face. "Because you would do the work well. And because you would not be alone."

The last sentence snagged in her. He could not know where it caught.

"I am not alone," she said, more quickly than was graceful. "I have always managed."

"Of course." He dipped his head the smallest degree, as if acknowledging the truth and the cost both. "My carriage will meet you in Marlow when you arrive."

His words, so calm and sure, and yes, arrogant, startled a sound from her that might have been a laugh. "You do not think very well of my chances with Mrs. Roche."

"I think very well of you," he said simply, and the ring of truth she heard in them confused her. "And I think you deserve employment befitting your skills."

The bell chimed when he opened the door for her, and again later when she opened it for herself, leaving after having been declined employment.

Days crawled past. Isabella attended at least two interviews daily and came away from each with nothing but a deeper pit in her stomach. Her spirits were sorely tested, her hopes dashed repeatedly. Desperation gnawed at her. Unpaid bills sat in a tidy pile on Papa's desk. The rent was paid on the house for only ten more days, and then she would need to find lodging as well as employment. Her first quarterly income since Papa's death would not come until Midsummer, and that was months away.

Resting her palms on the smooth wood of her father's desk she stared at the ticket to Maidenhead until it blurred, wondering if she dared accept Mr. Caradoc's offer. Wondering how she would survive if she did not.

Each letter of rejection, each humiliating interview chipped away at her confidence and hope, leaving her raw.

She began to pack, not because she had any idea where she would go but because the act of folding linens and sorting her father's belongings allowed her to pretend that she was in control of something.

Now, she opened the lower right-hand drawer of Papa's desk, intending to separate papers to burn or donate. Would anyone even want his monographs? Perhaps one of his contemporaries or a museum... Her hand closed on a stack of letters tied with black ribbon. Curious, she drew it out and set it atop the desk. She untied the ribbon and unfolded the letter at the top of the stack.

The parchment was fine, the script bold, the sentences constructed with precision and care. As she read first letter, then the next and the next, she realized these were the correspondences Mr. Caradoc had sent to Papa, and they were exactly as he had described: offers of employment, nothing more, nothing less. No veiled messages or threats. No offensive language. Nothing to raise Papa's hackles or send him into a rage.

Mr. Caradoc had not lied. The admission both relieved and distressed her.

She sank into the chair behind the desk, the bundle before her, the black ribbon clutched in one hand.

He had not lied about the contents of his letters, but she could not know if he had been truthful about the letters Papa had sent in return. And if he had been, then why had Papa used her as an excuse to refuse, why had he claimed she had a delicate nature?

She sent a note to Mr. Christopher asking for his opinion of Mr. Caradoc.

His reply was straightforward.

Mr. Caradoc is a gentleman, Miss Barrett, sharp of mind and possessed of considerable means. I am certain his offer is made in good faith, and you would do well to consider it most seriously.

The wording was careful. Too careful. Polished and smooth. The very fact that the note contained nothing specific, and certainly nothing revealing, lent it a hollow ring. Or was it only Papa's acrimony toward Mr. Caradoc that made her wary and mistrustful?

The wraith glided forward from the corner where she lurked, eyes fathomless and dark.

"Go away," Isabella whispered, then clamped her lips shut, appalled that she had acknowledged the creature in any way.

The air chilled, so cold that Isabella's breath puffed white before her lips. On a dry whisper, the wraith moved closer, stirring the letters on the desk. Mr. Christopher's note rose on an eddy of air, hovering a finger's breadth above the desk before falling flat.

And then the wraith disappeared.

Snatching up the note, Isabella stared at it. Elaborate scenarios spun through her thoughts until she landed on one where she imagined that Mr. Caradoc had some hold over Mr. Christopher, that he had somehow placed the letters ostensibly addressed to her father in the desk while she was away from the house, "proof" meant to lure her into a situation where—

Where *what*? What could his purpose possibly be? What storm gathered behind those gray eyes and that quiet, self-assured voice?

But try as she might, she could not conjure a motive

for Mr. Caradoc to create an elaborate scheme in order to lure her to his home.

Unless it wasn't *her* he wanted at all—but something *of* her. Something she *possessed*. Her fingertips traced the outline of the key through the cloth of her bodice.

He had never mentioned Papa's secret collection. Yet the possibility nipped at her and clung like a burr: what if the books in Papa's trunk were his true quarry?

A huff of incredulous laughter escaped her at the folly of her outlandish thoughts. She was not normally one for flights of fancy, and she did not enjoy the melodrama of a penny dreadful or a gothic novel, yet here she was, spinning a tale that would rival those of Radcliffe or Maturin.

She assessed her options. She had few, and none were pleasant. She had not the funds to continue living here. She had neither friends nor relations to turn to. She had thus far found no other options for employment.

Mr. Caradoc's offer was all she had. The truth of it settled, heavy as a damp cloak.

She rose and went to pack her things.

CHAPTER SIX

Monday dawned dreary, the low hanging sky a smear of charcoal and soot. It wasn't quite wet enough to be called rain or cold enough to be called snow, but it was miserable all the same.

Isabella refused to look back as the hired hackney carried her away from the narrow house she and Papa had called home all her life. The windows had been shuttered, the hearth gone cold. She had sold or given away everything she could not carry, her life whittled to two trunks. One contained Papa's secret books locked up tight. The other was stuffed with her clothing and accessories, her mother's silver brush and comb set, a kit wrapped in oilcloth containing the tools of her trade, and Papa's coat, folded flat at the trunk's bottom. She had been unable to leave it, just as she had been unable to stay.

Now, as the hack creaked to a halt, the station loomed before her, its iron-and-glass roof rising like the ribcage of a monstrous beast. It struck her that this place, all steel and steam and shrieking metal, could not be more unlike her father's book-lined study. He had hated trains, called them unnatural, noisy contraptions built to scar the countryside.

He would have hated this journey, and the destination even more.

Harrowgate Manor, home of Rhys Caradoc, a man her father had warned her about in the most strident terms. She could pretend that she had accepted his offer solely because there had been no other and because she had been desperate and afraid.

But while those things were true, they were not the only truths.

Beneath the grief and guilt and the echo of Papa's disapproval, there was a well of curiosity, vast and deep.

Something about Mr. Caradoc's visit had opened a wound in Papa that morning, one that had festered deep beneath the surface and gnawed at his spirit, igniting a darkness in him and sending him spiralling in a coil of despair and dismay. Ever since that visit, Papa had been afraid.

And now Rhys Caradoc wanted her under his roof. She intended to find out why.

Fog curled around her as she stepped down from the hack onto the damp stone. She paid the driver, and he dropped her trunks beside her, the smaller with a thud, the larger with a loud scrape and groan that made her ribs tighten.

A porter in a frayed waistcoat with a pencil behind his ear materialized with a handcart.

"Destination?" he asked.

"Maidenhead," she said.

He tied on a pasteboard label written in a neat, black hand and whistled up a second man.

"Guard's van for this beast, miss," he said with a

gesture at Papa's trunk. "You'll not want it crowding your compartment."

She watched with unease as the second man trundled the trunks away, wheels rattling over iron seams.

"Don't worry, miss. They'll be safe and you'll see them again when you reach Maidenhead," the porter said.

She palmed him a shilling and tucked the luggage claim in her glove, then followed the crowd into the station. Steam hissed from engines, mingling with the din of clanging luggage carts, shouting porters, and the screech of metal wheels.

Weaving through the press of travellers, Isabella strode forward. The air around her grew cold as cellar stones. Two wraiths glided at the corners of her vision, vague, spectral forms that drifted along the edges of the platform, untouched by the chaos around them. One turned its face toward her, mouth open in a soundless plea. The other lifted a beckoning hand, fingers tipped in curled talons. Isabella walked on, refusing to acknowledge them. Not here. Not now.

Heart tripping, she approached the Bristol train, its engine exhaling thick clouds of steam that curled around the wheels and drifted across the platform.

Mr. Caradoc had spared no expense; her ticket was for the first-class carriage. A porter opened the door for her, and she stepped into a compartment with walls of polished wood and green velvet seats that were deep and cushioned. A brass lamp swayed overhead. She took a seat by the window and watched the crowd surge past: a mother clutching the hands of two small children; a woman carrying a hatbox; an elderly man leaning heavily on his cane; a group of young men, talking and laughing.

But the compartment itself was empty, save herself.

She was alone. And though the seat was soft and comfortable, the emptiness pressed in on her, unsettling.

A sharp rap sounded at the carriage door. Startled,
Isabella turned as Mr. Christopher swung it open,
breathless from running the length of the platform. His
hat was askew, his cravat loose, his face flushed with
exertion.

"Mr. Christopher!"

"Miss Barrett," he said, his tone urgent. "I was afraid I
would be too late." He stepped inside, shutting the door
against the rush of steam and shouts outside. "I could not
let you go without warning you." The gravity of his
expression made her wary.

"I made inquiries," he continued, catching his breath.
"I hired a man, discreet but thorough. We have not the
time for me to provide details but suffice it to say that
while Mr. Caradoc is what he seems, a gentleman of
means, there is also a blight on his history. My man traced
him to St. Jude's Asylum. He was a patient there many
years ago."

The name struck Isabella in her heart, making it twist
in fear and remembered horror. Her palms went clammy
inside her gloves, her breath coming in short rasps.
Memories of St. Jude's clawed their way free. The reek of
carbolic acid and damp stone. The muffled cries that
haunted the corridors. Bars on the windows. Wired panes
in the doors.

And now she was to picture Rhys Caradoc there,
trapped in a windowless room, gray eyes dulled by the
shadows that haunted that place. If he had been a patient
there many years ago, he would have been a very young
man at the time.

Why had he been confined? What had driven him into

that place? And most of all, was it only happenstance that he had sought out Papa...and her?

Papa's warning came back to her with sudden force. He had wanted her as far from Rhys Caradoc as possible. And yet, here she was, about to deliver herself into his hands.

Mr. Christopher's eyes softened. "Your father was more to me than a client, Miss Barrett. He was my friend. I believe he would want me to watch over you." He studied her carefully. "I must ask...Are you certain this is what you want? To go to Harrowgate Manor?"

Certain? No, not at all.

Fear churned through her like quicklime. She opened her mouth to demand more—why Mr. Caradoc had been there; what affliction had chained him to those barred rooms—but the shrill of the guard's whistle cut her off.

The train shuddered beneath her feet, ready to pull away.

Mr. Christopher offered his hand. "Come now. Quickly, before it is too late."

Isabella rose, her body taut with indecision. For an instant, she nearly followed him, nearly let herself be guided back to the platform. Her pulse pounded in her ears.

But for all his concern and kindness, Mr. Christopher had offered her no other path, no other refuge. Where else could she go? What else could she do? And beneath those concerns sat a deeper truth. She needed answers. Needed to understand what had driven Papa to such despair, what had brought Rhys Caradoc to their door.

"No," she said, firm. "I must go."

Worry flickered across Mr. Christopher's face, but he only nodded once and said, "Then may God keep you."

His hand slipped from hers and he stepped down. Steam roiled up to swallow him.

Isabella lowered herself to her seat once more, her hands pressed tight together in her lap, the echo of Mr. Christopher's words and Papa's warnings tangling like thorns in her chest. Whatever waited at Harrowgate, she was bound for it now.

The train gave a lurch that rocked through the floor beneath her feet, and she braced herself as it began to move. Pulse racing, she watched the platform slide away, the glass-and-steel vault of the station vanishing into the fog.

The soot-streaked buildings of London gave way to countryside painted in shades of gray and green. The world grew quieter, the sky larger, the view unimpeded by buildings. In the distance, fields stretched beneath a pewter sky, their hedgerows frosted white. Smoke curled from the chimneys of distant cottages. Isabella rested her gloved hand against the windowpane, the cold of the glass biting through.

As the minutes gathered into miles, the cadence of iron on iron worked its slow spell. Her head sank back against the plush seat. The carriage lamp hummed. The train swayed. Her lashes lowered. Sleep slipped in on the next curve.

A wraith touched her nape.

The whispers grew harsh.

The rain fell, dripping off the edges of her umbrella.

Shivering, she looked down at her father's open grave then up again.

She looked to the hedge where Mr. Christopher waited just out of sight.

Mr. Caradoc was in the distance now, the fog swirling

at his back. She lifted her skirt and hurried after him, instinct guiding her feet.

But no matter how she quickened her pace, she could not catch him. She called out, but he did not turn or slow. She hurried past endless rows of gravestones, moss-covered and damp. The rows grew narrower, the stones taller, until she was forced to turn sideways to maneuver between them. Her heart pounded and her mouth grew dry, unease gnawing at her like vermin at a carcass.

The walls narrowed even further now, no longer stone but formed by the bent and twisted branches of burnt and blackened trees. Iron bars jutted from the trunks, wired windows hanging between them, windows ripped whole from St. Jude's itself. She saw her reflection warped in the glass, pale and desperate, as though she were the one trapped inside.

She pressed on, the way so narrow that it scraped her skin with every inch she gained.

Mr. Caradoc was there in the darkness, his form barely discernable far ahead, broad shoulders and an uneven gait, moving through the tunnel with far more ease than her. And she knew that if she did not follow now, she would never have this chance again.

The tunnel widened and she ran forward, the branches like talons as they tore her hair and scratched her face. Scorched roots sprang from the earth, catching her ankles, twisting in her skirt. She tugged and pulled until she heard the material tear, only to be caught again and again no matter how carefully she stepped. Sweat prickled along her spine. Her breath came in shallow gasps.

With a desperate yank, she tore herself free and ran, faster, and faster still, lungs heaving.

But she gained no ground. He was always too far away to catch.

Go back. Do not follow. The warning came in Papa's voice, rough and urgent. But Papa was gone, buried beneath the cold earth.

From somewhere far ahead came the crack and snap and roar of a fire she could not see. The fog grew thick and heavy, smelling of mildew and copper, of things dead and rotting, and underlying that, the stink of smoke and soot and tar. The damp cold sank into her bones. It stroked her cheeks, her lips, her limbs, like webs twining about her. She brushed them away, but they came again, thicker now, sealing her lips, covering her eyes, hissing softly, like dozens of whispering voices.

She struggled to lift her hands, but the webs were too strong, trapping her in a cocoon that forced her legs together and her arms to her sides. Sick with fear, she struggled against them, but they held her fast, growing ever tighter.

She was bound, unable to move, unable to see, unable to scream. Terror was her world. Her heartbeat became a hammer, each strike cinching the bindings tighter.

Voices came to her, soothing and soft. The wraiths pulled at her bindings, aiding her struggles, working the threads.

The sun flashed, blinding her.

With a cry, she sat upright, panting and drenched in sweat, cheek cold where it had pressed against the window. The scents of coal-smoke and hot metal stung her nose. Her chest heaved, her limbs shaking. The sound of her own breathing, loud and ragged, rasped in her ears.

There was no graveyard, no man, no webs, only green velvet and thin daylight bleeding through the carriage window. Yet the whump and roar of hungry flames and the scent of smoke and ash clung to her as real as the blood pounding at her temples.

Papa's key had bitten half-moons into the tender skin of her palm. She unclenched her fist and tucked it back beneath her bodice to lie warm against her chest.

It had only been a dream. A nightmare. And yet... the echo of her father's voice lingered in her ears, and she could not shake the feeling that the nightmare was a portent of things to come, a warning...or a summons.

Moments later, a uniformed guard leaned into the corridor to call, "Maidenhead! Maidenhead Station."

The train slowed and pulled into a modest station, the red brick walls dark with soot, the platform edged by cast iron lamps. Isabella gathered her things and stepped down onto the platform, her boots landing on the wood with a thud.

"Where might I find the post-chaise?" she asked a porter.

He gestured toward the exit. "Just there, miss. Man in the black coat with the gray bays."

Isabella stepped from the shelter of the station into the cobbled street, the porter following at a short distance, trundling her trunks on a hand cart. The chaise waited, its body black-lacquered and mud-splattered, reminding her of the carriage in which she had ridden to Papa's burial. The gray horses stamped and snorted, restless in the cold. The driver, a tall, stoop-shouldered man, touched the brim of his hat in greeting.

"I am Miss Isabella Barrett," she said. "I believe you are expecting me."

"Right then, Miss Barrett." He glanced at her trunks. "Those'll go in the luggage cart behind. My lad will fetch it round and follow us to Marlow. We're just waiting for two more, then we'll be off straightaway."

He opened the door, and she stepped up into the narrow compartment. The seats were worn but clean, the interior close and smelling of leather and horse.

She had barely settled when she saw two elderly women approaching. They were both short and plump, bundled in thick brown coats, matching bonnets tied beneath their chins.

Isabella slid along the seat to the far side as one of the women climbed in with surprising agility and settled opposite. The second woman followed more slowly and sat beside the first, the door clicking shut behind her. There was an odd symmetry to them, like two halves of a cracked porcelain doll.

"Off to Marlow, are you?" the first woman asked, her voice high and lilting, almost childlike.

"I am, yes," Isabella said.

"Visiting?" the woman pressed.

"I have a position waiting for me," Isabella murmured.

The second woman stared at her in silence. With her cocked head and brown clothing, she reminded Isabella of a wren perched on a branch, sharp-eyed and twitching. She tipped her head, first one way, then the other, pale blue eyes fixed on Isabella's face. There was something unsettling in her stillness, in the way her gaze never wavered, probing, assessing, as though Isabella were a curiosity laid out on a tray for inspection.

The chaise lurched forward then. The wheels struck uneven stone, then settled in a rhythmic clatter as they wove through the narrow streets of Maidenhead. The women stared at her in silence as the chaise passed beyond the outskirts of the town. Fields swept out on either side, hedgerows blurred by a low mist.

"I am Miss Viola Burns," the first woman said. "This is my sister, Miss Pansy Burns."

"Pleased to make your acquaintance. I am Miss Isabella Barrett."

"We live in Great Marlow," Pansy said.

"In the white cottage at the very end of Chapel Lane," Viola said.

"You must visit," Pansy said.

"We are always happy for company," Viola said. "Life in Marlow can be quite—"

"Boring," Pansy interjected.

"Uneventful," Viola said, ignoring her sister's interruption. "Going through our days without someone with whom to converse—"

"Other than ourselves," Pansy said.

"Is hardly exciting," Viola said.

They both leaned forward in unison, peering at Isabella expectantly.

"I..." Isabella looked back and forth between the two. "I do not yet know all the details of my position. I do not know when I will visit the village."

"*Visit* the village?" Pansy said.

"Is your employment not *in* Marlow?" Viola asked, then cast a speaking look at her sister, one that made Isabella wary.

"Near Marlow, I believe," she said. "I am expected at Harrowgate Manor..."

Both women froze. Pansy's eyes widened and her hand darted to her mouth.

"Harrowgate?" Viola said.

"Oh, my dear. You do not want to go there," Pansy said. "I suggest you turn right back around and go home."

Isabella stared at her, a bubble of uneasy laughter rising. She held it back. Something in Pansy's tone, intense and utterly certain, scraped against her nerves.

"Pansy..." Viola warned. "Do not gossip."

"Gossip?" Pansy's eyes gleamed and her lips curled in a tight smile. "It's hardly gossip when anyone in the village could tell the same tales."

"What tales?" Isabella asked before she could think better of it.

Pansy leaned forward, her breath smelling of cider and cloves. "Madness. Death. Scandal. Tragedy. And a curse," she said. "People die there."

"People die everywhere," Viola said. "Death is a fact of life."

The word *madness* made Isabella's stomach clench and her thoughts swirl to Mr. Christopher's revelation about St. Jude's. The asylum's wired panes flashed across her memory, and she pictured Rhys Caradoc's gray eyes staring through them. What had he endured in that place?

But she had not the opportunity to ponder because Pansy leaned closer still and said, "A maid from Harrowgate was found dead in the woods two years ago, her eyes open wide in terror, her mouth full of dirt."

Isabella's fingers curled into fists in her lap as the terrible image took shape, lodging cold and heavy in her belly.

Viola gave her sister a long-suffering look. "She took a fever, poor thing. She was not in her right mind and slipped out in the night, unnoticed. She was found the next day. It was very sad, a tragedy to be sure."

"They say you can see her ghost in the woods whenever there is a full moon," Pansy whispered. "That you can hear her cries of terror."

"*I* have never seen her ghost," Viola said to her sister. "*You* have never seen her ghost, either. Because there are no such things as ghosts."

"There most certainly are," Pansy said with a pout.

The two women stared expectantly at Isabella, as though waiting for her to side with one or the other. Instead, she looked to the window and said, "It seems the sky is clearing."

"It does," said Pansy.

"It certainly does," said Viola.

But Pansy was like a dog with a bone. She pressed her lips together, then said, "There is more to the tale. More death, more tragedy. The house is cursed, as is the house's master. Everyone knows it."

Isabella looked back and forth between the two women, certain that Pansy would have her say regardless of her sister's protests.

"The fire had nothing to do with any curse," Viola muttered.

"Fire?" Isabella asked, thinking of her dream, the roar of the flames she had heard but not seen.

"There was much death even before that. The curse taking all of them, one by one," Pansy whispered.

"Gossip and hearsay," Viola snapped.

"Then please tell me the facts," Isabella said.

"She still screams, Viola," Pansy said, her expression mulish. "When the wind is right. When the moon is full like it was that night. Her screams echo through the woods, but no one comes." She leaned forward and patted

Isabella's hand. "I doubt you'll last longer than a fortnight."

"Pansy!" Viola sounded truly aghast now. "Enough. You should not say such things to Miss Barrett when she is on her way there. That is unkind."

"It would be unkind not to warn her," Pansy said and flounced back against the seat with a huff.

Viola made a dismissive sound and cast a quelling look at her sister. "Pansy enjoys a good tale." Her expression grew somber. "But Harrowgate has long been a place of sadness and death."

"It *is* cursed," Pansy insisted.

"It is not," Viola said, firm.

"I don't believe in curses," Isabella said. She didn't *want* to believe in curses. They were the province of frightened children. But then, most people didn't believe in ghosts either, did they.

Isabella glanced at Viola, who sat ramrod straight, staring out the window, jaw set. Her gaze returned to Pansy, who stared at her with pale blue eyes wide and unblinking as she gave a tiny shake of her head. And so, they sat in silence as night fell, leaving the sky so black it looked like spilled ink across the heavens. The stars glittered sharp and bright, diamonds strewn with careless beauty. Never had Isabella seen the like. She had not imagined that the sky was different in London than it was elsewhere, but now she could see that London's sky was dull and closed. Here, the heavens stretched, open and unguarded, vast enough to swallow her whole.

After a time, the wheels struck stone once more. Marlow's streets wound narrow between low brick buildings and shuttered shops. The chaise entered the town square and drew to a halt. A sign for The Crown Inn hung above the door of a nearby public house, creaking in the wind. Oil lamps guttered on their brackets, sending an amber glow pooling on the cobblestones. Just beyond, the slender spires of a church pierced the darkened sky.

The coach rocked to a stop and after a moment the driver opened the door. "Marlow."

The sisters descended from the chaise first, their cloaks fluttering like dark wings. Isabella followed. A moment later, with a creak of wheels and the sharp jingle of harness, the chaise lurched forward and disappeared into the dark.

"It was a pleasure to make your acquaintance, Miss Barrett," Viola said with a gracious dip of her head. "Do remember that our door is always open."

Pansy reached out and caught Isabella's hand. Her grip was surprisingly strong. "Keep your wits about you," she said. "Harrowgate has a way of...taking things."

Viola made a soft sound in her throat, one that might have indicated agreement or disbelief or anything in between.

"Be careful," Pansy whispered and released Isabella's hand.

With that, they turned and walked away. Isabella watched until they disappeared down a dark lane, their footsteps fading into the hush. Pansy's warning hovered around her like mist, clinging to her skin.

The square was deserted, the last whispers of market day long faded. In the distance, a few windows flickered with hearthlight, but the shops around the square stood dark and silent.

A stray gust snatched at the hem of Isabella's cloak. Flexing her fingers inside her gloves, she stamped her feet, feeling the chill seeping through her clothing and boots. The lamps sputtered and smoked.

There was no sign of a cart or carriage, no lantern bobbing in the distance, no sound of approaching wheels, only the faint clatter of hooves far away and the restless sigh of the wind through the empty streets.

She looked again at the lanes that led from the square. If no one came for her, she would need to find lodging for the night. She glanced back at the inn and wondered how long she should wait. A fat fly battered weakly against the wavy glass, its droning thin in the cold.

Standing here alone in the unfamiliar darkness sent an odd sensation digging between her shoulder blades, sharp and intrusive, like a splinter of ice digging beneath her skin.

Pansy's voice seemed to whisper from the shadows. *Keep your wits about you... Harrowgate has a way of taking things.*

Cold scraped the back of her neck. She spun, her skirts twisting around her ankles, her pulse jumping.

No one was there.

She steadied herself, taking in a breath that did not settle easily in her lungs. She was tired, that was all. Tired and uncertain, the disquiet of too much change too quickly. Or perhaps it was the seed of Pansy's warnings taking root, growing sharp-edged in the darkness.

From behind her came the creak of wooden wheels and the soft clop of hooves. She turned to find a small donkey cart rattling into the square. The driver, a stooped man in a patched coat, set her trunks down. Then the cart rattled away, leaving her alone once more, the glow of the oil lamps a paltry sentry against the night. Around her were dim lanes, darkened windows, and silent buildings. With a sigh, Isabella eyed the door of the inn.

Almost did she go inside when hoofbeats carried through the night, slow, deliberate, followed by the metallic jingle of a bridle. A carriage emerged from the dark, its lanterns spilling wavering circles of light, the horses' breath steaming in the cold air as the driver brought them to a halt.

A wiry man with a weathered face climbed down from the driver's seat. His sharp eyes glinted in the lamplight.

His gaze landed on Isabella. "Miss Barrett?"

"Yes," Isabella replied.

"Tom Grange," he said, then he jutted his chin toward her trunks. "Yours?"

"Yes," she said again, watching as he turned to assess her trunks.

Tom's expression remained impassive as he hefted the smaller trunk and strapped it to the back of the carriage. Then he eyed the larger as if it had once wronged him before dragging it toward the carriage with a determination that suggested he had handled worse. With a combination of brute strength and calculated efficiency, he lashed it in place.

Tom handed her into the carriage and closed the door, leaving her alone as he clambered up top. A horse whinnied. The wheels creaked and they set out.

CHAPTER SEVEN

I sabella leaned close to the window, hoping to catch a glimpse of the world beyond, but the night was dark and there was little to see save the black silhouettes of trees and bushes. Every so often, branches arched close enough to scrape against the sides of the carriage, the sound dry and skeletal. The occasional lantern mounted to a post flickered past, fleeting and insubstantial.

In the end, she wedged herself into the corner and endured the jolts and bumps.

The road grew narrower, the surrounding trees pressing closer. After a time, the coach made a sharp turn. Its lamps threw shallow bowls of light to either side, revealing brick columns, their surfaces veined with ivy and moss. The road curved and dipped as they drove along. Isabella thought they had been travelling for about half an hour, which made Harrowgate Manor farther from the village than she had imagined.

Isolated. Solitary. Forgotten.

The trees thinned at last to reveal a clearing, and an enormous house.

Anxiety twisting through her, Isabella leaned forward, her breath fogging the window's glass.

Harrowgate Manor loomed before her, its silhouette stark against the night-black sky. Its high, gabled roof and angular chimneys gave it the appearance of an ancient crouching beast, poised and waiting. Lantern light caught the pale bands of sandstone in its brickwork, but rather than softening the structure, the effect only heightened its cold, unyielding presence.

Two of the six chimneys belched white smoke, pale trails rising like restless spirits. The windows were dark, their shutters closed tight against the wind, several of them nearly obscured by the overgrown ivy that crawled up the walls, its twisted fingers prying into cracks in the mortar, trying to claw its way inside.

Fatigue weighed on her, despite the excitement of arrival. She rubbed her eyes and when she blinked, colors danced before her. For an instant, an orange glow seemed to flood the far windows, as if a great fire raged within. Then it was gone, leaving the panes black and depthless.

The carriage continued along a lane that ran to one side of the house, then around to the back, which was no more welcoming than the front. Here, too, ivy shrouded the walls and the windows were dark.

Once he had brought the carriage to a halt, Tom opened the door and helped her down before rounding to the rear to see about unstrapping her trunks.

The air was thin and cold and still. An icy finger caressed the back of her neck. Frigid breath puffed against her cheek.

Isabella spun, expecting to see a wraith, surprised

when none emerged. The absence made the skin between her shoulders prickle worse than any apparition.

The night pressed close, muffling sound, swallowing light. The house stood in her peripheral vision, and she could not shake the feeling that someone—or something—was watching her.

But there was only Tom Grange, and no other mortal or ghostly companions that she could see. Yet uncanny awareness crawled across her skin like spiders. There were eyes on her, she was certain of it, hungry eyes, hidden from view.

Drawing the edges of her cloak tighter, she tipped her head back and examined the house. There, at the far corner of the third floor, a single candle gleamed in a window. The flame wavered before going still, as though someone had placed a hand to block the light. And then a shadow moved across it...a figure, barely discernible.

Isabella strained to see. The figure lingered for only a moment before the flame was snuffed out, plunging the house back into darkness.

Rhys stood at the upper casement, a candle cupped in his palm. The dark night beyond turned window into mirror, reflecting his own face back at him. For a heartbeat, another shape wavered there, a woman's silhouette, indistinct yet unmistakable, her presence shadowed and foreboding. He pinched the wick between his finger and thumb. The flame died, giving way to a thin stream of smoke that carried the scent of tallow. Somewhere within the walls in the vast runs of flue, a thread of metal shivered in mortar, tinkling like a distant bell. Then came the despised scrape he knew too well, metal on stone, a slow purposeful drag.

Below, a figure stepped into the wash of the carriage lamps, a woman in a dark cloak.

Isabella.

He felt pleasure at just the sight of her, and that shamed him. He had lured her here to use her as he must. It mattered not that his actions were for the dead he loved. He had set the snare and that made him the villain of the tale. But he was a villain with a conscience and if harm came for her, it would need to pass through him first.

Even at this distance, her presence made the ever-present clamor ease, not gone but muffled, its murmur low and patient.

Tom moved to the back of the carriage and set his shoulder to the straps. The smaller trunk came down first with a grunt and a thud. The larger he half-dragged, half-eased down, straining at the task. It was iron-banded and brass-cornered, too heavy for its size.

The tome Rhys sought had not been part of Barrett's collection, not listed in the detailed notes, not hidden in the sealed crates. But perhaps Isabella had brought it with her. She was the key he needed, but the missing half of the grimoire would be a welcome bonus. He would not scavenge through her belongings like a thief; if the grimoire lay there, he would earn it.

Isabella moved into the lantern wash, head tilted back to reveal the pale oval of her face and the vulnerable hollow at the base of her throat where her pulse would lift and race beneath his thumb. Her lips were parted in the cold. He remembered that mouth, wet with rain, as she knelt before him in the mud by her father's grave. Brave girl. Resilient girl.

Desire rose, unbidden. He eased back into the shadows.

Want muddied judgment and fed foolish decisions. But want her, he did.

The wind howled in a frigid burst, clawing at Isabella's skirts and bonnet.

A door creaked open, spilling golden light onto the drive. Then a woman stepped into view, her figure backlit by the glow.

"Miss Barrett? Are you Miss Isabella Barrett?" she called, her voice warm. "Come inside now, lamb. Come inside out of the wind. You must be famished, poor dear. Tom will see to your things. Come along now."

Isabella hurried forward, drawn by the promise of warmth and shelter, propelled by the desire to be away from the suffocating darkness that seemed to cling to her like a shadow.

Once inside, she followed the woman down a long, narrow hallway, boots clacking hollowly against the stone floor.

"I am Mrs. Abernathy," the woman said over her shoulder just as the hallway opened to a large kitchen.

The warmth of the room was immediate, almost smothering after the chill outside. The scent of roasted meat, herbs, and something sweet hung in the air. Bunches of dried rosemary and lavender hung from dark wooden beams that striped the ceiling.

"Sit down, my girl. Sit down." Mrs. Abernathy turned and gestured at the long wooden table that stood to one side. Isabella had her first good look at the housekeeper then. She was a tall woman with a round face and rosebud lips. Tufts of blonde curls escaped her frilled cap and curled around her temples and cheeks. Isabella was surprised to see that she was young, perhaps only five or six years older than Isabella.

But there was something else, something older etched into the lines around her mouth and the set of her shoulders. Mrs. Abernathy looked like a woman who carried her burdens in silence.

"Here is Miss Isabella Barrett," the housekeeper said to someone at Isabella's back, her voice firm and pleasant, as though announcing a guest of importance. "Come from London."

Isabella turned and found four sets of eyes staring back at her. Three of the sets belonged to young women dressed in black twill with white aprons, each wearing a white crochet cap. One set belonged to an older woman who turned to one of the maids and said, "Fetch her plate."

"That's very kind," Isabella said.

The older woman—Isabella thought she must be the cook—grunted in return.

"Pay her no mind," Mrs. Abernathy said lightly. "That's as friendly as Cook gets." She turned to the girls at the table. "Here are Mary and Emma." The other girl set a plate before Isabella. "And this is Peg. On with you, now, girls. Miss Barrett is far too tired to entertain the lot of you tonight."

The expressions that flickered across their faces as they hurried away were something between disappointment and relief. As Isabella watched them go, it struck her that they retreated in silence, no whispers exchanged, no murmurs or laughter, their footsteps soft on the worn floorboards.

"Mr. Caradoc likes a quiet house," Mrs. Abernathy said. "Especially at night. Was that explained to you?"

A flicker of sadness wove through her. Perhaps quiet had become a discipline for him, *institutional* quiet, the kind enforced by keys and seclusion cells. The thought pressed hard against her breastbone, leaving a dull ache within.

"No, but I see no difficulty," Isabella said. "My father liked a quiet house, all the better to read and study." The exception had been when they entertained his contemporaries; then, the conversation had often grown quite lively and boisterous. "I can be quiet as a mouse."

Mrs. Abernathy nodded, but her gaze lingered too long on Isabella, as though weighing her worth, or perhaps her resilience.

Finally, she said, "Will you want the water closet?"

Grateful, Isabella went and performed her ablutions before returning to the table. She sat before the plate of beefsteak pudding and boiled turnips the maid had set out for her, the meal plain but comfortingly warm and filling. Mrs. Abernathy sat on the opposite side of the table while Isabella ate, asking innocuous questions about the journey and London. But the housekeeper was not comfortable. Isabella saw it in the way the woman clasped her hands, in the tone of her voice, and in the way she gnawed on her lower lip.

"Is something amiss?" Isabella asked, recognizing the small languages of worry.

"No...not amiss, not precisely," Mrs. Abernathy said, drawing out each word. "We have a large house but a small household here. There's only Mr. Caradoc and... And the staff. A smallish staff. There's Cook, the three maids you met when you arrived, and Tom Grange. You met him, too."

"The coachman," Isabella said.

"Coachman, groom, stable hand all rolled into one. Oh, and there's Matty. The houseboy."

"And you," Isabella said.

"And me."

Isabella thought of the enormity of the house she had seen from outside, its windows staring down at her like empty eyes, vast and unfeeling. The staff, as described, seemed swallowed whole by the place, too few souls to warm so many cold rooms. Pansy's warnings drifted back to her, weaving a curl of unease through her belly.

"Does Mr. Caradoc have a valet?"

"He does not. There was a footman, Robert Kent, but he left for London a half year ago," Mrs. Abernathy said.

The silence that followed felt heavy, weighted with something unsaid. The fire crackled, and a draft whispered across Isabella's ankles, cold as an ice house floor. The housekeeper pressed her lips together as if holding back words she had not yet decided to set free.

Isabella wondered if those words pertained to the departed footman or to the issue that was "not amiss, not precisely," as the housekeeper would have it. She did not wait long for an answer.

"You see... The thing is..." Mrs. Abernathy drew a deep breath and finished in a rush. "You're an in-between."

"I beg your pardon?"

"An in-between," Mrs. Abernathy said. "You're not quite a servant, but neither are you family or a guest. I didn't quite know where to put you in the order of things, if you take my meaning. I don't know how things are done in London, but we are simple folk here."

Isabella was quiet for a moment. Papa's household had been small and intimate with a level of familiarity with the staff that was uncommon. She was surprised by the housekeeper's admission that she wasn't certain how to proceed. But the genuine concern in Mrs. Abernathy's expression had Isabella hastening to reassure her.

"I have no wish to be set apart. I am an employee, and I will gladly share the duties and table of the household."

"Alone isn't always better," Mrs. Abernathy said softly, almost to herself. Her gaze darted around the room before snapping back to Isabella. The shadows cast by the fire stretched along the walls, long fingers reaching into dim corners.

"Then you don't take it as an affront?" the housekeeper asked. "As I said, I don't know London ways. Never been there. I wasn't certain..."

"I have no London ways," Isabella said. "At this point, I'm merely grateful for the warm welcome, the warm fire" —she gestured at the hearth—"and the warm food."

Mrs. Abernathy smiled a little, the corners of her mouth twitching upward, though the hint of sadness in her eyes did not fade.

"I hope you'll find warmth here in other ways too, Miss Barrett." Her voice was quiet, almost wistful, and Isabella couldn't help but feel as though the housekeeper was speaking of things beyond hearth and home. She gave a decisive nod. "Then you'll have meals with us rather than alone in the dining room."

"Alone?" Isabella said. "Does Mr. Caradoc not eat in the dining room?"

The housekeeper shook her head. "He's never taken a meal there that I've seen. Not in the years I've been here."

A habit spawned by regimented days and nights behind locked doors?

After a moment, Mrs. Abernathy asked, "What were your other posts like?" She pressed her finger to her lips. "Oh, dear. Was that rude? I meant no offense, lamb. I'm just a curious sort."

"I was my father's secretary before he died." Sadness tugged at Isabella's heart as she said the words. It was still difficult to believe he was gone, to think that she would never see him again, never hear his wheezing laugh.

"My mother died when I was ten," Mrs. Abernathy said, covering Isabella's hand with her own. Isabella looked up to find sympathy and kindness in the woman's expression and in that instant, she was glad she had come here, glad she had made this journey.

"Once she was gone, I grew up quick. I saw to my father's small household for many years. When my father died, I married my husband, Mr. Abernathy. Then he died only a month later and I wasn't at all certain what to do. I suspect my circumstance then was like your own now."

Isabella had no need to inquire as to the nature of the circumstance. She was not the first woman to be left without enough funds and few options.

"Mr. Caradoc offered me a place here. As housekeeper. I was far too young and inexperienced for the role, but I learned quickly." Mrs. Abernathy gave a soft laugh. "We're all here with a similar tale. Mary and Emma are sisters. Orphaned. Sixteen and fourteen they were when they started here. Matty's father had a heavy hand. The boy was always sporting a black eye or bruised cheek.

One day, I passed him on the road, both his eyes blackened and him wearing nothing but trousers and shirt in the cold wind. Mentioned it to Mr. Caradoc, I did, and he went off with an angry face and came back with the boy."

"Mr. Caradoc collects strays," Isabella said. The words were neutral but the thoughts and questions behind them were not.

Was it merely happenstance that desperate people lived here, the generous impulse of a man with a conscience? Or did he gather around him only those with nowhere else to go, people whose gratitude could be relied upon, whose dependence on him could not easily be broken? Those who had no one and nothing else, people who would be grateful and beholden to him?

She had no proof of such a motive, but Papa's dislike of the man was not something she could easily forget, and suspicion was a difficult seed to uproot once planted. Nor could she fully discount Pansy's warning...

"Collect strays...I suppose he does," Mrs. Abernathy said with a laugh. She rose and took up a candle before handing a second one to Isabella. "Come along. I'll show you to your room. We'll take one of the servants' staircases tonight only because it's closest. In the morning, I'll show you the house and the main stairs."

"How many servants' staircases are there?"

"Two in the east wing, two in the west wing, and one in the old section to the north but we don't use that one. That part of the house is closed." The housekeeper sent her a speaking glance. "No one goes there. It isn't safe."

Because of the fire. Isabella almost asked about it, then decided again that excessive curiosity was a poor introduction to a new position. She held her tongue and followed the housekeeper along the passage to a staircase. It was narrow and steep, the handrail smooth, the wooden steps worn, creaking under their weight as they began their climb. The darkness was punctured only by the candles they carried, the flames wavering with each step, their glow too weak to banish the suffocating shadows that clung to the corners and ceiling.

They went up a flight and then another. As they climbed, Isabella had the strangest sensation that the wall to the right was moving toward her, that the space grew narrower the higher they went, as if the house was leaning in, listening.

"This way," Mrs. Abernathy said, her voice more a breath than a whisper.

They walked along a wood-paneled hallway, the oak floor covered by a thick runner that made their footsteps muffled and soft. The combined light of their candles made only a small dent in the darkness. The shadows seemed thicker here, like ink stains spreading outward, swallowing all they encountered.

"Why does Mr. Caradoc prefer the quiet?" Isabella asked, her voice low.

Mrs. Abernathy glanced back, her expression unreadable. "He values order," she said after a pause. "He dislikes disruptions." Her gaze flicked forward. "It is a large house. Noise carries."

Her answer felt incomplete, as though she had held back far more than she had revealed. Isabella wondered what sort of disruptions Mr. Caradoc sought to avoid, and what sounds would carry in a house like Harrowgate. She supposed she would find out in time.

Mrs. Abernathy turned down a second hallway, then a third. Isabella tried to memorize the way, thinking she would be hard pressed to find her way back to the kitchen in the morning. Left, then right, then left again...already the turns slipped like quicksilver through her grip.

The third hallway was cold. Isabella glanced about, looking for a window or an open door that might be letting in a chill. But all the doors were closed and there was no window in sight. Her breath hung in a pale cloud as she exhaled and then dissipated as she continued after the housekeeper.

A sound came from behind...footsteps, soft and measured. She glanced back, feeling wary, the fine hairs at her nape prickling, unease pinching her skin. But there was nothing but darkness, thick, oppressive, swallowing every corner and crevice. The absence of any wraith made it all the more unsettling.

"Miss Barrett?" The housekeeper's voice drew Isabella's attention, snapping the thread of her rising unease. She realized that the woman had asked her something and she had neither replied nor heard the question in the first place.

"I'm sorry. I must have been wool gathering," she said.

"There now, lamb. No harm done. You must be exhausted," Mrs. Abernathy said. "Sleeping on your feet with your eyes open. Come along, then."

She turned and continued on, her candle flickering, throwing dark shapes to twist and curl against the wood-paneled walls.

Finally, she stopped before one of the doors and pushed it open. "This one. It has a lovely view of the garden."

Isabella stepped inside. A fire burned in the hearth, and she saw that her trunks were already there. One was

set on the floor at the foot of the bed and the other—
Papa's trunk—was pushed into a corner. The walls were
dark paneled like the hallway, the floor dark wood,
covered in part by a large rug. A heavy armoire stood
against the wall opposite, its surface polished to a dull
gleam, its brass handles glinting in the firelight.

Mrs. Abernathy sidled past her and crossed to the
window, pushing it shut with a firm click.

"That Peg," she said with a sigh. "I told her to air the
room, and she must have forgotten to come back and
close the window." She shook her head. "It's a bit chilly
but the fire should warm it up soon enough."

Isabella set her candle down on a small table by the
bed as Mrs. Abernathy pulled closed the heavy velvet
curtains.

"Is there anything else you need tonight, Miss
Barrett?" the housekeeper asked, turning to face her.

"No, thank you," Isabella said, forcing a weary smile.

"I'll leave you to yourself, then," Mrs. Abernathy said,
her expression softening. She hesitated in the doorway,
her face half-illuminated by candlelight. The shadows
deepened the lines and hollows around her eyes and
mouth, making her look older, wearier, and somehow…
haunted.

"The house is old," she said, her voice low, almost
conspiratorial. "There are drafts and cold places, and the
wind finds its way inside. It can sound like whispers. Like
sighs. But it is only the wind."

Her gaze held Isabella's and the silence stretched
between them.

The wind, Isabella thought, could not explain the
feeling in her chest, the deep and unshakeable sense of
dread.

And Mrs. Abernathy didn't sound as though she believed the wind was the source of the whispers and sighs. Not at all.

"Then this house is much like my home in London. It was full of whispers and sighs," Isabella said, the irony lost on the other woman. "I am certain I will be most comfortable here."

"Sleep well, Miss Barrett."

With a smile, thin and too brief to be comforting, the housekeeper left, closing the door behind her.

Isabella was tempted to curl up on the bed in her dress and close her eyes until morning. Instead, she opened the armoire. The faint scent of lavender wafted from its dark interior. And underlying that, a different smell...something acrid and unpleasant. Memory clung to the edges of her thoughts, just beyond reach. She tried to think why the scent was familiar, and why it forced a chill down her spine. *Limewash and closed rooms. Old pennies. Wet stone.*

She exhaled sharply then drew a slow breath through her nose, only to discover that there was only lavender now. With a shake of her head, she returned to her trunk and began to unpack her belongings, smoothing out each dress before placing it in the armoire. She was just closing the lid of her now-empty trunk when there came a knock at her door.

She opened it to find one of the three maids standing in the hallway, carrying a fresh pitcher of water and a warming pan. The girl was small but sturdy, with bright green eyes, red hair tucked beneath a crooked cap, and freckles scattered across her nose and cheeks. With an awkward bob, the maid said, "Sorry, miss. I forgot to bring these when I made up your room. May I?"

"Of course," Isabella said and pulled the door wide.

The girl set the pitcher on the washstand, then slid the warming pan between the sheets before turning back.

"Are you Peg?" Isabella asked.

"I am. You remembered my name."

She seemed so pleased that Isabella decided against clarifying that it was Mrs. Abernathy's muttering about "that Peg" that had given it away.

Peg's eyes darted around the room, and her teeth sank into her lower lip. Then she offered a stiff smile. "Is there anything else you need, miss?"

"Not that I can think of." Isabella expected her to take her leave. Instead, Peg scuffed her toe against the carpet and chewed on her lower lip once more.

"Are you the sort to walk the halls at night?" she blurted, her voice barely above a whisper. The way she asked the question, accompanied by a wary glance toward the dim hallway, made Isabella wary.

"I do not make a habit of it," Isabella said. "Why do you ask?"

Peg shook her head and crossed to the door. "I'm sorry, miss. I shouldn't have said anything. It's just..."

Isabella waited her out. Either the girl would say what was on her mind or she would not.

Finally, Peg said, "It's this house, this place. You feel it, don't you? The strangeness of it?"

"Strangeness?"

"It isn't right. You walk down a corridor or carry something up the stairs, and the walls feel odd, like they're closing in. Mary and Em don't feel it, but I do. I feel it so strong sometimes I think I might retch. And at night, I hear things. Knocking from inside the walls. Or moans. Or cries." She pressed her lips together, then whispered, "I hear them. And as soon as I saw you, I thought you might hear them, too." She hesitated, then added in a rush, "And if you wake to find the door open when you know for certain you closed it—" She stopped, blanching and shook her head. "Best not to say more."

Isabella stared at her. Never before had she encountered someone who saw the things she saw, heard the things she heard. For a brief, shining instant, she considered trusting this girl with her confessions, sharing the burden of the wraiths that haunted her. The words rose to the back of her teeth, *Yes, I hear them.*

But a level head and years of caution won out. She held her silence and only waited for Peg to say more.

"I don't tell you this to make you upset or afraid," Peg hastened to reassure. "That isn't it at all. I tell you because when you hear it, I want you to know I hear it too, and I've been here nigh on a year and nothing bad has happened to me. Sometimes it does scare me." She shook her head and offered a small smile. "But my mam always said that ghosts aren't really here and even if they were, they couldn't hurt you. Only being afraid of them can do that."

The girl fell silent and after a moment, bobbed an awkward curtsey and edged toward the door.

"Peg," Isabella said.

The maid stopped in the doorway and looked back at her over her shoulder.

"Thank you for telling me about..." Isabella pressed her lips together. "I won't be afraid."

Peg offered a wavery smile, nodded once, and slipped out, closing the door with a soft click.

The quiet that followed felt heavy, leaden. The fire's

embers glowed in the hearth, battling the cold and the creeping dark that pooled in the corners like black treacle.

The armoire loomed, its polished surface reflecting a smudgy, distorted version of Isabella's face, the warped image bending and swaying with each flicker of the flames. Her gaze slid to the dark gap between the doors. She could have sworn something shifted within.

Pansy's words slid through her thoughts. *Keep your wits about you... Harrowgate has a way of taking things.*

From somewhere deep within the house, carrying through the walls, came a faint, deliberate knocking. Three measured beats, then silence.

Isabella turned a slow circle, trying to determine the direction of the sound.

It came again, closer now, a little louder. *Knock. Knock. Knock.*

Her skin prickled, the fine hairs on her arms lifting. She strained to hear it again, but the silence was heavy and absolute, thrumming in her skull.

Still, she felt it, the certainty that somewhere in this vast, cold house something had stirred, something that knew she was here.

CHAPTER EIGHT

Isabella lay still, her breathing shallow, her eyes open to the heavy dark. Something had woken her...

There. A sound. A deep, resonant scrape of metal across stone.

The sheets, which had been warmed by the pan when she had climbed between them, cocooned her in the scent of clean linen and lavender. At some point, her candle had guttered out and the fire had burned low, leaving only a scatter of glowing coals in the hearth. Shadows pooled thick in the corners of the room, shifting with the uneven flicker.

The sound came again, harsh and grating, reverberating through the house.

She pushed back the covers. The cold in the room felt wrong, unnatural, piercing her skin and muscle, surging deep to scrape at her lungs. Her wrap hung over the end of the bed, and she drew it tight around herself as she rose, tying it at her waist with stiff fingers.

Crossing the room, she then pulled back the heavy drapes, allowing silvery moonlight to spill across the bed,

the armoire, the dark-paneled walls. The shadows sharpened their teeth.

There, again...the sound, harsh and grating.

Don't listen. Don't answer. Her father's voice echoed in
her mind.

Isabella's hand froze on the edge of her wrap. How
many times had Papa warned her? How many times had
she feigned blindness, feigned deafness, while the wraiths
brushed her skin with fingers of frost and whispered their
spider silk words in her thoughts?

But ignoring them never made them vanish. Ignoring
them had never stopped their burning eyes from
watching her, their icy breath from chilling her skin,
their whispers from curling around her like gossamer
webs.

The rasping scrape carried through the stillness,
closer now, louder, nothing like the whispers she had
grown accustomed to all these years. This felt different.
Frightening.

She squeezed her eyes shut. She should crawl back
into bed, pull the sheets over her head and shut out the
world until morning light bled pale gold across the room.

But she could not.

She knew that Papa had meant the very best for her,
but he had been wrong. Acknowledging the wraiths
didn't make them appear and ignoring them didn't keep
them away. They came whether she wanted them or not.
And if she ignored them, they only grew bolder.

Heart pounding, she relit her candle and crossed to
the door. The corridor stretched before her, lit only by a
streak of silver moonlight slicing through a high window
at the far end.

She hesitated, her breath coming in shaky rasps. *If you*

follow them, Isabella, they will only take you deeper into the dark.

But the sound, deep, grating, impossible to ignore, pulled at her. She thought of an iron poker dragged against the stone of a hearth but could not say why that particular image came to her.

Breath fogging in the cold air, footsteps barely a whisper against the carpet, she stepped forward.

Then the house fell still, silence descending, heavy and watchful.

Almost did she turn back. Almost.

But that would mean hearing the sound again tomorrow night, or the night after, until she finally answered the summons. Better to choose to pass the threshold now than be dragged across it against her will.

And so, she walked on.

She turned a corner, then another. She let her fingertips drift along the wall, guiding her, the rise and dip of doorframes marking entryways to locked rooms. Each knob held fast.

The corridor grew narrower, the walls closing in, leaning toward her.

It is not real, she told herself. But it felt real.

Icy breath drifted across her nape. A whisper of laughter, high and childish, danced at the edges of hearing. She smelled roses, sweetly floral with just a hint of honey.

Isabella turned and froze.

A girl stood at the far end of the hallway, her slight frame swallowed by an oversized nightgown tied with thin, pink satin ribbons. Pale hair hung in damp, tangled strands, spilling over her narrow shoulders. Her eyes, too large for her delicate face, fixed on Isabella with unblinking intensity.

The girl did not move. Not even the hem of her night-gown stirred in the draft that sighed along the floor.

She was no wraith, for her form was as solid as Isabel-la's own.

Isabella took a cautious step forward, her pulse thrumming like the wings of a moth caught in a spider's web. "Hello?"

The question was greeted by silence.

She was no servant; Isabella was fairly certain of that. The gown was fine, the fabric delicate and expensive, yet...*wrong* somehow.

The girl's pale face gleamed in the moonlight, her expression vacant, eyes dark and endless as she stared at Isabella with an eerie intensity, her head tipped to one side.

"Do you need help?" Isabella asked, taking another step forward, an uncomfortable wariness crawling through her. "Are you lost?"

The girl's head twitched sharply, a convulsive move-ment, the angle unnatural, like a doll's head knocked loose. Isabella's pulse stuttered. A small, thin sound escaped the girl's lips, not a word or even a moan, just... breath.

"Who are you?" Isabella whispered, every instinct screaming that something was terribly wrong.

The girl blinked slowly and took a single step forward, the movement odd and stiff, disjointed, as though her limbs argued the command of her mind.

Isabella's breath caught. The cold deepened, sharp as thorns against her skin.

She saw now the dark halo surrounding the girl's form, writhing like oil slicking across water.

And then she knew. Impossibly, the girl was a *wraith*,

though unlike any she had encountered before. Solid. Dangerous.

A sudden, wind howled down the hallway, kettle-hot, breathy with ash and scorched oak, whipping Isabella's hair across her eyes. Heat scored her cheeks and the backs of her hands.

As if a grate had been flung open and a bellows put to work, the sounds of a fire raged around her, quick, greedy crackles and pops and snaps accenting a gathering roar. A rippling wave of scorching air stole her breath.

The flame of her candle sheared flat, then clawed upright once more, hissing and spitting.

In the next instant, the heat was gone. The sounds and smells and horror of the fire were gone.

And the girl was gone.

The corridor stretched before her, empty, silent.

The air was thin with cold, heavy with the scent of metal and rot. Somewhere close, something tapped inside the wall. *Tap...tap...tap.*

Isabella's heart thundered. She had seen wraiths all her life, but never one like that, never one that looked so real, as if it could step fully into the world.

She stumbled forward, desperate to escape this place, to return to her room, to what paltry sanctuary it might offer. Her heel caught on the edge of the carpet. With a startled cry, she fell, bracing for the impact—

But she never hit the floor.

A hand caught her wrist.

Warm. Solid.

She looked up into the shadowed face of Rhys Caradoc. His hair, dark and thick and sleek, framed his face. The moonlight painted his bare shoulders in silver, the hard planes of his chest rising and falling with slow, measured breaths.

"Miss Barrett," he murmured, his voice low and smooth, the sound wrapping around her like a cocoon of velvet and silk.

She stared at him, stunned, unsteady, her pulse tripping violently. He yet held her wrist, his hand warm, his body close, the faint rasp of his breath stirring against her temple.

"Mr. Caradoc!" she whispered, the sound barely more than a breath. For a heartbeat, she saw him not here in this corridor, but in another place, trapped behind iron bars and wired glass. She pushed the vision away and gathered herself. "It seems you are always catching me when I fall."

She meant to look away, to compose herself, to remember that she was alone in the dark with a man she barely knew, a man who was only half-dressed and standing entirely too close.

But her gaze betrayed her, tracing the dusting of dark hair on his chest, the hollow that marked the center of his throat. She imagined the pulse there, steady against her lips if she but dared to lean in, to press her mouth—

Heat flashed through her, and something clenched low in her belly. She jerked her gaze away, stunned by her own wayward thoughts, unsure what had elicited such an uncharacteristic desire.

"What are you doing wandering the halls at this hour?" he asked, his tone quiet, intimate.

She swallowed, her throat dry.

"I..." She could not tell him about the wraith she had seen. The entrenched caution of a lifetime stayed her tongue.

He would think her mad. Of course he would.

Oh, the bitter irony. She could neither ask what madness had once confined him to St. Jude's, nor reveal her own.

Years of her father's warnings rang in her ears, yet another reason to keep her secrets.

"I could not sleep," she said, wondering if he would challenge her lie.

He did not. He only studied her in the darkness, his fingers still wrapped around her wrist, the sound of her breathing too loud in her ears.

After a moment, she tugged against his grip. He set her free, his thumb grazing the inside of her wrist, lingering there for a breath too long, the touch so slight she might have imagined it.

"You could not sleep," he said softly. "A situation in which I find myself quite often." His lips twitched, though the movement never quite became a smile. "And so you sought...what, precisely? A midnight stroll?"

There was no censure in his tone, no mockery, only a quiet curiosity that felt more disconcerting than any accusation.

"I heard something," she whispered.

He exhaled through his nose, a sound partway between amusement and resignation. "This house is filled with strange sounds, Miss Barrett. It groans, it whispers, it shudders and clanks. May I suggest that you not chase after every sound you hear?"

She should have felt chastised, cowed. Instead, she felt *angry*—angry at his dismissiveness, angry at his effortless calm while she still felt as though her skin was stretched too tight over her bones. Worse, she felt a spark

of something sharp and enticing, as though his very indif-
ference dared her to provoke him.

"In future, I will be sure to chase only those noises
that promise certain danger," she said, acerbic. "What is
the point of wandering in the night if there is no threat?"

His huff of laughter was low and warm. Unsettling.

"I, too, wander when I cannot sleep," he said, then
glanced down at himself before meeting her eyes once
more, his expression sardonic. "I had not expected to
meet anyone in my nocturnal wanderings, or I would
have dressed with more formality. Please excuse the state
in which I find myself."

His words only served to draw her attention to his
naked skin, the ridges of his belly, the thin, dark trail of
hair that descended—

Pressing her lips together, she dragged her gaze away.

He took a step closer. The scent of his skin teased her,
a clean hint of citrus and...mint. It felt illicit to breathe it
in; even so, she did, letting the scent stroke her senses.

Her mouth grew dry, her pulse racing.

She took a hasty step back.

"Come," he said, his voice low, his gaze locked on
hers. "I will take you back to your room."

"No need." She shook her head, stepping away.

He watched her, expectant, amused.

"No need? Then please lead the way, Miss Barrett."

She edged around him and paused as she took in the
hallway, trying to remember how she had arrived at this
spot. Finally, she took an awkward, sliding step to the
right.

His voice was a low murmur behind her. "Other way."

She turned, her movements rigid.

Without another word, he led her through the darkened corridors. As they walked, her senses betrayed her, focusing on the subtle sway of his gait, the faint rasp of linen over his hips, the warmth radiating from him in the cold dark. She was acutely aware of everything about him, his height, the breadth of his shoulders, the muscles of his back shifting beneath his skin as he moved. His state of undress. She had never seen a man without his shirt.

Oh, she had read Papa's books of anatomy, seen the drawings therein, but nothing had prepared her for this.

Rhys Caradoc was...beautiful.

As they turned down yet another hallway, her shoulder bumped his arm. He made no indication that he even noticed. But *she* noticed, her skin tingling beneath her wrap.

Her pulse beat a frantic rhythm, her every sense painfully aware of him in the velvet-dark corridor, that unfamiliar twist low in her belly gnawing at her like hunger.

When they reached her door, he turned to her, his gaze lingering on her face. The shadows softened the hard lines of his jaw, but his eyes, those piercing gray eyes, held an intensity that made her stomach flutter.

"Why did you buy my father's collection?" she asked, both because she wanted the answer and because she wanted to prolong their moment together. "Are you an antiquarian?"

If he was surprised by her questions, uttered here in the dim corridor while they stood improperly close, he made no indication.

"The answer to the second question is no," he said. "The answer to the first is that I wanted to gain his good favor."

"Because you wanted something from him." Her

thoughts drifted to the key around her neck. It lay beneath her bodice against her skin, the metal cold. "You wanted his private collection. How disappointed you must have been when those books were not included in the material you purchased. Doubly disappointed when he refused to part with them that day when you came to call."

Mr. Caradoc took a step closer. His shadow swallowed her, the air between them crackling until she could feel the whisper of his breath on her cheek.

"I know only what I received," he said. "If there was something your father kept apart...something uncata-logued...I have no direct knowledge of it." He paused. "Do you?"

Isabella stiffened. "No," she said, too quickly. The lie felt brittle on her tongue.

He tilted his head, watching her with an unsettling calm. "Next time you hear something in the night," he murmured, "stay in your room."

The warning in his tone sent a shiver down her spine. And then, before she could reply, he leaned in and tucked a stray lock of hair behind her ear, his knuckles grazing the angle of her jaw, his fingertips lingering at the sensitive skin just beneath her earlobe. The world narrowed to that single point of contact. The warmth of his touch combined with the way he looked at her sent heat spiraling through her veins.

She swayed toward him.

They were separated by mere inches, his gaze fixed on her mouth in a way that made her edgy and nervous, wanting...no, *needing* something she could not name.

Her pulse raced. Her lips parted. She couldn't breathe, couldn't think. He filled her senses. The heat of his body, the rough texture of his fingertips, the weight of his gaze—

He stepped back.

"Goodnight, Miss Barrett," he said.

A small bow. A turn.

And then he was gone, swallowed by the darkness.

Isabella stood there for a long moment, forcing her ragged breathing under control. She entered her room and closed the door behind her then pressed her forehead against the wood, her body trembling, not with fear or cold, but something else, something unfamiliar and exciting. Desire, she thought. It pricked her like pins from the inside. Confusion lapped at its edges.

She made a soft, shaky laugh, unsure which haunted her more, the wraith or the man who had walked her through the shadowed dark.

A buzz drew her glance to the floor. A crisped fly lay on the rug at her feet, its wing giving one last brittle flutter before falling still.

Rhys strode along the dark corridor, the feel of Isabella's skin lingering in his palm like a brand. With each step away from her, the thin, needling susurrus he had learned to endure crawled back into his ears. But the noise was a pale imitation of itself, as if someone had draped wet muslin over a violin and bid it play. Just having her in the house made the hum bearable but *touching* her made the sound weak and toothless.

He told himself that was the reason his pulse had stumbled when she swayed toward him, the only reason his thumb had found the hollow beneath her ear and rested there as if it belonged.

He had meant to keep his distance. He had meant a hundred sensible things.

She had looked at him, a proper little scholar with a straight spine and threadbare wrapper. She had *seen* him and not looked away. That had surprised him, as had the truth of it: desire arrived not as a blaze but as recognition, the clean, undeniable sort a man feels when a key finds the lock he's been turning bloody for years. He dismissed the metaphor before it could fully form. She was not a key, not a tool to be used. She was a woman who did not flinch.

And he was a man who had already decided what he must ask of her, how he must use her, though she deserved better.

At his door, he stilled, recalling the round, steady drum of her pulse beneath the delicate bones of her wrist when he'd held it. Had he not released her, the chorus might have stilled altogether. A seductive thought. A dangerous one. A man might do unforgivable things for quiet.

A child's cry carried from inside the wall, a thin warble that might have been his name. Or not. The sound was tinny with distance, heavy with despair. Another cry followed, a woman's wrenching sob that sat heavy on his heart. Then the scrape came low along the skirting, nails on stone, chasing the others away, sharpening itself on his regrets.

He opened the door and stepped inside. The fire had fallen to red embers and ash. On the table lay a half-sorted sheaf of notes...dates, marginalia, the diagram he had sketched of a half-circle and its broken twin. Two halves, the grimoire had stated.

Two willing halves joined, and the gate would open.

Two halves, one of them a living conductor that could reach into the ethereal place not quite of this world when the gate began to sing.

He had chased that promise—the promise of freedom for the souls of those he loved—through ink and rumor until it had brought him to a man in London and the man's daughter who steadied a haunted house simply by being in it.

As he set the papers in order, he made a silent vow. He would keep her safe and he would have what he needed of her. Both truths could live in the same space. He could keep her here, arrange her circumstances so leaving felt unthinkable, pay her well and call it mercy, pretending all the while that he was not the villain in this tale.

"She is staying," he said aloud, and only then allowed himself to acknowledge the truth. He wanted Isabella Barrett for more reasons than he cared to admit. And if he could keep his hands from her, if he could do what needed to be done, then the weeping in these walls would at last go quiet for good.

CHAPTER NINE

The air carried the faint scent of smoke and ash, the last remnants of the fire that had burned itself out during the night. The morning light crept through the narrow crack in the heavy curtains, painting thin, bright lines that stood out like scars on the dark wood floor and the carpet that covered it.

Isabella sat on the edge of the bed, her dark hair tumbling in loose waves over her shoulders, her nightgown pooling around her legs. She had tossed and turned after returning to her room, falling asleep only in the early hours.

The events of the night before clung to her still.

The girl. A wraith unlike any she had previously encountered, too solid, too real.

The man. Rhys Caradoc. Barefoot. Half-dressed. His voice like brandy poured over gravel. His eyes, gray as a winter sky, fringed in black curling lashes, lingering on her face, making her pulse race.

Her body remembered the press of his fingers against her wrist, the graze of his knuckles below her ear, the heat of his touch before he had released her. He had stood so close she had breathed in the scent of his skin, a clean bite of citrus over linen.

Her reaction disarmed her, confused her. The racing of her pulse. The unfamiliar dryness in her mouth. The yearning ache that had unfurled deep in her belly. Dark. Thrilling.

She did not know what she might become beneath his gaze, beneath his touch, and that not knowing was its own peril.

With a sharp breath, she pushed herself to her feet. Enough of this. She was not some schoolgirl mooning over a beau.

The faint ache in her legs told her she had been tense even in sleep, every muscle drawn tight like a piano wire. She exhaled then drew a deep, slow breath, forcing her lungs to expand, using the moment to remind herself that she was still here, still herself, still in control of her own body and choices despite the man who made her feel unmoored. She held her breath, counting to four as she had when Papa's hands had shaken and she had needed to be the steady one.

Her gaze flicked toward the heavy velvet curtains, and she crossed the room to pull them open. Daylight spilled in, revealing a room that now seemed so ordinary, stripped of last night's shadows and secrets. The walls were paneled in dark oak, carved with intricate designs of vines, flowers, and leaves. The heavy armoire loomed in one corner, its polished surface reflecting her pale face back at her, warped at the edges. For a heartbeat, the reflection appeared to double, like two versions of herself occupying the same place, before merging into a single image once more.

Her gaze drifted across the large four-poster bed with its thick canopy and heavy drapes. A dark blue and gold rug stretched beneath her feet, its pattern faded and threadbare in places, worn away by countless footsteps.

And there, against the farthest wall, stood her father's trunk, its brass fittings glinting. The keyhole was a dark mystery, waiting...waiting.

Not today. The thought clanged like a gong.

The weight of the key against her chest was like an anchor, heavy and unyielding, cold as frost. But she was not ready to know. Not yet. Maybe she never would be. She thought of Papa, kneeling by the trunk, books and manuscripts scattered all around him, desperation a thick cloud sitting on his shoulders. There was nothing good to be found in that trunk.

Shaking off the seedlings of a sour mood, she went to the window and pressed her palm against the glass, her breath fogging the cold surface.

In the distance, the gentle rise and fall of hills rolled out toward the horizon, their edges swathed in morning mist. Below her was the garden. Once, it must have been a marvel, an ordered labyrinth of beauty. Now, it lay in disarray, vines creeping like dark veins, rose bushes grown wild and untamed, symmetrical green grass paths stretching between squared hedges and shrubs, their shapes undone by years of neglect. Stone statues leaned at odd angles, features softened by moss, eyes watching.

Isabella lingered for a moment longer, her fingertips against the cold glass, then she drew away and turned back to the room.

There was no going back. Not to her father's study, not to the life she had known.

She dressed, her gown of black wool warm against her

skin, then she rolled her hair into a loose knot at her nape. A glance in the looking glass revealed pale cheeks and purple shadows beneath her brown eyes, but nothing more. No wraiths with burning pits for eyes, no translucent hands reaching for her.

Still there was something about the reflection that did not feel like her own. For the briefest moment, she thought the glass rippled, as though it were a deep, dark pond and something had shifted below the surface. She blinked, and the illusion was gone. Gone...or hiding.

Isabella turned away from the mirror, wrapping her arms around herself before squaring her shoulders, resolute. She would carve out a place for herself here. She would build a life.

But first, breakfast.

She opened the door with confidence, but as she stepped into the hallway, doubt began to creep in. The manor's hallways were an unforgiving maze, their corners sharp, their lengths shadowed even in daylight, the air smelling of beeswax and old smoke.

Isabella hesitated at the first junction. Left, or right? Each direction seemed equally unfamiliar, equally uninviting. The paneled walls and faded tapestries gave no hints, no guidance. The echoes of her own soft footsteps followed her as she chose the left corridor.

She paused again at a fork in the hall, pressing the tip of her tongue against the backs of her teeth. She should have paid more attention when Mrs. Abernathy led her upstairs last night. A pang of irritation flared within her, at herself, at the manor, at the way these halls seemed to still and listen, leaning toward her as though cupping an ear.

Determined to find her way, she was relieved to find

the servants' stairs, surely the same ones she had ascended the previous night. She followed them down and then the clink of porcelain and the low murmur of voices reached her ears proving she had chosen the correct path after all.

She turned toward the sound, her skirts brushing against her boots with every step. The scent of eggs and toasted bread grew stronger as she rounded another corner. Her stomach answered with a mortifying growl.

At last, she saw the wide doorway to the kitchen, the warm glow of firelight spilling out like a golden beacon into the dim hallway.

Peg stood by the entryway, wiping her hands on her apron. The maid's head snapped up when she saw Isabella, her round face brightening.

"Oh, miss! I was just about to come fetch you," Peg said, bobbing an awkward curtsey. "Mrs. Abernathy said you might not remember the way."

Isabella offered a faint smile. "I managed, eventually. With only one or two wrong turns," she said, lighter than she felt.

Peg gestured for Isabella to enter.

The warmth hit her immediately, along with the thick scent of bread, the crackle of the fire, the faint sweetness of boiled eggs. Isabella felt her shoulders relax.

Mrs. Abernathy stood by the hearth, speaking softly with Cook, who stirred something in a copper pot. The housekeeper glanced over her shoulder as Isabella entered, her expression softening into a smile.

"Good morning, Miss Barrett. You must be chilled half to the bone wandering those halls. You've surprised us all by finding your way. Took me a week when I first arrived before I stopped feeling lost at every turn. Come and sit, lamb. I'm fair certain you're famished."

Breakfast was a quiet meal of tea, bread, and boiled eggs taken in the company of Mrs. Abernathy, Cook, and the three maids. Tom Grange and the boy, Matty, had already breakfasted. As conversation flowed around her, Isabella listened more than she spoke, the small jokes and easy rhythm of the women's interactions setting her at ease.

Peg and Mary teased Emma about lingering too long at the scullery door when the butcher's boy made his delivery. Cheeks red, Emma sputtered denials until Cook rapped the table with her spoon to restore order. Mrs. Abernathy shook her head and rolled her eyes at Isabella, drawing her into the moment.

Isabella had never been part of such easy warmth. Papa's tiny staff had always been unfailingly kind to her, but kindness was not the same as inclusion. She had always been solitary by nature and circumstance. Here, the rhythm of voices overlapped, teasing and familiar, the sound of women who trusted and liked each other. A fragile sense of belonging brushed against her.

As they finished their meal, Mrs. Abernathy turned to Peg. "Run up to the press and fetch clean kitchen cloths." She glanced at Isabella. "And take Miss Barrett along. She ought to know every way through the house."

Isabella blinked at being included, but she was glad of it. The house's passageways tangled like knotted threads, and the chance to learn another staircase felt like seizing a strand to follow.

Peg rose and smoothed her apron, then led the way to a set of stairs Isabella had not seen before. They climbed, the way narrow and steep.

Halfway up, a hollow knock reverberated from inside the wall. Peg stopped short, clutching the banister. The air grew heavy and damp, the walls leaning and shadows swelling until it felt like the entire staircase was collapsing in on them.

Again, came the knock, louder, nearer.

Peg squared her shoulders and whispered under her breath, "Iron to bind. Hearth to keep. Shadows hush. Spirits sleep."

She repeated the words, her voice steadier the second time.

"What is that?" Isabella asked.

Peg glanced back at her over her shoulder. "A charm my mam taught me when I was little more than a babe." She gave a small nod. "It works, too," she said.

Then she drew a long breath and resumed climbing.

Isabella followed, silent but thoughtful. She had never before seen someone else meet fear in the same fashion she did, not by pretending it was nothing but by pushing back against it with whatever tools she possessed. Peg had her rhyme. Perhaps that was enough.

After they returned with the folded cloths, Mrs. Abernathy gave Isabella a brief tour of the house, or rather, the parts of it that were "safe" for her to see. Drawing rooms and parlors, the dining room, corridors lined with faded portraits and sconces. But not the north wing.

The tour ended before a tall, arched double door at the far end of a dimly lit hallway. Heavy curtains veiled a narrow window nearby, muting the daylight and casting elongated shadows across the carpet. Cobwebs hung in the corners, testament to her suspicion that the small staff could not possibly maintain a house this size at its best.

"The library, Miss Barrett," Mrs. Abernathy said with a faint smile. "Mr. Caradoc instructed me to leave you to your work here. He trusts you'll know where to begin."

The doors were grand, but the corridor leading to them felt oddly neglected, as though the library had been pushed away from the heart of the house, exiled to this forgotten corner where the chill seemed sharper, the silence deeper.

"The north wing lies just beyond this wall," Mrs. Abernathy said. "Sometimes I imagine I can smell the smoke through stone and mortar."

"I have read that smoke binds to the resin in wood," Isabella said. "It can be trapped there for decades, released anew with every change of weather."

Mrs. Abernathy glanced at her. "So not my imagination, after all."

She reached down to her chatelaine where a collection of keys hung heavily from one of the chains. The faint jingle of metal against metal cut sharply through the quiet corridor as her fingers selected a key from the crowded cluster, her movements careful and deliberate.

For a moment, she simply held it, turning it between her fingers, her expression contemplative.

"Here we are," she murmured at last, holding up a long, blackened key with an ornate bow shaped like a serpent eating its own tail.

"Ouroboros," Isabella said.

The housekeeper sent her a questioning glance.

"An Ouroboros is a serpent eating its own tail. It is a symbol from ancient Egypt."

"Is it?" Mrs. Abernathy studied the key. "What's it a symbol of?"

"Eternity," Isabella said softly. "But eternity is only a

circle that devours itself. My father found references in old texts that said it marks completion, warding, a safe ring where nothing escapes."

"What is safe for the living can be a prison for the dead. Imagine being trapped in the in between, unable to escape," the housekeeper murmured, then gave a start, as if her own words distressed her.

Isabella made no reply, thinking that the wraiths were trapped exactly like that. Memory flared of herself at fifteen, pointing out the symbol to Papa. "Life feeds on death and makes more life," she had said, bold with theory. "Ghosts are where the bite halts, where the circle cannot close. Break the ring, open the smallest gap, and the restless will slip from repetition into rest—"

Papa's pen had jerked, blotting the page. "Hush. Do not speak of such things, Isa." His eyes had begged her silence. She had still been learning then. *Never say it. Never show it.* Papa was adding a new rule to the list. Never speak of it, even obliquely, even in philosophical terms.

Now she said gently, "Continuity, Mrs. Abernathy. Beginnings swallow endings and turn them into beginnings again."

The housekeeper turned the key in her palm, thoughtful. "A comfort, put that way."

She slid it into the library door's lock, the metal scraping softly before the mechanism gave way with an audible click.

The doors groaned as they swung inward, revealing a cavernous room beyond. A draft rose to meet them, dry as sand, carrying the scent of dust and neglect.

Mrs. Abernathy hesitated for just a heartbeat, just long enough for Isabella to take note.

"There you are, Miss Barrett," she said.

Isabella stepped across the threshold into the library. Mrs. Abernathy did not join her.

When Isabella glanced back at her over her shoulder, she had the odd impression that the woman was listening for something. The housekeeper's gaze flicked to the lintel, then Isabella's eyes, then away.

"Well," she said softly. "I will leave you to it."

With a nod, she turned and walked away, the heavy ring of keys clinking as she turned the corner at the end of the corridor.

Isabella stepped deeper into the library's waiting gloom. Inside, the air felt heavier, as though it carried centuries of secrets trapped between the rows of towering shelves.

The room stretched vast and hollow, its corners lost to shadow. The floor was laid with wide planks of ancient English oak, the brown surface darkened over the centuries to near black, the rich patina lending a sense of silent grandeur. High windows, partially veiled by brocade curtains, let in thin slashes of light.

Shelves climbed toward the arched ceiling. To Isabella's surprise, they were mostly empty. A thick coating of dust had settled in the vacant spaces where books had once rested.

Against one wall sat dozens of crates, lids pried open and leaning, nails half drawn, straw spilling across the carpet. Volumes lay strewn across the floor or perched precariously in disordered piles. Papa's collection, rifled in haste.

On a side table was a deliberate heap: Agrippa's *Occult Philosophy*; Barrett's *The Magus*; Kircher's *Ars Magna Lucis et Umbrae*; pamphlets on angelic alphabets and natural sympathies. The pile included only titles that touches on the supernatural. She knew every spine at a glance. All were part of Papa's collection, as were the books left on the floor in disrespectful disarray.

Anger rose beneath her ribs at such rough handling, bright as a blade.

Had Mr. Caradoc created this mess himself? Or had someone else unpacked the collection, someone unfamiliar with the delicate nature of aged tomes? Instinct bid her immediately begin setting all to rights, but practicality made her finish assessing her surroundings first. She could not put the books on the dusty shelves and packing them back into the crates only to unpack them once more after she had properly cleaned the room would be a ridiculous waste of her time.

A lone desk sat at the far end, angled toward one of the tall, arched windows. A straight-backed chair waited beside it, its wooden seat worn smooth, the armrests polished to a subtle shine from years of human touch.

The desk bore evidence of recent occupation. A leather-bound ledger lay closed, a crimson ribbon marking an unseen page within. Scattered papers, their edges bearing smudges of ink, rested like fragile wings across the polished surface. Beside them sat an empty glass decanter, the bottom stained amber, and a tumbler etched with faint fingerprints.

Isabella approached, dust motes dancing around her. Her fingertips grazed the desk's surface, leaving trails in the layer of dust. The scent of leather and aged paper filled her senses, mingling with something very faint, something that made her pulse quicken...citrus and mint.

Her hand hovered over the closed ledger, her index finger brushing lightly against the crimson ribbon. A flicker of temptation curled through her. What secrets lay bound within these pages?

They were not her secrets to know.

A glimmer of metal caught her eye. Nestled in the corner of the desk, almost hidden behind the pile of papers was a small, ornate box.

Isabella lifted it, its weight surprising in her hand.

The box was rectangular, its brass surface tarnished in places. She turned it this way and that, examining the etchings carved into its surface. They were sharp and intricate, winding along the edges and curling around the keyhole at the front like coiling serpents. At each corner, a scarab was engraved, wings splayed open, tiny eyes almost lifelike. A central motif dominated the lid, a sun disk flanked by two uraei— cobras rising tall and regal with their hoods flared. The craftsmanship was exquisite, the details impossibly fine.

Her breath hitched. The scarabs. The serpents. So familiar.

Closer now, she saw a maker's mark, no wider than a thumbnail: a tiny bee in a cartouche, *T and S* stamped beneath. She knew that mark. It hid on the escutcheon of Papa's trunk. *Thorn and Sons, Ludgate Hill.* She remembered filings in the carpet when Papa had the lock replaced, and the locksmith saying he would cut the wards to match the key.

Her free hand rose to her collarbone, her fingertips grazing the hidden key resting beneath her dress. Slowly, she drew the chain over her head, letting Papa's key dangle before her eyes.

The bow was circular, decorated with an engraved Eye of Horus at its center, the lines impossibly delicate. The shaft was etched with tiny spirals that echoed the same sinuous shapes carved into the brass of the box.

The similarities were unmistakable.

Papa's key appeared to match this box in Rhys Caradoc's library. It was possible enough; warded locks were often cut to common patterns. Still, the coincidence made her pulse count out a warning.

Almost did she slip the key into the waiting lock, almost did she turn it and let whatever secrets lay hidden within spill free.

But the creak of a floorboard in the corridor startled her, followed by the shuffle of steps as though someone lingered just beyond the door. Her breath caught, the box balanced in her hand. In that suspended instant, the metal warmed against her skin, eager, waiting.

Then, with a prudence Pandora had lacked, she carefully set the box back onto the desk. The metal kissed the wood with a soft, decisive thud.

The key, she tucked back beneath her dress, where it lay heavy and cold against her skin.

She turned instead to the drawers. Their handles were tarnished brass, shaped like curling ivy leaves. She pulled at the first drawer, its resistance giving way with a reluctant scrape.

Inside, she found what one might expect in a desk: an assortment of neatly arranged quills, ink pots with dried rings staining their bases, brittle sheets of unused parchment. The smell of ink and aged wood rose to meet her, familiar and soothing. There was nothing unusual here, nothing secretive.

Closing the drawer, she then moved to the next, driven not merely by curiosity, but by a vivid certainty that there was something to find. Inside the drawer was a collection of ledgers bound in cracked leather, the edges stained with use, the spines marked with faded lettering. Accounts. Inventories.

The third drawer was slightly off kilter in its frame, the handle loose, splintered at the edge as though it had been wrenched open in haste at some point. The drawer slid free with a reluctant groan, protesting her intrusion. Inside was a stack of correspondence in an untidy pile.

The topmost letter caught her attention. Her father's handwriting slanted across the page. She froze.

Reaching into the drawer, she fanned the pile and saw that there were several letters written in Papa's distinctive hand. The fine hairs on the back of her neck prickled and rose.

The letters she had discovered in Papa's desk had been letters *from* Rhys Caradoc. These must be Papa's replies.

She unfolded the first.

Sir,

I must once again decline your invitation and your offer. Whatever it is you believe I possess, or whatever qualities you perceive in my daughter, I assure you they are of no value to you.

My daughter is a good girl. She is innocent, kind, and with no knowledge of the darkness that shadows this world. Her delicate health will not permit a move, nor would I wish her burdened by further strain. I must therefore implore you to cease your inquiries and to refrain from contacting us again.

I trust this will be the end of the matter.

Yours faithfully,

Thomas Barrett

The ink had smudged near the end, and Isabella could almost see her father's hand trembling as he'd signed his name. The hint of a thumbprint ghosted the margin. Her throat tightened. Whatever her father had been protecting her from, it had been enough to rattle him, enough to make him refuse Rhys Caradoc, a man who clearly did not accept refusal lightly.

And yet, in this at least, it seemed Mr. Caradoc had not lied. Papa *had* claimed her health would not allow him to accept the position.

She reached for another letter, this one shorter, more desperate, its ink uneven as though written in haste.

Sir,

You must cease this at once. You have no understanding of what it is you ask, and if you persist, you risk unleashing something neither of us can hope to control.

I will not grant you access to her. You will not have her.

Do I make myself understood?

Thomas Barrett

Her hand fell to her lap, her pulse thrummed, her breathing uneven. *You will not have her.* The words clanged in her mind like hammer blows.

The meaning was clear, sharp as broken glass. It wasn't her father's skills or knowledge that Rhys Caradoc had wanted. It was *her*.

Papa had been afraid, not for himself, but for her.

A draft threaded icy fingers under her collar. She tucked her chin and held still until the shiver passed, then she sank down onto the chair, confusion and dismay rolling through her. But layered beneath those emotions was something else, something raw and angry.

What did Rhys Caradoc want with her, and why had it frightened Papa so? Did it have something to do with Mr. Caradoc's time at St. Jude's, or the reason he had been treated there?

But then why had Papa claimed *she* was unwell?

The instinct to flee, to run from this room, this house, rose sharp and hot.

She surged to her feet once more, a thousand thoughts whirling, colliding. Answers. She needed answers, and the man who held them wore a mask of civility.

As if her thoughts had conjured him, the deep timbre of Mr. Caradoc's voice resonated from the doorway, wrapping around her, silk and velvet. "Miss Barrett."

Isabella froze, her grip tightening on the letter in her hand.

Rhys Caradoc stood framed in the doorway, impeccably dressed, coat buttoned, cravat secured, waistcoat crisp, one hand braced against the carved wood. He looked every inch the gentleman he was supposed to be.

"Forgive me," he said after a brief pause, his voice soft and low. "For my inappropriate lack of attire last night."

She blinked, startled by his apology. "You needn't—"

"I must," he interrupted gently. "It was unforgivably improper."

His words brought the image of their encounter to the forefront of her thoughts. The hard planes of his naked chest and shoulders, painted silver in the moonlight. The trail of dark hair bisecting the ridges of his abdomen, disappearing into the waistband of his breeches. The way his hair had fallen loose around his face, framing those sharp cheekbones and that mouth...severe, full, sensual. She had wanted to press her mouth against his throat, feel the thud of his pulse beneath her lips, taste his skin beneath her tongue.

Heat washed her cheeks. Something about Rhys Caradoc made her think things, *want* things, she had never wanted before.

As if something in her expression betrayed her inner secrets, his attention sharpened, his gaze flicking to her lips then back to her eyes. The air between them seemed to crackle, charged and electric. For one raw, unguarded moment, his expression was not that of a gentleman, but of...something else. Something hungry.

Isabella wet her lips, snared in his silver gaze. Heat coiled low in her belly, her pulse fluttery and uneven. It was inappropriate, even indecent, and yet she couldn't stop herself.

His gaze pinned her, and she was certain, absolutely certain, that he *knew* what she felt.

She hated that he knew. Hated that she wanted him to.

CHAPTER TEN

Rhys took a step closer.

The pulse at Isabella's throat fluttered against her skin.

Then his gaze flicked to the letter in her hand.

"Am I interrupting something?" he asked. The words were laced with dangerous amusement, but there was a steel thread of something sharper running beneath them. Something that should have felt like suspicion, or anger, but sounded more like...satisfaction.

But that made no sense.

"I—" She pressed her lips together then continued, "I was only beginning my work, Mr. Caradoc. Familiarizing myself with the space."

His eyes swept across the desk, the open drawer, the scattered letters, the ornate box sitting askew at the corner.

"Familiarizing yourself, indeed."

He stepped further into the room, slow and deliberate, his limp doing nothing to diminish his sinuous grace. For an instant, pain ghosted his features when his weight shifted.

Isabella's breath hitched as he drew closer, his eyes fixed on her face with an intensity that made her stomach tighten. She inhaled sharply, the faint scents of lemon and linen coiling around her.

"You rose early this morning, Miss Barrett," he said, his voice low, each word shaped with precision, the hint of a rasp at the edges. "I would have expected you to sleep late, given your... adventures during the night."

Her cheeks flamed.

"Tell me." His voice was softer now. "Was it the light that woke you? Or something else entirely?"

The questions were innocuous enough, but she felt as if he was looking for a depth of reply she was not willing to offer. She swallowed hard, straightening her spine as though it might steel her against his perusal. "The light, I suppose."

His lips twitched, not quite a smile, more a suggestion of one.

"The light," he echoed, his gaze dipping briefly back to the letter in her hand before returning to her face. "Yes, I imagine it reveals quite a great deal, doesn't it?"

Isabella could barely breathe. The game of cat and mouse he played with his words, his proximity, the way he looked at her, it was too much...yet not nearly enough.

With a sharp motion, she tossed the letter onto the desk, breaking the invisible thread strung taut between them.

"Why do you keep these letters, Mr. Caradoc? Why did you keep Papa's words, when you had already decided to disregard them?"

The air went still, dense with things unsaid.

His dark brows lifted. "I do not disregard the words written by a man as intelligent as your father."

"But you *did*. You persisted when he denied you," she said, her voice rising, anger and fear twining together in her chest. "Why couldn't you leave us in peace?"

"Peace." The word came out soft. His jaw tightened, and for a moment, something unreadable flashed in his eyes, something raw and untamed. Then it was gone, replaced by that cold, enigmatic mask he wore so well. "Because there are certain truths one cannot turn away from." He tilted his head, studying her as if he were measuring something within her, calculating how much she could bear before she broke. "Your father knew it, even if he denied it."

She blinked against the sharp sting of tears.

"You speak of truths and what my father knew," she said, her voice low and steady. "You barely knew my father, yet you claim to understand what he did and did not know? All I see is a man who wants something he cannot have."

Almost did she ask him about St. Jude's then. That was a truth he could not turn away from. But she could not make herself be so unkind, confronting him with a memory that surely must be terrible for him to revisit.

Silence stretched between them, vibrating with tension.

Mr. Caradoc took one more step forward, and now there was barely a breath of space between them. The light from the window cut across his face, silvering the edges of his hair and painting shadows in the hollows of his cheeks.

His jaw tightened, a muscle twitching beneath his skin, but his voice remained calm, almost lazy as he said,

"And yet, here you are. In *my* library. With *my* secrets in your hands."

His gaze dropped to her lips, his pupils dark and dilated, surrounded by only a thin rim of gray. For one breathless instant, Isabella thought he might close the distance, might claim her mouth.

Her breath caught. Her chest rose and fell in sharp, uneven bursts. She ought to step back, step away. She ought to turn and flee. Instead, she stood perfectly still, her own gaze dipping to his lips before jerking back to his eyes.

"And if I were to tell you to leave this library right now, Miss Barrett?" His voice was barely more than a whisper, soft, intimate. "To go back to London. If I were to offer a full year's wages and pay your way home, would you go?"

Would she?

She *ought* to.

But she couldn't leave. Not yet. Not without answers. Not without understanding this man and the intricate knot of secrets surrounding him. Because she suspected that his secrets were tangled with her own, that she would find answers here that had eluded her all her life.

The truth settled, sharp and heavy. Her lips parted, but no words came.

He seemed to see it, her answer, written plainly on her face. His head tilted ever so slightly, and his lips parted as though he might say something vital.

A second ticked past. Then two. The moment closed like a book. He offered no revelation. Instead, he stepped back. The absence of his nearness felt cold, hollow.

Finally, she said, "I have no home. Not anymore. Papa was my home."

"Then we are alike," he said quietly.

"In what way?" She gestured to indicate their surroundings. "Is this not your home?"

"Harrowgate is my duty. What made it home is lost to me."

His words struck like a bell. Home was the people that made it so, not the walls and floors and roof.

She thought of the life she had left behind, and an ache of bittersweet regret and loss tinged by guilt swelled in her heart. Because she had loved Papa, loved being part of his world, the days filled with books and learning and fascinating conversation. But sometimes, in quiet moments, she had imagined something else. A different life. *Her* life.

Something in his expression acknowledged that ache, as if he recognized it, knew it, lived it.

His gaze pierced her, unblinking, unyielding. "Do you ever wonder what your life might have been like if things had been different?"

"Different how?" she asked cautiously.

"If you could have chosen it yourself. If there were no debts to pay, no secrets to protect, no shadows to chase. What would you have wanted?"

She gasped, startled by how closely his question mirrored her secret thoughts.

Seconds ticked past. Almost did she deflect, deny, refuse to answer. Then for reasons she could not name, she found herself telling him the truth.

"Sometimes I dream of a cottage somewhere warm and quiet, with flowers spilling over the edges of painted window boxes and sunlight pouring in through lace curtains. Sometimes I dream of Paris, a city I have only read about, the wide boulevards lined with trees, the air thick with the scent of fresh bread and roasted chestnuts. I imagine walking along the Seine in a dress the color of cornflowers, a book tucked under my arm, free to go wherever my feet might take me."

Free from the wraiths that were her forever companions. He waited in silence for her to continue.

She offered a sad smile. "But those were the dreams of a girl who had not yet buried her father, who had not yet felt the crushing weight of unpaid bills and unanswered letters."

A girl who had not yet been drawn into a house like Harrowgate Manor, a house that seemed to breathe and shift in the darkness, a house where the shadows pressed too close and whispered things she had no wish to understand.

A muscle moved in his jaw. "Perhaps you will find new dreams. Perhaps you will find something here worth staying for."

His words hung between them for an instant and then she whispered, "And you? What do you dream of?"

"I cannot afford to dream," he said, something like longing in his eyes. "Dreams are for men unfamiliar with the cost. I want no dream. I want an end."

His gaze touched her lips again. Her pulse stumbled and she gathered it back.

"An end to what?"

The softness flickered and was gone, a shutter dropping over his expression. Deliberately, he shifted his attention toward the open drawer.

"Tell me, Miss Barrett, what were you hoping to find in my desk?"

She hesitated, baffled by the rapid shift in both mood and topic. "Answers."

"And what if you do not like the answers you find?" he asked.

"I think..." She swallowed hard, forcing herself to hold his gaze. "I think I need to know them anyway."

For a long moment, he said nothing. He simply stared at her, his expression unreadable, his eyes deep and endless.

"Then I suggest you tread carefully." His tone was cool now, a sharp edge of authority coloring the words. "The library is yours to work in."

He turned, his coat sweeping behind him as he walked back toward the door. At the threshold, he paused, one hand resting on the carved wood frame.

"You think you want knowledge," he said over his shoulder, his tone regretful. "But knowledge, Miss Barrett, has fangs."

And then he was gone, the heavy door clicking shut behind him, leaving Isabella alone with the silence, the dust, and the severed ends of the fragile threads that had connected them for one fraught moment.

Her lips tingled with the ghost of a kiss that had never happened.

The pull was undeniable now, the sharp edge of fear softened by something else.

Desire. For him. For the feel of his hands on her skin, his lips on her own.

It was a heady thing, wild and overwhelming.

The breathless anticipation, the prickle of awareness across her skin...she recognized these feelings for what they were. After all, she had read the poetry of Byron, Shelley, Keats. Their words had awakened a trembling awareness, unfamiliar and thrilling, though not even a pale shade as thrilling as what Rhys Caradoc stirred in her veins.

But she could not allow these emotions to color her thoughts, her logic, her decisions.

Was she safe here? What exactly did this enigmatic, magnetic man want from her?

She exhaled a shaky breath, her hand rising to her throat, fingertips resting lightly over the key that sat just beneath the fabric of her dress.

After a long moment, she turned back to the desk, her gaze flicking to the ornate box and the stack of her father's letters.

Slowly, carefully, Isabella set the letters back into the desk drawer and slid it closed.

The library stretched out before her, quiet, shadowed, and filled with secrets. Secrets her father had tried desperately to shield her from. Secrets Mr. Caradoc guarded with a sharp edge of possession in his voice and a glint of something unreadable in his eyes.

Papa had been afraid—*for* her, yes—but also *of* her. Of what she might become if she stepped into the madness he had worked so tirelessly to keep her from. She saw that now.

But was it madness?

What of Papa had been wrong? What if the wraiths were not the conjurings of her unstable mind, but something else entirely?

What if convincing her that she did not see them was the mistake Papa had alluded to?

There was no turning back, not without answers. Not without knowing what her father had sacrificed so much to keep hidden, and why Rhys Caradoc had pursued her with such persistence.

She was not certain what haunted her more, the secrets, the ghosts, or the feeling that he, with all his dangerous knowledge, saw something in her that she could not yet see in herself.

When Isabella returned to the library the following day, she found that cleaning had begun. The layers of dust had been wiped away from the desk, the chair, the narrow table near the multitude of open crates. The tang of beeswax polish and the faint bite of smoke lingered. The remainder of the room was still cloaked in a veil of dust and decay, Papa's books exactly where she had seen them the previous day, scattered about in random disarray. She felt certain that Mr. Caradoc had been searching for something specific in those crates.

Light crept hesitantly through the tall, freshly washed windows, casting thin, angular streaks across the dark wood floor. Dust motes swirled and scattered and danced. Somewhere in the walls, a faint chime threaded through the hush, too thin for a bell, too regular for pipes.

The space felt cleaner, yes, but not lighter. The air still carried a weight, a solemn hush, a sense of secrets coiled tightly in the shadows, waiting. It felt like walking into a cathedral a moment before a sermon...or a crypt moments before the last stone sealed it shut.

Isabella's gaze lifted to the towering shelves and the carved wood ceiling above, her breath hitching as her imagination painted eyes in the carvings, mouths hidden in the dark knots of wood.

Near one of the lower shelves, Peg knelt with a feather duster clutched in one hand and a rag in the other. Her red hair, damp with sweat and barely tamed beneath her white cap, glinted like molten copper in the morning light. Her shoulders were hunched, her head down, as though she were trying to make herself small.

"Peg?" Isabella called softly.

The girl jolted upright, clutching the duster to her chest as though it might ward off some phantom threat.

"Oh! Miss Barrett!" Peg's cheeks flushed crimson. "You startled me, miss. I thought you were Mrs. Abernathy come to scold me for dawdling."

"You're working hard, Peg. No one could accuse you of dawdling." Isabella hesitated, her eyes drifting around the room, seeing all Peg had accomplished as well as the vast array of chores yet to be done. "May I join you?"

Peg's green eyes widened. "You mean to help me clean, miss?"

"I do." Isabella began to roll up her sleeves. "There's more work here than one person can manage alone."

Peg hesitated, then a shy, grateful smile tugged at her lips. "Well, if you say so, miss. Mrs. Abernathy sent me in before dawn. Mr. Caradoc said the room wanted cleaning."

They worked side by side, Isabella taking up a clean rag while Peg wielded her feather duster.

The quiet between them was fragile, threaded through with faint creaks and the distant groans of the old house settling. Occasionally, Isabella would glance up at Peg, only to find her sending a sidelong glance at one of the shadowed corners of the library, her brow furrowed.

"Are you all right, Peg?" Isabella asked gently.

Peg hesitated, her teeth sinking into her lower lip. "I don't like this room, miss. It's like..." She paused, her voice dropping lower. "Like it's holding its breath."

Isabella studied her a moment. "You've been here at Harrowgate for a year, haven't you, Peg? And you told me nothing bad has ever happened to you. You told me not to be afraid."

Peg gave a tiny nod. "Aye, miss. Nothing bad has happened. And I'm not afraid, not even when the house cries in the night. But this room..." She glanced around, her eyes darting to the shadows. "Sometimes it feels like these walls are listening. Like they're leaning in, close enough to hear us whisper."

Isabella's rag stilled against the wood. Peg was the first person she had ever met who seemed to experience things as she did, to feel things, sense things. Isabella could not help but wonder if the girl *saw* things as well. Her words came careful and cautious. "Have you ever seen anything unusual here, Peg?"

Peg froze, her fingers tightening around the feather duster.

"I mean," Isabella continued softly, her voice level, "a person...or something that looked like one. Someone who... shouldn't be here."

Peg's face paled, her freckles standing out starkly against her skin. She opened her mouth, closed it again, and shook her head.

"Best not to ask such things, miss," she said, her words hushed and frantic. "Best not to stir them up." She turned abruptly back to her task, her small shoulders tense and drawn tight as bowstrings.

Isabella's rag stilled again on the carved wood, her chest tightening with words she very nearly let slip, the truth about the things she saw, the cold brush of hands that should not be felt. The urge to confide pressed hard, desperate to be shared with someone who might understand. Peg's wide green eyes and the things she had said seemed to invite it.

But caution and Papa's long shadow clamped her mouth shut. *Never say it. Never show it.*

Peg glanced at her and their gazes held for a heartbeat, as though she waited for words yet unsaid. Then she set her jaw and bustled toward the hearth. She snatched up the iron poker, carried it to the threshold, and laid it flat across the sill. The metal rang as it slapped wood.

"There," she said with quiet conviction. "That keeps them out."

"Them?" Isabella asked.

Peg pressed her lips tight. "Whatever listens. My mam says iron's good for doors and sills. And window—" She glanced at the windows framed by brocade curtains. "So the walls can't breathe on us."

Soft, almost imperceptible, the silence thickened, and the air shifted...a sigh or the settling of timbers.

The two women stilled. Then, at the same time, they laughed, too quick, too quiet, the sound edged with nerves. Peg clamped a hand to her mouth, freckles dark against her pale cheeks. Isabella shook her head, startled by her own reaction.

When their laughter faded, the oppressive weight had eased. The library was no less shadowed, but the air felt less dense. And Isabella looked at Peg with fresh eyes. She was not merely a skittish servant repeating tales. She was an ally armed with iron and stubborn resolve.

Peg's gaze flickered toward the north side of the library. "There are parts of this house, miss, where no one goes. Where no one *should* go."

"The north wing?" Isabella prompted gently.

Peg nodded, eyes wide.

"What happened there, Peg? Do you know?"

"Fire," Peg whispered. "A terrible fire." Her gaze darted around the room as if the fire might still flare in the corners. Isabella marked the fear and chose another path, one that would soothe rather than stir.

"Tell me, Peg, do you have any brothers or sisters?"

Peg's expression softened.

"Oh, aye, miss. Three brothers and a sister, though I'm the youngest of the lot. They all think I'm spoiled, mind you. Being the baby and all."

Isabella smiled faintly. "And are you?"

"A little, maybe. But it didn't stop them from sending me here to earn my keep." Peg's lips twitched into a grin. "My eldest brother, Danny, he's the worst for it. Acts like he's my father sometimes. But he writes me letters, every month, like clockwork. Full of gossip and nonsense. You'd think the whole village was on fire the way he tells it." She paused. "Glad I am now that Mam taught all of us to read and write."

Isabella let out a soft laugh. "Your brother sounds like quite the storyteller."

Peg nodded, her smile lingering before she turned back to her work. The silence that followed was softer now, less suffocating.

After a time, Isabella turned her attention to one of the crates. It sat apart from the others, its lid cracked open, nails bent and splintered. She went to stand before it, her hand hovering over the splintered wood. With a huffing exhalation that felt too loud in the stillness, she pushed the lid open.

Inside lay books. Dozens of them. Their shapes were familiar and welcome, cracked leather spines, gilded titles faded with time, corners softened by years of careful hands. They should have been wrapped carefully in oilcloth and twine, for that was how they had been packed. Instead, there was a snarl of twine off to one side and the books were stacked in a random way.

She took care to wipe her hands on a clean cloth before lifting one carefully. *Philosophiæ Naturalis Principia Mathematica.*

She knew this book, and every other in this crate. She brushed her fingertips lightly over the embossed letters on the spine before placing it gently on the table.

Another followed, then another. Titles in Latin, French, Arabic. Symbols that seemed to twist and writhe on the page if she stared at them too long.

"That's an awful lot of books," Peg said. "And those just from a single crate." She looked around at the piles on the floor. "So many books."

"These belonged to my father," Isabella murmured.

"They look old. Older than books ought to look."

"They are very old," Isabella said, memories of Papa summoning a bittersweet smile.

Peg set down her feather duster and lifted the heavy bucket of dirty water, her arms straining with the weight. The water sloshed as she adjusted her grip.

"I need to fetch fresh water," she said.

Isabella nodded. "Of course, Peg. Take your time."

The maid hesitated at the threshold, her freckled face pinched with worry, her gaze darting around the room.

"You'll be alright, miss? Alone in here?"

Sweet girl. Whatever ghosts she imagined in the dim corners of the library, they were no worse than the wraiths that had been Isabella's companions all her life, certainly no worse than the wraith she had encountered her first night here.

"I will. Go on," she said.

Peg cast one last wary glance around the library before slipping out the door. The echo of her footsteps faded.

Isabella turned slowly, her eyes sweeping across the room. The silence stretched around her, vast and unyielding, like the weight of the centuries pressed into the stone walls and carved wood panels.

And in that silence, something moved.

Not footsteps. Not the creak of settling wood. Not the whispers of unseen wraiths.

It was more a shift in the air, like breath stirring dust. She felt that breath on her cheek, stone cold, cellar damp. Heat without flame licked across the floor. The scent of roses filled the air.

Then came a thud as a book tumbled from the shelf across the room and struck the floor.

Isabella froze. All the spirits she had seen her entire life were insubstantial remnants, unable to influence the physical world. All save the girl in the moonlit hallway who had looked so very real.

Was she here now? Had she tossed the book to the floor?

Isabella turned, her gaze searching every nook and cranny for signs of a wraith. She saw none.

The book lay sprawled open, its pages twitching in the draft that curled through the room. Slowly, cautiously, Isabella stepped toward it and bent until her fingers brushed the leather cover.

A whisper.

Not a voice, not quite, but something else. A sound that slithered through the silence like cold breath against the back of her neck.

The book's pages fluttered. The library door slammed shut.

Isabella turned sharply and crossed the room. The door handle was icy beneath her touch. When she tested it, it would not turn.

She gripped it tighter and twisted. Still, it held fast.

The air around her was frigid now, her breath puffing white before her lips.

She rattled the handle and yanked.

Then something brushed against her wrist. Not the air. Not a draft. Something slithered, cold and damp and solid, smelling of soot and wet stone, the aroma of roses turning sulfur sharp.

On instinct, she yanked her hand back, a strangled gasp catching in her throat. The sensation lingered, wet and slippery, a phantom touch that should not have been there.

Her heart beat hard and fast. Her breathing turned ragged.

And then the door swung open on its own.

Isabella stumbled back, her pulse stuttering. She squared her shoulders and lifted her chin.

"It will take more than that to frighten me," she muttered, hating the tremor that betrayed her. Her gaze swept across the crates, the shelves, the desk. The quiet was unnatural. The cold doubly so. But it was the brief blast of heat that unsettled her.

Wraiths were cold, always. Yet this wraith seemed determined to alter the rules.

Isabella took a step toward the door, but her limbs felt sluggish, heavy, the very air resisting her progress. A shiver traced down her spine on centipede legs, pooling in her stomach, heavy as lead.

With a sharp inhalation, she shook off the feeling and stalked toward the now open door. But as she crossed the threshold into the hallway, she could not escape the feeling that something did not want her to leave. That it would wait here for her return.

Then came a whisper. Not a breath. Not a voice. Something else.

"I...s...a...b...e...l...l...a...."

Papa's voice.

But Papa was dead. Gone.

Grief and horror tangled in her breast until she could scarce draw breath. The syllables crawled along her skin as though the malevolent thing that shaped them meant to sink claws and drag her back through the library door.

Always had she heard the whispers but never had they called her by name.

The air in the hallway felt warm against her chilled skin. Too warm, like the unnatural heat of a fever. She paused, crossing her arms and rubbing her palms up and down.

Her wrist prickled. She glanced down and froze.

Both her skin and the hem of her sleeve were slippery and wet. A single droplet slithered along her pulse and fell. As it hit the floor, the air turned sour with the reek of water thrown on a fire...wet ash and scalding steam.

CHAPTER ELEVEN

Isabella slipped out onto the terrace, skirts skimming the stone. The sky was darkening, the air clean and fresh without a hint of dust or beeswax or old paper. She walked down into the garden, past box hedges gone leggy, bristled and black rose canes, and a sundial covered in lichen. Still, she could taste the house on the back of her tongue. She took a deep breath, letting the wash of cold air ease her nerves.

As always, she heard them, the whisper of the wraiths, murmurs without words, quieter than they had been in London, but still there at the periphery of her senses.

But other than the girl, she still had not seen one here at Harrowgate, a lack that left her uneasy.

From behind her came the crunch of gravel.

"Miss Barrett."

Mr. Caradoc stood just beyond the terrace steps, a lantern in one hand, casting a golden circle around him. His other hand was tucked in his coat. A lock of his sleek, dark hair had fallen across his brow.

"You should take a lamp if you plan to walk the garden after dusk," he said. The words could have been censure or concern. She did not know him well enough to decide.

"Is the garden so dangerous, then?" Her chin tipped up.

He glanced to the thicker growth and darker shadows to the north. "Not all dangers strike quickly," he said mildly. "Some prefer to wait."

She ought to have thanked him and gone inside. Instead, she stayed.

As he came to stand beside her, the lantern threw their shadows long across the ground. The ever-present hum at the edge of her senses quieted, as if a hive had settled after swarming. Beside her, he went still and drew a slow breath through his nose, as if he felt it too.

Then he said, "It is quieter."

She turned to face him fully, surprise warring with wariness. He could not mean the voices, the whispers. Surely, he could not mean that.

She swallowed and asked, "What is quieter?"

He studied her for a long moment, his eyes locked on her own. Then he said, "The wind. It dropped at sundown."

A deflection, neatly done. Her mouth curved. His gaze flicked to her lips, then back to her eyes.

"Do you always lie so easily, Mr. Caradoc?" she asked. She surprised herself with her own temerity. She dared much to speak to him so, and had she been pressed to explain herself, she did not think she could have.

"I do not lie," he said. "I omit."

She could have laid bare the unspoken fact he had

omitted, his time at St. Jude's. But just as he had not revealed his experiences there, she had not revealed hers. She did not owe him that, nor did he owe her. He did not owe her a revelation of his pain.

"Ah," she said softly. "A distinction."

"A useful one." One corner of his mouth curled as if at some inward jest.

He lifted the lantern and turned, light skimming the ruined, overgrown beds. "My mother planted rosemary there. Rue there." He indicated a tangle off to one side. "The plants hold their shape only so long after the hand that cared for them is gone."

Grief lived in the words, the tone, the set of his shoulders.

"Rosemary and rue," she murmured. "Memory and warning."

He glanced at her, quick and sharp.

"You miss her," she said, thinking of Papa, thinking in that moment how much she missed him.

"She remains," he said, and paused. "In my heart."

The breath he let stretch between the first words and their gentler correction pricked at her. For an instant, she had thought he meant his mother remained here in more than memory, in walls and drafts and a watchful hush.

A thread of heat swirled around her ankles, like the heat of a fire breathing against her skin. The lantern flame leaned. From the house came a sound, a rhythmic tapping. Mr. Caradoc stiffened, a muscle in his jaw clenching.

"You hear it," Isabella murmured.

"The settling of the house?" His tone was mild.

She wanted to believe that was all she heard.

The heat receded, replaced by a chill blast that left her shivering. He lifted the lantern toward her, wrapping her in the circle of its light. "Allow me."

He set the lantern on the sundial and shrugged out of his coat. He settled it around her shoulders, the wool still warm from his body, smelling like citrus and linen and him.

His knuckles grazed the hollow at her throat as he drew the lapels together. Her pulse jumped and danced. For a heartbeat, they stood like that, his hands on the lapels, her skin thrumming under his touch, the space between them sparking like the air before a storm.

The weight of the garment felt like a claim.

From the house came the scrape of metal on stone, the sound she had heard before, eerie and disturbing. He moved closer, his gaze scanning the dark reach of the north beds.

"Come," he said. "It grows cold."

He reached for the lantern. Their fingers touched, no accident, and the shock of it skittered along her skin.

They walked in silence, the lantern swinging a bowl of light ahead of them. He opened the terrace door and stood aside to let her pass, his coat still draped over her shoulders. As she crossed the threshold, the whispers grew a fraction louder, though still soft, negligible in the face of what she had known in London.

She slid his coat off and held it out to him, a part of her hoping their fingers would brush once more. But he was careful as he took it. It mattered not. The air between them crackled all the same.

A child's voice carried through the walls, a sob, a plea, then a woman's answering cry. The house was never silent, not completely. The dead pressed close, reminding Rhys what bound him here. Their cried were his burden, their rest his only absolution. Whatever else Mr. Christopher thought to interfere with, that truth remained.

She knows

Rhys stared at the letter that lay open on his desk, creased and rumpled from the closing of his fist when he had crushed it. He had thought to fling it into the fire, to watch Christopher's careful hand dissolve into ash, but instead he had smoothed it flat, rage still thrumming in his blood. The words endured, implacable beneath their scars.

His jaw tightened. He should have expected Christopher to meddle because meddling was all he could manage. He had sent an investigator sniffing after shadows best left buried and thought himself noble for it. Noble for burdening her with St. Jude's, as though she had not grief enough already. Weakness dressed as virtue.

And now, this letter, Christopher's attempt at virtue. A confession of his interference, cloaked as courtesy. A warning to Rhys, perhaps. More likely a plea for absolution should she suffer for knowing.

Where had been the solicitor's gallantry when she shuttered her windows against hunger and cold? Where was his protection when the first disbursement of her quarterly funds was still months away? Advice he had provided, yes. But no food, no coin, no fire. He had left her adrift, and only now, when Rhys had reached for her, did Christopher find courage to interfere.

And yet, despite it all, she had come. Knowing what she knew, she had still stepped aboard that train. The thought curled through him, part satisfaction, part torment. Satisfaction that she had not turned away, not his brave Isabella, fierce in her own quiet way. Torment that she had chosen to lean upon his honor when in this he had none.

He was no safe harbor. He was a murderer dressed in a gentleman's coat.

Christopher's meddling altered nothing.

His plan stood. He would not be turned aside.

But the image of Isabella swaying toward him, eyes lifted to his, lodged deep. It steadied him. And broke him. He had no right to such a tether, no right to wish she might see past his shadows. Yet the wish coiled tight within him, undeniable as breath.

Isabella settled into a rhythm at Harrowgate. Each morning began with a quiet breakfast in the kitchen, sharing the long table with Mrs. Abernathy, Peg, Emma, Mary, and sometimes Cook. Though the food was simple —porridge with a spoonful of honey, eggs, kippers, warm bread, tea brewed dark and strong—it gave her a sense of normalcy and calm, kept her from drifting too far into the strange undercurrents of the manor.

She was determined to pretend that nothing unusual had happened in the library, that the door that refused to open had only been stuck, that the dampness of her sleeve had a reasonable explanation. And yet...

The house was not right.

There should have been wraiths. She could not remember a time where there had not been. But other than the girl in the nightgown, she had seen no other spirits. For a house as old and layered with history as Harrowgate, this seemed impossible. Ghosts should haunt its corridors, its crumbling wings, its forgotten staircases. Yet, while the house creaked and groaned and settled, and while she heard the whispers, muted and soft, any sighting of wraiths themselves was absent.

That absence left her wary and anxious, waiting for the moment when her fragile peace would shatter, wondering if they were somehow being held at bay, and if so, by what? In the dark of night, she had had the terrible thought that the house swallowed its dead.

One evening, when the kitchen had gone to embers and whispers, she came upon Mrs. Abernathy sitting with a clean cloth, working with small, relentless circles the bowl of a spoon she seemed determined to coax to a shine.

"The repetition soothes me," the housekeeper said without looking up. "Will you take some tea?"

"Yes, thank you," Isabella said, taking a seat across from her.

Mrs. Abernathy already had the kettle set on the hob where it hissed and spat. She lifted it with a folded cloth, poured a little boiling water into a squat earthen pot, swirled it to warm, and tipped it out. After measuring two scant teaspoons of leaves, dark and dry, she poured the water over them. Then she set aside the kettle and covered the pot with a folded cloth.

"That Peg," she said as she set two pottery mugs on the table. She cracked two lumps of coarse sugar from the loaf with iron nippers and dropped one in each mug before adding some milk. "She's abed now, but she had a day, she did. Swore up and down that the walls of the back stairs meant to crush her."

After a few moments, she poured the drawn tea, dark ribbons clouding into the milk, then slid a mug across the table. Isabella wrapped it with her palms, grateful for the warmth. The scent of the tea drifted up, smoky sweet.

"My first night here," she said, "Peg told me not to be afraid. That her mam said ghosts can't hurt you, only being afraid of them can."

"That child," the housekeeper said, half-chiding, half-protective. "Sees spirits in every corner, claims she isn't afraid, but trembles like a leaf." She stirred her tea, her spoon ringing soft against clay. "Mind you, I wouldn't call her a liar." Her tone was thoughtful now. "Some folks' eyes are set to see what others can't."

The words sparked along Isabella's skin, bright and perilous. She studied the other woman over the rim of her mug. *She believes Peg. Would she believe me?* Her pulse skipped a beat, a quick, betraying flutter.

"Have you seen such things?" she asked carefully.

The housekeeper took a sip of her tea and set her mug down. "When I was a slip of a thing with more bones than sense, my mother sent me to the miller's to ask for flour on tick. I came back late, dusk making a bruise of the lane. A man walked ahead of me with his hat tipped just so, the way Mr. Briggs always wore it. He turned at the stile and lifted two fingers by the brim. Polite as Sundays." She smiled, but it was the kind of smile that didn't brighten anything. "I lifted mine back. I knew him. Everyone knew him."

She took up the cloth and began polishing the next spoon. "In the morning there was church-bell talk and my mother's sharp whispering. Mr. Briggs had taken fever and gone to God two nights prior. They'd laid him out with pennies on his eyes right while I was lifting my hand in greeting the evening after." She gave a soft, dismissive click of tongue and teeth.

"Did you tell anyone?" Isabella asked, lifting her mug to blow across the top.

"My mother said to hold my tongue. 'There's things you'll only make worse by naming,' she said. So I kept it."

Isabella's chest ached. To see and be told one had not, to hide the tale, to smile and lie and pretend...That was the shape of her own childhood. Her own *life*.

Mrs. Abernathy's mouth firmed. "I've never seen such a thing again. But I won't call a girl a liar for having eyes set different from mine. Peg sees something. She's no mischief-maker."

"No, she is not," Isabella said, too quickly. Heat rose to her face; she bent to sip and let the mug shield her. The truth swelled in her throat...the wraiths, the voices, the way the house leaned close to listen. It would be the easiest thing to set the cup down and tell this woman who polished spoons to a moon-bright shine about the dead who would not leave her be. So easy. So ruinous.

Never say it. Never show it.

Mrs. Abernathy reached across and, with the dry gentleness of a mother smoothing a child's hair, straightened the cuff of Isabella's sleeve where it had folded.

"Some folk see more," she said. "Doesn't mean they're broken."

The words rang like a bell tolling in a fog.

"My father..." Isabella began, and the room seemed to lean nearer, the coals shifting as if to hear. The words lay sharp on her tongue. Duty. Promise. Grief. She swallowed, and the swallow hurt. She wrenched the truth into a different shape, safer, smaller. "My father would have agreed with your mother, about the keeping of some things." She made herself smile. "But Peg will be the safer for being believed, and feel less lonely for it, too."

Mrs. Abernathy set the second spoon aside and reached for a third, content with what had not been asked for. "Aye," she said. "Belief costs little. *Not* believing can cost a world."

They sat a while, quiet, bound for a moment by something perilously near trust. When Isabella rose, the mug left a pale ring on the scrubbed table. Mrs. Abernathy wiped it away with her cloth and a nod. How easily some marks could be erased.

By the end of the following week, Isabella had made headway in unpacking her father's books and arranging them on the shelves like watchful sentinels. The familiar scent of beeswax polish and aged paper surrounded her. She worked by habit and rule, first creating a rough shelf-list in a ledger's front pages, then a fair copy in the catalogue book, including title, author, language, date, provenance, any notable marginalia, her hand neat and even. Fragile atlases and folios she laid beneath boards with a stone weight to coax their buckled leaves flat. Torn joints she tied with narrow cotton tape. Dog-eared corners she smoothed and touched with the lightest smear of paste. When mold freckled a board, she wiped it with a vinegar-dampened cloth. When she came upon a leather cover that was powder-dry, she breathed on it and polished with a square of soft flannel until it took on a healthy glow. Everything was done precisely as Papa had taught her, and she found comfort in the familiarity of the tasks.

There were dozens of other crates she had not yet

examined, ones she believed were filled with the manor's own books. Those would need ordering by subject, then language, then size...mathematics and natural philosophy together, voyages and antiquities, sermons, and so on.

For now, she focused on her father's collection. Each title she placed on the shelves felt like restoring a piece of him, bringing him back to life in small, fleeting moments. She asked Matty to bring the tall stepladder, and the boy obliged with solemn care. Noting his interest, she taught him to set out clean blotters at her elbow and bring a small pot of fresh paste, the surface covered with damp muslin so it would not skin over.

She set a regimen against the room's old damp, drawing the curtains when the sun was fierce, then opening them for an hour to air. She kept the fire to a steady glow rather than a blaze. She wrapped small cones of camphor in linen and nested them in drawers and empty nooks to keep nibbling things at bay.

She was not always alone in her work. Sometimes, Matty would help her fold thin runs of paper and lay them on the shelves so the book bottoms would not wick splinters or soot. Peg would slip in to brush dust from carved cornices with a feather whisk.

And as the days passed, no wraiths came to show themselves. Not one.

Only once, as she slid a folio home, a cool damp kissed her wrist and left a brief, bitter reek of quenched coals, the whispers rising to a roar before settling once more.

She could not recall a time in her life when wraiths had not dogged her every step. The reprieve ought to have been a relief. It was not. She could only think on how terrible it would be when they returned, when she had to once more guard her every movement, every glance.

Rhys Caradoc appeared daily, his timing unpredictable but his presence always commanding. Oh, aloud, she was formal and polite, addressing him as Mr. Caradoc. But in her thoughts, she allowed herself to call him Rhys, to imagine her lips shaping his name as she spoke it aloud. She was neither a child nor a fool. He was handsome, charming when he chose, and she was—she admitted it—a little enamoured. And she recognized the danger in that.

His visits were usually brief, punctuated by an exchange of polite words that felt anything but polite. He spoke to her with an intensity that left her heart fluttering and her thoughts clouded. Always, his gaze lingered on her longer than it should, and always, Isabella felt her cheeks flush in response.

Today, the fire in the library hearth crackled, its warmth spreading through the room as Isabella leaned over a crate, carefully lifting out books. The smell of aged tomes rose like a faint, dusty sigh as she removed the first, its leather binding cracked but sturdy.

Behind her, the door creaked open.

"Miss Barrett," came that familiar, low voice. The sound slid through her, as smooth and dark as velvet.

She straightened and turned, her heart skipping a beat when she saw Rhys standing just inside the doorway. His dark coat fit him impeccably, its cut accentuating the breadth of his shoulders, and a faint shadow darkened his jawline as she had noticed it did when the day aged.

"Good afternoon, Mr. Caradoc," she replied, hoping her voice did not betray the sudden hitch in her breath. "You find me once again covered in dust."

"I see you've made progress," he said, stepping closer.

His eyes swept over the neatly arranged books on the shelves, then drifted back to her. "You do your father's collection justice."

The warmth in his words surprised her, and for a moment, she didn't know how to respond. He drew something from his pocket, a small oval chemist's tin, japanned black, with a thin gilt rule circling the rim.

"Do you enjoy sweets, Miss Barrett?" he asked.

She blinked, caught off guard by the question. "I... I do."

She stared at the tin in his hand, a sense of familiarity nagging at her.

The tin... Her gaze snapped to his, understanding dawning. "It was you."

His head tilted, amusement flickering in his expression. "Me?"

"You left the baskets of food," she said, the words falling from her lips before she could stop them. "After my father died. The same tin of sweets was in one of the baskets you left on my stoop."

For a moment, Rhys said nothing, his gaze steady and unreadable. "I have never liked the taste of grief." He paused. "After meeting you, I found that I disliked the thought of you swallowing your tears, alone in that house."

The words sent a flush rising to her cheeks, and she looked away, suddenly overwhelmed by the weight of his attention. Then the implication of what he said dawned. *I have never liked the taste of grief.* That suggested he had known grief and loss, more than once. She wanted to ask, to know, to ease his burden by sharing it. And that made no sense. He was practically a stranger to her.

Except...he wasn't. Not anymore. She saw him every

day. They spoke of things that mattered on occasion, but mostly things that did not: whether the chimneys drew properly after the last storm; whether a torn folio binding could be mended with paste or if it required new thread. Once, he told her of his favorite place to walk, a half-wild orchard at the edge of the grounds. Another time, he lingered to ask what she read, his tone mild, his questions pointed, as if he sought not only the title but her thoughts upon it. And in the midst of such small exchanges, the distance between them had thinned, thread by thread, until she thought she might touch the shape of him beneath his mask.

When she finally glanced back at him, his expression had softened, the sharp edges of his face tempered by something gentler.

"Mr. Caradoc—"

"Call me Rhys," he said quietly. The words hung in the air, intimate and improper.

Isabella hesitated, her breath catching. In her thoughts, she already called him by his given name. But to do so aloud? "That would be inappropriate."

A faint smile ghosted across his lips. "And yet, here we are. Isabella."

She had not invited him to make use of her given name. Yet, the sound of it, uttered in his low, masculine voice—

The air between them crackled, charged with something unspeakable. Isabella's pulse thrummed beneath her skin as she struggled to find her footing, to steady herself in the face of his relentless presence.

Her teeth gnawed at her lower lip. And then, she whispered, "Rhys."

He went very still, his eyes fathomless, sliding to her

mouth, focused there. He looked away first, as if catching himself, and opened the tin he held, then offered it to her, revealing pale yellow lozenges dusted with fine sugar. "Would you like one?"

Hesitating only a moment, Isabella plucked a lozenge from the tin. The taste of lemon burst bright, a mingling of citrus and sweet. Her tongue darted out, catching the dusting of sugar that clung to her lower lip.

His eyes darkened as he stared at her mouth; a muscle flexed in his jaw.

Her breath locked. Her pulse raced. The way he looked at her—

"May I?" he asked, his voice rough.

Confused, she stared at him then nodded.

His hand lifted, hesitated, then he brushed the pad of his thumb across her lower lip.

"Sugar," he murmured.

She froze, entranced by the way he looked at her, as though he were hungry and she a morsel to be devoured.

With his gaze locked on hers, he leaned in, slowly, so slowly.

Her breath hitched but she did not step away. Her world narrowed to the inch of air between them. Heat gathered in the pit of her belly, low and bright, a tremor skimming her skin, her blood thrumming in her veins. Her fingers curled into her skirt as she fought the need to lean in, to close that paltry space that separated them.

A low sound escaped her, a plea, and then his mouth was on hers, his lips pressed to her own, a brief, restrained touch, lemon sweet.

It was not enough. She yearned for more. She rose to the kiss, untutored but certain.

His mouth answered hers, once, twice, then the kiss

deepened, stealing her thoughts, her will. The room fell away. There were only his hands steady at her arms and the velvet slide of his lips on hers.

Then, as if something in him caught and locked, he pulled back, breath unsteady, the inches between them too distant for her liking. His thumb traced the line of her jaw.

"Isabella," he said, the sound rough as though he offered her name as both warning and apology.

A draft nosed through the library, though no window stood open. Somewhere on the shelves, a book fell against another with a soft thud. His gaze flicked past her shoulder and his expression shifted, all softness gone.

"This is...ill-advised." His voice was steady, smooth as he stepped away, putting distance between them as if it were a kind of shield. "You are in my house, under my protection. I must honor that." He paused. "Forgive me."

She wanted to tell him that the only apology he need make was for ending the kiss, but she could not trust her voice.

He took a step back, then another, leaving her feeling cold and somehow bereft. He settled his composure around himself like a cloak, the gentleman once more.

"If you require anything," he said softly, his gaze lingering a heartbeat too long on her lips before lifting to her eyes, "ring for Mrs. Abernathy."

He turned. At the threshold, he paused. Her heart stuttered as she waited for him to say something true, something honest, something...to leave her feeling less alone.

He did not. The door clicked shut behind him, leaving her with the taste of him still on her tongue.

Rhys closed the library door and stood with his palm pressed to the paneled wall until the ache in his leg outshouted the urge to go back. Not only because being near her made the prickles of sound drop to a hush. And not only because he wanted her. The urge to return was not desire's work alone.

He had wanted women before. He knew the shape and swell of appetite and how easily a man could mistake hunger for more in that moment. This was...different. He *liked* her. Liked her mind, the questions she asked, and the way she ordered chaos without complaint. Liked her steadiness—no simpering, no artifice. Liked her stubborn dignity, even when there was mud on her hem and grief clogging her throat. He respected her.

Respect sharpened the danger.

He had left Barrett's letters where a curious mind would find them, the drawer left slightly askew. A snare baited with truth. He had known the words written by her father would show her only what he had assured her was the basis of their correspondence. What she read in those letters would make his own word worth something to her.

He had burned the letters that did not support the narrative he wove, the angry letters refusing him access to Barrett's grimoires. Refusing him access to Barrett's daughter.

On his desk in the library, the small box waited. He had left it there knowing she would look inside that, too, and the contents would tell her what she needed to know when the time was right, would lure her along the path he had set for her. A snare baited with truth was no less a trap for being honest.

He loathed himself for laying such snares, but he would not falter. The faces of the lost were etched in his mind, in his heart. He would not fail them in death as he had in life.

CHAPTER TWELVE

Early the following morning, Isabella woke with a gasp, her breath sharp and ragged as though she'd been running. Her chest heaved as she pressed a hand to her racing heart, the remnants of a dream slipping away like water through her fingers.

She had been chasing someone. No, not someone—*him*. Rhys Caradoc. His dark coat had whipped behind him as he strode away, always just out of reach, disappearing into a tunnel formed by the twisted, barren branches of blackened trees. Her bare feet had slapped against the ground so hot it seared, smoke clawing her throat as she tried to follow. Sparks rained down. Ash stung her eyes. She had called his name, her voice lost to the roar of the fire. But he never turned back. He never slowed.

Then, just as she had slowed, choking on smoke and despair, he had stepped from behind the charred trunk of an ash tree and caught her, as if that had been his goal all along, as if he had lured her by staying just out of reach until he had led her into the very heart of the blaze.

The dream faded, leaving behind an unsettling wariness. She had had a similar dream before, on the train to Maidenhead. Then, as now, she had had no explanation as to why.

She pushed upright in the large four-poster bed, her nightgown clinging to her damp skin, her hair stuck to her forehead in tangled curls.

The dream slipped away, and in its place came something sweeter.

Closing her eyes, she lifted her fingers to her lips. Rhys had kissed her. She had wanted him to. The memory came in fragments: the velvet heat of his lips, the steadiness of his hands when the world had tilted and she had become unmoored, the clean bite of his scent, citrus with a note of mint, the sharp ache low in her belly.

Shame did not come, though perhaps it should have.

But reckless wanting did, bright and insistent, battling the sobering certainty that she ought to keep her distance. She traced her lower lip with her fingertip, remembering the feel of him, the taste of him. A treacherous part of her wished the moment back, ached for his arms around her, his body flush with her own.

"Enough," she whispered and opened her eyes once more.

The fire had long since burned down in the hearth, leaving the air cold and sharp. Isabella swung her legs over the edge of the bed, the chill seeping up from the floor through the carpet to bite at her bare feet.

She washed and dressed in a black wool gown, her movements brisk. Once her boots were laced and her hair gathered into a loose knot, she hesitated at the door. A glance toward her window revealed thin fingers of dawn reaching through the heavy curtains. Papa's key hung around her neck, warm against her skin. Her gaze skidded to the trunk in the corner. Then she thought of the brass box on the desk in the library, questions humming in her mind.

For a moment, the room was silent. Utterly silent. Until a sound carried from within the walls, faint and distant, a rhythmic *tap...tap...tap.* Slow. Deliberate. She held her breath, listening, but the sound had already melted away.

With a final breath, she opened her chamber door and stepped into the hallway.

There, she walked softly, her boots muted against the thick runner. The grand staircase loomed ahead, broad and imposing, spilling down into the cavernous entrance hall like the spine of some great sleeping beast. She hesitated at the top.

The thought of descending into that wide-open space, with its yawning darkness and towering portraits, sent an uncomfortable prickle down her neck. Besides, she was uncertain that she would find her way to the kitchen given that she had only ever used the servants' stairs to reach it.

Instead, she retraced her steps then turned down the side corridor. It took only a moment to locate the small wooden door tucked between two tapestries, half-hidden in shadow.

The servants' stairs were steep and uneven, but she welcomed the closeness of the narrow walls, the sense of familiarity, and oddly, even the feeling of being enclosed and hidden from the yawning emptiness of the grand hall.

When Isabella stepped into the kitchen, she was greeted by a wash of warmth and the luscious scent of baking bread. The fire crackled in the hearth, its warm glow chasing away the predawn chill that clung stubbornly to the stone floors. Copper pots gleamed from their hooks, and steam rose in faint curls from a kettle set near the fire. A long dresser held blue-and-white crockery; pewter plates shone dully in the half-light.

Cook stood at the great black range, sleeves rolled up, forearms dusted with flour. She spared Isabella a quick nod before sliding a peel beneath a waiting loaf and turning the bread with practiced hands.

Mrs. Abernathy sat at the long wooden table, her cup of tea cradled in both hands. She glanced up at Isabella's entrance, her sharp blue eyes softening. Wisps of fair hair escaped her cap and curled at her temples, her rosebud lips curving in a smile.

"Well, good morning, Miss Barrett," she said, her voice carrying the rasp of early hours. "You're an early riser today."

Isabella lingered in the doorway for a moment before stepping forward, her skirts brushing against her boots. "Good morning, Mrs. Abernathy. I hope I am not intruding."

"Not at all, lamb." Mrs. Abernathy set her tea down and gestured toward the bench near the table. "Sit yourself down. There's tea in the pot, and Cook's just pulled bread from the oven. You'll want something warm in your stomach before the day begins."

Isabella hesitated before lowering herself onto the bench. As she poured herself a cup of tea from the stout pot, her gaze drifted across the kitchen. Matty, thin-shouldered and quick, slipped in through the scullery door, a bundle of kindling under one arm and a bootjack in the other. He bobbed his head to Mrs. Abernathy and set the kindling by the coal scuttle before continuing on his way.

"Did you sleep well?" Mrs. Abernathy asked Isabella.

"I... I think so. But I woke early. And I—" Isabella faltered. "I dreamed..."

"What did you dream about?"

"A man," Isabella said softly, willing to admit only that and no more. "I was chasing him. Calling after him. But he did not stop, did not turn."

Mrs. Abernathy's lips pressed into a thin line. "Perhaps it was not a man you were chasing in your sleep but rather your old life. Settling in to a new place can tangle the mind."

Isabella glanced down at her tea, her brow furrowed. "Do you think dreams are tricks, then?"

"My mother said dreams are wishes or warnings," the housekeeper said.

Isabella's cheeks warmed at the memory of Rhys's mouth on hers. Wish, warning...perhaps her dream had been a little of each.

"Pish posh," Cook said, her tone brusque. "Dreams are just dreams."

Mrs. Abernathy reached for the pot to pour herself another cup of tea. For a moment, the only sound in the kitchen was the faint splash of liquid into the mug. Then, with a click of the scullery door, Peg edged inside, balancing the ash pail, cinders ticking as they cooled. A curl of soot rode the air like a black snowflake.

"Tell me about the fire in the north wing," Isabella said to Mrs. Abernathy, deciding a direct approach was the best. She had questions. The housekeeper might have answers.

The woman's eyes widened, and her gaze flicked to Peg.

Not wanting the maid to be scolded for carrying tales, Isabella hastened to add. "I heard about it from the Burns sisters. We shared a carriage from Maidenhead to Marlow."

"I stay away, miss. I don't go near that wing," Peg blurted. "Not if I can help. You can hear—"

"That will be enough, Peg," the housekeeper warned.

The maid ducked her head and busied herself at the grate, but her words had already escaped, hanging in the air.

Isabella set down her cup. "Why was that part of the house never repaired after the fire?"

"Because the men who were hired to do the work would not finish it," Mrs. Abernathy said, turning her cup, aligning the handle precisely to the right. "They said the stone would not keep. They said their tools were moved or went missing. They said they heard...things. Fools, the lot of them." Her gaze held Isabella's. "Mr. Caradoc had the doors barred after that. That wing is not safe."

"What sorts of things did they hear?" Isabella asked.

"Whispers down the flue," Peg said. "Knocking in the walls. The howl of the wind on a still day. I've heard all those things, too, and more." She shuddered.

"Peg," Mrs. Abernathy said, sounding exasperated but not unkind.

"Well, I have," the girl said, mulish. "And the draft there is wrong. Comes hot when the weather's cold and there's no fire anywhere nearby."

"Peg," she said again, her tone sharper now. "I've buried one maid already, poor thing. Fevered she was and terrified, swearing she heard things in that wing. Snuck out in the night and was found dead the next day. I'll not bury another for the sake of curiosity." The housekeeper shook her head and said to Isabella, "There are places in Harrowgate, Miss Barrett, that are best left undisturbed. The north wing is one. There are shadows in this house that have been here far longer than either of us. Some doors, once opened, cannot be closed again. Do you understand?"

Isabella's brows lifted. "I understand that oblique answers invite curiosity."

Mrs. Abernathy hid the hint of a smile.

"I wondered if you might accompany me to the village on Wednesday," she said, her tone lighter.

"The village?" Isabella blinked. "Why?"

"You spend every day in the library, breathing in mildew and dust and old paper," Mrs. Abernathy said gently.

"Well...yes," Isabella said. "I've been hired to set the library to rights..."

"Of course." Mrs. Abernathy nodded. "But you've been here for weeks now and not taken so much as a half-day. A bit of fresh air will do you good, lamb. Besides, Wednesday is market day. So many people milling about. One never knows what one might see...or hear."

Isabella studied Mrs. Abernathy carefully. The woman's expression was calm and placid, but there was something in her eyes, something watchful.

"And one never knows what answers one's questions might yield?" Isabella asked cautiously.

A flicker of approval crossed the housekeeper's face.

"People talk at market, Miss Barrett. They speak freely when they think no one is listening. Stories spill like grain from a broken sack." Mrs. Abernathy's lips pressed into a thin line. "But not all stories are true. And not all truths are meant to be heard." She rose, smoothing her apron with her palms. "Not *everything* you hear in the village will be true. But some things will be. And it's knowing the difference that makes all the difference."

Evening gathered in the library, the fire sunk to a velvet glow. Isabella capped her paste pot, set a blotter beneath two dampened boards, and smoothed her palm over the ledger to press a fresh line of ink flat. The room had learned her habits these past weeks...straightened piles, swept hearth, the consoling breath of beeswax and old paper.

She rolled her shoulders, her day's work done. Again, she had lost herself in her tasks and worked without pause. Now, her neck and shoulders cried their protest, and the growl in her belly reminded her that she must eat. She tidied the desk and rose. In her fatigue, she knocked the brass box with the back of her hand, sending it tumbling to the floor.

She hurried around the desk and bent to retrieve it, the weight of it settling in her hands. Tiny scarab eyes looked back at her. The key at her throat felt warm against her skin. Would it fit? Would it turn? Would it unlock whatever secrets the box held?

The keyhole beckoned.

"Don't," she told herself. "They are not your secrets."

As if in agreement, the lamp flickered, once, twice, the flame shrinking small and sullen. A draft crept along the floor and breathed across her fingers. The whispers thinned, not coaxing but cautioning, a hush settling with a start, like a palm had been pressed across a mouth.

Isabella set the box on the desk and pulled her hands away. When had she become a woman who would open a drawer and read a man's private correspondence? Who would try to unlock his possessions and rummage through his life?

When she had come under his roof, under his power, she answered herself.

She stared at the box. Almost did she turn away. Then she set her hand upon it again.

Rhys had wanted her here at Harrowgate. He had tried to entice Papa and when that had failed, he had enticed *her*. He was a man with secrets, as was his right. He had no obligation to share them with her. Unless they involved her, and she felt certain they did.

Her thumb stroked a scarab at the corner of the box.

She should leave it. The right thing to do was leave it. But courtesy was a luxury, safety was not.

She could not be sure that his secrets, in the end, would not do her harm.

Her fingers disobeyed common sense and decency. She drew the chain over her head, freeing Papa's key. It slid into the escutcheon with indecent ease.

From the corridor came the creak of a floorboard, a weight shifting just beyond the door, like a warning, one she had heeded when last she held this box in her hand. This time, she chose to ignore it, the key biting cold between her fingers.

The turn was smooth, the click soft as the lock yielded.

At the sound, the draft grew hot, the whispers bolder,

clear in their disapproval. Which made her want to view the contents all the more.

Heat suffused the brass as if the box sat in full sun. She lifted the lid.

Inside lay a careful stack of letters. The paper was creamy wove, edges worn from handling, the ink gone tea-brown with age. On several of them, a second slant of cross writing ran over the first. All were written in a feminine hand, an elegant, right-leaning copperplate, with narrow ovals and capitals looped like ribbons.

Guilt surged. She closed the lid. Opened it the smallest crack. Closed it again.

But written words were witnesses. Ink told tales. Just as Rhys's letters to Papa and Papa's replies had offered her clarity and certainty, so, too might these letters offer her insights.

She opened the lid and the name on the topmost letter caught her eye. Rhys.

Curiosity surged. She set the box down, drew forth the top letter, and read.

Harrowgate, 4th October 1830

My dearest Rhys,

I write at once, though I scarcely know how to set down what must be told. Your aunt, our sweet Helena, is gone. A fall upon the stair. The physician says she missed her footing and, oh, my dear, I cannot bring myself to say more. Your uncle is quite undone.

Your cousin, though no child and older than yourself, cannot be brought to sense. She wanders after him, calling for her mother.

We shall manage until you can be spared, though your father insists you must not be sent for, that you have examinations and obligations, and all that business men make of propriety when their hearts are breaking.

Forgive so plain a recital. If I knew how to soften it, I would.

Your most affectionate Mother

P.S. Your father bids me add that you are to attend to your books and keep to your hours. He will write in a day or two. If you have need of anything, send word to me directly.

Isabella read the woman's grief in the lines she had written and those she had not, the kind of grief that comes when news arrives and there is nothing to be done but bear it. She pictured a boy in a narrow school chamber, a single candle guttered low, the letter open beneath his hand, reading it then as she read it now. But for him, the world had tilted under news he could not fix.

She lifted the next from the stack. The hand was the same, clear and feminine, the descenders long and steady. The wafer's red shell had cracked and reset when someone had opened it before. She smoothed the fold and read.

Harrowgate, 14th November 1830

My dearest Rhys,

It grieves me more than I can say to tell you that your Uncle Owen has gone after our sweet Helena. The physician calls it an Apoplexy, taken on Tuesday, yet I think it was sorrow that struck him under his ribs. We laid him yesterday beside her. The earth was iron hard and the bells very soft. I know how dear he was to you, and I fear this blow will find you where your studies cannot shield you. Your father is sorely struck by his brother's death. He does all that must be done, but I see the blow in the set of his mouth and the long nights he keeps.

Your cousin Catrin is with us now. She is brave to outward show, but her grief is profound.

Will and Ned are very quiet. Both ask me daily when you will come home. Your brothers miss you sorely. I have told them you will come to us at Christmas.

Your most affectionate Mother.

P. S. If you have the heart, write Catrin a few lines addressed here. Your hand will do her more good than physic.

The library blurred and steadied. Sorrow rose, clean and unexpected.

He has known grief, she thought, not the gentleman's abstract kind, but the raw kind that leaves fingerprints on a life. She pressed her thumb to the tidy signature, then folded the sheet along its old wound and laid it back as she had found it. Her fingers hovered over the next letter, one corner already bent back as if in invitation, or dare.

As her fingertip made contact with the letter, the fire gave a quick, low crackle. A wave of heat rolled through the room then fled, leaving the air cold as a mid-winter night. The lamp at her elbow flared and guttered. Somewhere in the walls, a metal flue ticked.

Across the room, a book toppled from a high shelf and hit the floor with a solid thud. Another slid after it, landing atop the first. Beneath her hand, the brass box shuddered, and she snatched her fingers back as the lid snapped shut. The skin of her palm prickled as though it had been kissed by steam. The air grew heavy with the stink of wet ash and old roses rotting on the stem.

Isabella surged to her feet and turned toward the library door.

The girl she had seen before stood between Isabella and escape. She looked older now, not a child anymore, but neither was she an adult. Her nightgown hung straight from narrow shoulders, pink satin ribbons at the throat and cuffs, the hem singed black. She lifted one pale hand and at the lazy sweep of her fingers the nearest shelf bucked and swayed, pitching volumes from their places, leather and paper drumming the floor with muffled blows.

Fear rose cold and clean to shiver along Isabella's skin. All her life the wraiths had been a constant, thin as frost, insubstantial, sighing and silvery, there but not there, unable to so much as lift a curl of hair. She had borne them, endured them, pitied them sometimes.

This one was not that. This one had weight. It occupied air. It cast the faintest shadow where no shadow ought to be. And it could move items in the physical world at will.

"Who are you?" Isabella asked. "What do you want of me?" Because there was the truth of it. This creature wanted something from her.

The girl stared at her with fathomless eyes. Her head turned to the right, chin grazing the line of her shoulder. Then, obscenely, it kept turning, slow and deliberate, until her nose pointed toward the small bumps of her spine. From her wrist, a pink ribbon slipped free and slithered to the floor, crawling across the carpet to touch the tip of Isabella's boot. There it lay like something shed, pale satin against burgundy nap.

The wraith's head unwound and with a sharp snap faced Isabella once more.

The ribbon struck, snake fast, coiling Isabella's ankle, climbing her skirt, biting tight at her wrist. With a gasp, she jerked back. Heat and cold flared together. Pain lanced to the bone. A stink rose, like tallow and charred meat and for a terrible instant, she thought it was her own flesh.

A crackle ran the ceiling followed by a roar. A wall of heat slammed her. Isabella jerked her arm up to shield her face and stumbled back.

"Enough," she said, and heard her father's tone from that day at St. Jude's in her own voice.

The ribbon slackened; the heat dropped away. Somewhere, a latch lifted with a soft click and the crushing pressure in the room released. Isabella steadied herself with a hand against the desk and looked about.

The library was empty.

Would that she could pretend she had imagined the whole of it. But the books from the nearby shelf lay scattered across the floor and a single length of pink satin ribbon lay at her feet, burned black at one end. She bent with shaking knees, wrapped it once around her fingers, and slid it into her pocket.

Anger bled through what fear remained.

"You want something of me," she said into the hush. "Whatever it is, you will not win by terror."

She went to the box and turned the key, locking it once more then slipped the chain back over her head and tucked it away so the metal lay against her skin. Lifting the lamp, she set her shoulders and left the library.

Somewhere deep in the house, metal scraped along stone once, twice, and then stopped, satisfied as a cat that had trapped the mouse.

CHAPTER THIRTEEN

Night in Harrowgate did not so much fall as gather. It descended on the long gallery like a fog settling in the hollows of the stairs. Isabella's candle made a small, stubborn light the shadows tolerated but did not welcome.

In her chamber, the fire had burned low and small. In the corner, Papa's trunk crouched, waiting, always waiting. The key lay against her throat, a paltry weight that made its presence known, nonetheless.

Setting down the candle, she stood a moment, listening. Somewhere in the walls, pipes ticked. And all around her, the whispers hovered like moth's wings.

She looked to the brass-bound trunk and silently acknowledged why she had skirted it for so long, not for the lock but for the dangers of what might be found within. The contents of that trunk had swallowed Papa whole. If she opened it, might it take her too? That fear had kept her circling like a moth at a candle. She straightened, decided. She would not be ruled by a box or by the terror of the unknown.

She had dared to unlock Rhys's secrets. How could she do less with her own?

Taking the key from around her neck, she knelt and fitted it in the lock. The wards turned. When she lifted the lid, the trunk exhaled a breath tinged with dust and old paper. Inside were oilskin bundles, neatly stacked. She thought back to how distraught Papa had been, sitting on the floor before the trunk, books and folios strewn around him. Even in his despair, he had packed everything away with care.

She drew out the first packet. Papa's tidy hand marched down the folios between marginal notes that cut across with urgency. *On Methods for Quelling Unquiet.* Dates. Parish names. A curious symbol repeated in the margins: two semicircles, nested but not touching. She brushed it with a fingertip and felt a faint prickle on her skin. She remembered seeing it before, remembered Papa hiding it with his hand.

Another bundle held clippings from journals and newspapers—accounts of apparitions, cautions against spirit-rapping—and a leaflet from a lecture on "manifestations."

"Papa," she said softly, confused. He had always viewed such things with a jaundiced eye. Why harbor such a collection, then?

She withdrew more packets, unwrapped them to find more books, some of which she had seen before. *Petit Albert. Dragon Rouge. Grimorium Verum.* Some were journals rather than tomes, diaries of spells and conjuration.

At the bottom of the trunk lay a book that had once been whole and now was not. The binding had been cleft clean down its spine, so that she held one board and half the gatherings while the other half either lived elsewhere

or had been destroyed. The surviving leather was worn and scuffed. The vellum leaves clung desperately to tattered cords. One showed a sketch of a room...lamps, a bowl, what appeared to be the chalked outline of a door on a stone hearth, and notes in the margins, old and faded.

Leafing onward, she found diagrams and more notes, circles within circles, and adjacent notations crossed out, only to be made again. At the torn gutter, the lines broke off, a paragraph snuffed, sentences missing half their clauses.

Someone, not Papa, had written in a small, cramped hand: *Two halves...willing...joined...living conductor required.* The words made no sense to her, but the rest was missing.

Tucked in was a single leaf in Papa's hand, *Quelling the Unquiet* written across the top. Beneath it was a terse litany: *Bar the chimneys with iron. Mark lintels with chalk. Salt the thresholds. Keep rowan at the hearth. Name nothing you do not mean to bind.* In the margin, he had added, smaller: *I have tried each. Some held for a night, some only an hour. Not enough. Never enough.*

In another place, a single line caught her eye, the ink faint as though Papa's pen had been nearly spent was the note: *Sensitives anchor the aperture. Without the anchor, the chorus shards into harm.* And further down the page: *A gate to continuity, to let the trapped end the endless circle. Cost unknown.*

Those final two words chilled her.

And at the very bottom Papa had written, *For Isa. When she is ready.* He had struck out *if* and replaced it with *when.* That small correction, that quiet certainty, made her heart knot with grief.

Her eyes stung and the note blurred. In the press of

Papa's script, ink blotched where his hand had paused, margins crowded where there had been little room, she saw what she had missed before. In those final weeks, he had known his time was short and he had hurried, not for himself but for her.

He had not thought her mad.

Iron and chalk. Rowan and salt. Everything he had tried was not a cure for delusion but a defense against what was real. He had believed her all along. He had believed in the things that breathed at the edges of her sight, and he had worked to banish them.

What Papa had feared were those who would not believe, the pity and censure and remedies and pain they would force upon a girl who spoke of voices and wraiths.

Suddenly, she understood that fraught breakfast the morning Papa had chased Rhys away, the way he had asked if he had made a mistake, if he had been wrong. Not wrong about her, not wrong about what she heard and saw, but wrong to keep this knowledge shut inside a box and ask her to pretend nothing moved in the shadows. Wrong to think silence would save her.

Never say it. Never show it.

His admonition took on new meaning. Never let others know what she truly saw because they would not believe, and she would pay a terrible price.

But Papa had believed.

He had meant to understand it and then teach her, but he had run out of hours.

Rhys had not lit the fire. Cold made a clearer edge for his thoughts. The lamp drew a narrow circle across the desk.

Beyond it, the paneled walls gleamed dully. The shelves of his study were lined not with books but with ledgers, almanacs, and neat piles of correspondence tied with twine, an archive of obligations, not curiosities.

He had written a single line and blotted it twice before setting down the pen. The page accused him with its emptiness.

"Mr. Caradoc." He looked up to see Mrs. Abernathy lingering at the threshold. "You sent Matty to fetch me."

"I did. Please come in."

She stepped in, shut the door softly, and waited with her hands folded against her apron. She wore her reserve like armor, her quiet a presence as commanding as any spoken word.

"I understand you've asked Miss Barrett to accompany you to the village," he said. His voice came too flat, too formal, and he despised the stiffness in it. But better to protect himself with cold formality than to hazard warmth and have it turned against him.

"I have. She's not taken so much as a half day since she's been here, and I reckoned a turn in the village might do her good."

The woman's practicality had always been her armor, as his silence was his. He let the quiet stretch until it bit, then forced the words out. "I have a request to make."

Mrs. Abernathy's eyes widened, but she stayed silent, waiting for him to speak.

"I want her to hear the truth," he said. The syllables felt like a stone dragged up his throat. "Not from me. From others. From those who remember what this house was, what this family was, and what was lost here. The fire. The deaths that came before it. The whispers people still trade across the green." He kept his gaze fixed on the lamplight haloing the blotter. To name the fire aloud was to peel back his own armor, to lay bare the raw wound of memory. "The sexton. Widow Pritchard. The ferryman…" he said, thinking aloud. And then, "No. The Burns sisters would be best."

"Pansy likes to tell a good tale," Mrs. Abernathy said. "And she doesn't always stick to truth."

"Viola will rein her in," he said.

"I could speak with Miss Barrett…" Miss Abernathy offered.

She could. But she was loyal to him and she might gentle the telling because of it.

No. Isabella must hear versions of events in other voices, voices not his own or those obligated to him. Soon, he must ask her to make a choice. She had a right to hear the variations of truth that would come from the mouths of others.

"The sisters," he said, decided now. "She has met them before. And she will be welcomed. I want open doors and willing mouths. But it must not smell of design." His hands curled on the desk. "If she hears it from me, she will take it for manipulation. If she hears it from you, she might wonder why you suddenly gossip when it is not in your character. The Burns sisters will do."

Mrs. Abernathy's gaze stayed steady. "Of course, sir."

The lamp guttered, flame bowing, then righting itself. He imagined the questions tumbling through Mrs. Abernathy's thoughts. In the end, she asked none of them because it was not her place and because she surely knew that he had already sacrificed much, asking for her help at all.

He met her eyes and held them. "I trust you with

this." The word twisted in him, bitter as gall. He did not trust. Not since betrayal and fire and ash had taken everything. And he would not tell her why this mattered; the ghosts were his burden alone.

Her face softened by a hair's breadth. "I'll see it done, sir. The Burns sisters are always at their window, eager for visitors. She'll not miss them."

He should have dismissed her then. Instead, he found himself saying, low and unfamiliar, "You think me a good man."

"You've been good to me." Mrs. Abernathy tilted her head, studied him a moment. "And I think you've borne more than most could and not soured past repair."

"Thank you," he said, and the words cost him.

She dipped a curtsey that was acknowledgment more than deference, then withdrew, leaving him to the cold and the silence.

The air was sharp and fresh as Isabella stepped out into the courtyard on Wednesday morning, her breath puffing white. The scent of damp earth and hay filled her lungs as the horses snorted and stamped, their flanks steaming in the chill.

She slipped her hand into her cloak pocket and rubbed the length of pink ribbon coiled there between her thumb and forefinger, the burned and blackened edge stiff. The ribbon was proof she had not imagined the events in the library. Proof she was not mad. She had carried it with her since but had not been visited again by the wraith.

Mrs. Abernathy stood with Tom Grange near the

carriage, the low murmur of their voices threading with the creak of leather harnesses and the click of metal buckles.

But it wasn't the housekeeper or the coachman who held Isabella's attention.

Rhys stood at the lead mare's shoulder, one gloved hand skimming the sleek rise of her neck, the other tucked in his coat pocket. He was dressed in a sharply tailored black coat and waistcoat, the crisp folds of his cravat stark against his throat. A lock of dark hair had shaken loose and fell across his brow. He looked every inch the gentleman he was meant to be, yet something untamed ran beneath the surface, restrained energy in the set of his shoulders, the balance of his stance, one boot angled as if he might pivot in an instant.

He turned his head, his slate-gray eyes meeting Isabella's across the courtyard, the intensity of his gaze making her feel as though a wire stretched between them, pulled taut. For a moment, neither of them moved.

"Miss Barrett," he said at last, his voice low and smooth, unspooling into the cold morning air. "Out for an excursion, are we?"

"Yes," she said, hating that her voice went soft. "Mrs. Abernathy invited me to the village."

His gaze dipped to the housekeeper and back, a not-quite smile shaping his lips, sharp and cold. He stepped nearer, gravel crunching beneath his boots. The mare's ears flicked then flattened.

"The village is a place of many voices," he said. "Some truthful, some false. All loud. You would do well to be careful about what you ask, and whom you ask."

Her chin lifted, a prickle of defiance straightening her spine. "Are you warning me, Mr. Caradoc?"

"Consider it advice." The almost-smile visited the corners of his mouth, not so cold now. There was amusement there, yes, but something else as well. Calculation. Wariness. A guarded wall. "Advice I suspect you'll disregard."

He was close now, close enough that she could see the faint shadows beneath his eyes, the tightness in his jaw, the crease between his brows, as if some less than pleasant thought pressed there and would not ease. The scents of citrus and leather folded around her.

Heat rose, traitorous and bright, as memory supplied the taste of lemon on his lips and the slow, deliberate weight of his hands on her arms.

"Will I regret going to the village?" Isabella asked, her heart beating too fast.

He studied her, the silence filled with the thrum of her pulse.

He reached out, so slowly she might have stepped away had she wished, and brushed a loosened strand back from her cheek. His gloved fingertips barely grazed her, yet his touch felt like an ember sparking against her skin. Her world narrowed to that small, shameless trespass and the weight of his gaze.

She ought to protest. She did not.

"You may regret many things before your time here is done, Miss Barrett," he said, the words low and deliberate. "But I doubt visiting the village will be one of them."

His thumb hovered near her cheekbone for just a breath longer than was proper, then withdrew, the space between suddenly feeling both too vast and too narrow all at once. His gaze dropped to her lips, lingering there for a single stolen second before lifting once more. Knowledge struck her with bright, dangerous clarity. He *wanted* her.

Her own want was a tightening low in her belly, an ache that made the cold air feel thin.

This desire between them unraveled something fragile inside her. Her life had been quiet, careful, filled with ink stains and orderly shelves. She was not the sort of woman a man like Rhys Caradoc wanted. But when he looked at her as he did now, she thought the air itself might catch fire.

From the corner of her eye, she caught Matty's quick, curious glance, the housekeeper's stillness. Impropriety had witnesses.

Heat stained her cheeks.

Rhys took a step back, the cold wind swirling into the distance he'd made. The lead mare tossed her head; steam drifted from her nostrils.

"Safe travels," he said, his tone civil and measured. He strode toward the manor, his gait favoring his left leg, his coat flaring behind him. At the foot of the stairs, he paused without turning, the line of his back stiff.

"Miss Barrett," he said, then paused. "Do return."

The command hummed in the air as he disappeared inside, the door closing behind him with a click.

Isabella stood on the gravel drive, feeling as though she had been hollowed out and refilled with something restless and alive. Her skin tingled where he had touched her cheek. Her lips felt sensitized, as if his look alone had been a caress.

"Miss Barrett?" Mrs. Abernathy called from near the carriage. "If we're to reach market early...."

"Yes," Isabella said, forcing her feet to move.

Tom handed her up, and as the carriage jolted

forward, she allowed herself to glance back at the looming façade of the house. The rows of long windows stared back at her, unblinking.

Two words danced through her thoughts, winding tight.

Do return.

Not an invitation. A command she had no wish to disobey.

Rhys listened to the carriage roll away, carrying Isabella with it. Hoofbeats struck the ground, wheels creaked, and the house changed its breathing. Her absence unspooled the hush she carried; the needling susurrus rushed back like a blow.

He stood a moment in the entrance hall with his hand on the newel, riding out the swell.

He thought of her.

The dusting of sugar beneath his thumb. Lemon on his tongue. Her mouth had been soft and willing, and he had forced himself to let her go.

Send her away, said the last decent part of him. *Put her in the coach and keep her on the road until London takes her in and Harrowgate forgets her.*

But decency was the smallest part of him now. Without her, the dead he loved would go on as they were, trapped in the circle that eats its own tail. He would not doom them to that. He would sacrifice morals and honor to give them rest.

He went down the passage to the library. The knob turned under his hand and a breath of wet ash met him. The brass box sat on the corner of the desk, the lid closed.

He had no proof, but instinct assured him...she had opened it.

He had wanted her to open it. He had baited the snare.

He had purchased the damned box because her key would fit.

His gaze went to the toppled books and the faint scorch licked into the nap of the carpet. The thing had come to her here. It had shown its teeth.

"You will not have her," he told the empty room, and the house answered with a steady tapping in the wall.

He crossed to the desk and touched the box. Cool under his palm. He could all but see the letters inside, his mother's elegant hand, the perpendicular cross-writing when she'd run out of space.

How many had she read? Some? All? If not yet, then soon. She was too curious not to want the story in its entirety.

Let the gossip in Marlow tell her what he could not: locks set after the fire, masons who would not finish, tools that walked, and most damning of all, that a girl had burned behind a door others swore was barred from without. Wasn't that precisely why she had gone to Marlow? To discover his secrets...his and Harrowgate's. But they were one and the same.

The chorus in the walls thinned and gathered, listening.

He looked toward the door and thought again of the coach, of Mrs. Abernathy's sensible obedience and the ease with which he could command it: Take Miss Barrett to see the Burns sisters.

What she heard there would turn curiosity into hunger and send her back starved for answers. He would make certain they lay in wait for her to discover.

He left the library and climbed. On the landing the air was warmer by the wall, wrong as breath in a sealed room. He paused outside Isabella's chamber, set his hand on the latch, and let his knuckles rest there without pressing. Boundary. Courtesy. He had already trespassed against both in both thought and design. He eased the door open and stepped in.

The bed was neatly made, the heavy curtains parted an inch, allowing a spill of daylight onto the carpet. Against the far wall, the trunk waited, iron-banded, brass-cornered. He crossed to it and crouched, ignoring the clutch of pain in his left leg.

Thorn & Sons, Ludgate Hill, the cartouche read, bee and all. The same mark adorned the brass box in his library; the same hand had cut both wards.

He sat back on his heels and studied the trunk. He could unlock it now, while she was away, rifle through the contents, find the grimoire if it was there. Doing that might win him the book, but he would lose the prize if she discovered his trespass. Her trust. Her willing collaboration.

"Not today," he said. If he breached her privacy and she learned of it, there would be no coming back from that.

He rose and left her room as he had found it.

In his workroom, the half-grimoire lay where he'd left it, brass inlay shaped like a broken coin gone dull with handling. The diagram at its heart named two halves, hands joined. Two willing halves joined and the gate will open. He had chased that promise for years until it brought him to London and to the girl who quieted the house's noise simply by breathing in it.

Willing was the hinge. If he told her what he wanted,

what he needed, she would think him both mad and monstrous. She had spent a lifetime being taught not to see what she saw, not to hear what she heard. Push too soon and she would flee.

No, she must tease the threads apart herself, discover the pieces and solve the riddle on her own. Only then might she be willing. Only then might they end this.

The wall at his back ticked. A child's thin cry threaded the sound; a mother's sorrow shaped the air, thick and heavy. He set his teeth until his jaw ached.

"I hear you," he said. "I am coming."

CHAPTER FOURTEEN

The carriage rattled into Great Marlow's High Street, wheels clacking on the cobbles. Isabella paused as she stepped down, looking about. Red brick fronts and timbered gables pressed close; painted signboards creaked on their irons. A brewer's cart went by and left malt on the air.

People were out, but welcome was not. Heads bent, steps quick, they cut sidelong glances at the carriage, wary.

As Tom helped Mrs. Abernathy down, Isabella's gaze fell on a little boy standing by the horse trough, hair plastered to his head, clothing wet, the building at his back showing clean through him.

Her breath hitched, then steadied. Habit returned, and she let her gaze pass over him as if he were not there.

Relief and unease tangled in her chest. After Harrowgate's drought, the ordinary presence of wraiths was almost a comfort, or at the very least a familiar discomfort. The house was starved of them, save the ribboned girl. What lived in those walls that barred every other ghost but made that one so terribly strong?

"Miss Barrett?" Mrs. Abernathy's voice was gentle. "Shall we?"

As they walked, the market unrolled with greens and eggs and wool, bolts of fabric, neat stacks of staves, a peacock bolt of worsted that caught the eye. Isabella noticed that conversations paused as they drew near, resuming once they had passed; she realized she was unlikely to garner any answers here.

After had walked a bit, Mrs. Abernathy paused and glanced at Isabella. There was a flicker of deliberation in her eyes. "I recall you mentioning that you shared the post-chaise from Maidenhead with the Burns sisters, did you not?"

"I did," Isabella replied.

"They'll be glad of a visit, I'm certain," the house-keeper said. "Cheerful company, those two."

A visit with the sisters would be a perfect opportunity to ask questions. "Do you think I ought?"

"I do. Their cottage is but a short walk from here." She pointed the way, and after taking her leave of the house-keeper, Isabella made her way down a narrow lane where the noise thinned to the soft slap of boots on stone and the drip from a gutter beating time.

The Burns sisters' cottage sat at the end of Chapel Lane. Ivy clung to the walls, lace curtains crowded the windows, and china teacups made a regiment along the sills. Isabella rapped twice.

The door creaked open on Pansy, pink-cheeked and flustered, flour on her apron. "Oh! Miss Barrett, you've come!"

"I hope my visit is not inconvenient," Isabella said.

"Not at all." Pansy fussed her in, warning her, "Mind the step. It will kill us all one day!"

Inside lay tidy clutter: bunches of drying thyme and mint, a narrow hearth, books stacked where a table would have been sensible. Viola sat by the fire, feet tucked under her, needles clicking.

"Miss Barrett," she said, warm and glad. "How lovely to see you. Sit you down, do."

"Mind your skirts," Pansy added, fluttering toward the kettle. "The hearth spits."

On the far wall hung four small watercolours. One was hedgerows under a bruised sky, another the river clotted with reeds; a third a lane in late afternoon with light like honey in the ruts, and, last, the square in summer, bursting with color.

"They're beautiful," Isabella said.

Pansy's hands flew to her mouth. "Oh," she said, voice breaking on the single syllable. "Our Hazel painted those."

Viola's needles paused. "Our sister," she said sadly. "She passed—"

"A year ago last Michaelmas," Pansy finished for her.

The room cooled, though the fire held steady. A figure stood at the edge of Isabella's sight, an older woman, hair in a tidy bun, cheeks round. Hazel, Isabella thought, looking at her sisters with a love so simple it made the air ache. It was longing that kept her. Love, and the habit of staying. Isabella turned her face slightly and let her gaze slip past as if no one was there.

"Tea?" Viola said, recovering, and set out the cups. "Milk? Sugar?"

"Both, please."

They spoke first of small things. Viola mentioned the

baker's new boy. Pansy mentioned how the river had swelled after last week's rain, then told the tale of the vicar's cat learning to open doors with her paw. Viola eased the talk along, smooth as butter on bread.

Pansy tipped her head, peering at Isabella with those pale blue eyes that missed little. "How do you find Harrowgate, Miss Barrett?"

And here it was, the entrée to the topic Isabella most wanted to broach. "Large," she said, deciding how best to word her inquiries.

"My dear Miss Barrett," Pansy said, kind but incapable of leaving a thing on the bone. "You did not come all this way for cats and weather. Ask your questions. Best to have them out."

"Pansy," Viola cautioned.

"Well, she's here now. She might as well have what she came for."

Isabella stared down at her tea. She thought of locked doors, the scrape of metal on stone, a girl in a gown tied with ribbons whose head had turned past the limit of its hinge. "I don't know precisely what to ask," she said honestly. "Only...what you know. Of the house. Of the... fire."

Viola's gaze slid to the hearth. "It's an old place," she said. "Old places hold—"

"—echoes," Pansy cut in. "And more than echoes."

"Fire leaves scars," Viola murmured.

"—as deep as caverns," Pansy finished. "Folk remember. And not just the fire." Pansy leaned forward, her voice a quick whisper meant to carry. "That house has known too much darkness, too many graves dug in too short a time."

"So much sorrow," Viola said.

Pansy nodded. "But there's more." She lifted a finger and tapped the air to emphasize her point. "The men sent to mend the north wing after the fire say their lines went wrong and their tools walked. The chimneys howled down a cold flue. Hot breath burned the backs of their necks though no fire was near. In the end they packed their carts and wouldn't go back for love or money."

"Stories," Viola said. "Tales told one to the next until they grew themselves a second head."

"These didn't need growing," Pansy said. "They came up quick as nettles and true as the north star."

"I've heard some of that," Isabella said carefully, recalling Peg's words.

Pansy drew a breath and Isabella found herself holding her own. "Kin of Mr. Caradoc's died in that fire. His father." She leaned closer. "His cousin. Catrin."

Isabella went very still. A line in a letter: *Your cousin Catrin is with us now. She is brave to outward show.*

"They say," Pansy went on, voice dropping, "he barred the door. Locked it from without."

The words landed like a slap. Rhys's coat warm on her shoulders. Rhys's mouth sweet with sugared lemon. Rhys's hand steady when the air turned wrong. The picture would not fit the frame Pansy built.

"People say all manner of things when they are afraid," Isabella managed.

Viola's needles clicked once, hard. "That they say it doesn't make it true," she said. "We don't know who barred that door."

Isabella's heart skipped a beat.

"We don't know that it wasn't him," Pansy replied, mulish. "What we do know is what they found when the fire cooled. Lock and latch scorched. The poor girl by the door, nails torn, wood gouged. And her—" She stopped, swallowed. "Burnt black, she was."

Heat tore through Isabella like a wave, then fled, leaving her cold. The singed pink satin in her pocket seemed to pulse against her thigh like a second heart. The back of her throat burned with bile. Still, she could not make the picture fit. But the North Wing had burned, and a girl had died whether or not she believed the rest.

"And that poor maid died there as well," Pansy said.

"She took a fever and wandered out," Viola snapped. Then her gaze shifted to Isabella. "There was no harm done her by anyone."

Pansy sniffed but did not argue the point. "Still and all," she said, "folk around here have no liking for Harrowgate." She spread her hands. "That house is not right."

Viola's needles clicked, steady. "Old houses carry their histories."

"Their ghosts," Pansy said.

Viola only rolled her eyes.

"Our Hazel used to say some hauntings are greedy," Pansy said. "Take all the air from a room and call it peace."

Isabella thought of the hush that fell like a shroud when Rhys Caradoc was near. The closest to peace she had known. Was it a reprieve or a mark of danger?

"And then there's the doctor," Pansy went on.

"Oh, hush now," Viola said. "He had nothing to do with anything. He only came to Marlow years after the fire."

"You hush," Pansy said, and turned back to Isabella. "A doctor from London he was, once a man of consequence before scandal clipped him. Took a post here in Marlow."

Viola nodded. "He kept rooms—"

"—off the High Street," Pansy said. "When he died, men with wagons came for his things at dawn, quiet as thieves."

Isabella sipped her tea, only half listening, her thoughts spinning with what they had revealed about the fire.

"Carried off every cabinet, bottle, ledger, and book," Viola said.

"Men Mr. Caradoc hired," Pansy said. "That's what folks say."

Isabella nodded, trying to look interested.

"Don't know what he wanted with Dr. Hargreaves's things—"

"Dr. Hargreaves?" Isabella interrupted, the name catching in her throat. The room tipped a fraction.

Tap...tap...tap. Doors with wired windows. Screams echoing from the bowels of the building. A door slamming shut, trapping her inside. *I have consulted my colleagues. I know what you've claimed. Hearing voices. Seeing people that are not there.* No, surely not. It could not be the same man.

"From London? From St. Jude's?" she asked, her voice strained.

"Indeed," Pansy said. "Do you know of him?"

"Oh, my dear Miss Barrett, are you quite alright?" Viola asked. "You've gone pale."

"Yes, I'm fine," Isabella managed. She lifted her cup once more and forced a sip. She smiled and nodded as the two women nattered on. She managed a few more minutes, then rose. "Thank you for the visit. I will not overstay. And I must not delay Mrs. Abernathy."

Both women rose, looking disappointed.

Viola said, "Of course. We understand. But—"

"—you will return?" Pansy said.

"I will," Isabella assured them, anxious to be away.

Outside, she drew a breath but found herself choked by all she had learned. For a man like Hargreaves, Marlow was a far step below London. How had he come to be here, and how had Rhys Caradoc felt about his presence? Had Hargreaves been his tormentor, his gaoler, or his savior? The questions bubbled in her mind.

She had come for gossip over tea, and left with poison steeping in her veins.

The return to Harrowgate felt longer than the ride down. The road curled along the river, gray water scudding under a sky the color of old pewter. The village fell away. Fields rose and folded. Hedgerows snagged the mist and held it like uncarded fleece. The carriage rocked and sighed, each turn of the wheels winding Isabella tighter until her skin felt a size too small.

Dr. Hargreaves.

The name had cracked something she had sealed years ago. She pressed her gloved fingers to her knee and willed them still. He could not be the same man, she told herself. And yet she knew it was he. The London doctor with a narrow mouth and a showman's cruelty, fallen into disrepute, fetched up in Marlow like flotsam. And upon his death, Mr. Caradoc—Rhys—had sent men at dawn to take every bottle, ledger, and book.

Why? What had he wanted to find among the dead man's effects?

The carriage rattled into the yard. Harrowgate rose

before her, windows blank as eyes, chimneys inked against the sky. *Do return.* The command sang in her, bright and thin as a wire. She did not quite know whether the words comforted or bound.

She thought of the Burns sisters, Viola's steady kindness, Pansy's appetite for rumor. She thought of Hazel's small watercolors and the soft ache of love that had kept a woman in a room where she no longer lived. She thought Catrin clawing at a barred door until her nails ripped free. And she thought of Rhys's father. She had not known he died in that fire.

All of it left her mind churning with a slurry of suspicion, pity, and confusion.

Tom jumped down. Mrs. Abernathy gathered her shawl closer. "You'll have a sit-down first," the housekeeper said, a question folded into the certainty.

"In a moment," Isabella replied. She tried for lightness, but the words took effort. "I'll go up and put my things by."

Mrs. Abernathy's eyes narrowed a fraction. "Very good, lamb. I'll see to Cook."

Her chamber was dim when she entered, the fire laid but not yet lit. She had just slipped off her gloves when a soft knock came and Peg edged in with a fresh ewer of water.

"Thought you'd want this, miss, after a carriage ride," Peg said, crossing to the washstand.

"Thank you." Isabella managed a smile though she felt as though her nerves were flayed after all the Burns sisters had revealed, and all they had held back. Questions slithered through her thoughts like eels.

Peg set down the ewer.

Isabella smelled roses and charred wood. Then a

frigid breath swirled through the room. Ice bloomed across the surface of the water, crackling in the silence.

With a cry, Peg jumped back. "Miss—"

The cold was swallowed in an instant by a blast of heat. The walls seemed to swell inward, the air pressing down, heavy and thick.

Peg. A whisper without sound, ricocheting through Isabella's thoughts, oily and sly.

Peg's eyes went wide, her freckles stark, her skin white. She flung an arm over her face, stumbling back, mouth open in a soundless cry.

Peg. The whisper came again.

The maid's braid tugged taut as if an unseen hand had yanked it. With a cry, she grabbed her hair, her breath turning to frost before her lips. Whimpering, twisting, she tried to wrench free.

Isabella caught her by the wrist and pulled her close. Rage struck through her like flint to steel. How dare it touch this girl. Her pulse thundered, her throat raw as the heat seared her. The room shuddered around them.

"Iron to bind. Hearth to keep. Shadows hush. Spirits sleep," Peg said, the words running together, her voice so low as to be barely audible. "Iron to bind. Hearth to keep. Shadows hush. Spirits sleep," she said again, and then again, each repetition faster, thinner.

"Let her be," Isabella snapped, her voice harsh, unsteady, but loud in the stifling room.

For a heartbeat, the weight deepened. Smoke curled low across the floor, veiling their skirts. Peg whimpered against Isabella's shoulder. The whisper came again. *Peg.*

Isabella's fury steadied her fear. "Enough!"

The air cracked, sudden as a whip and the smoke tore apart. The heat dropped away. The room was still.

Peg clung to her, shivering. "You felt it. You heard it," she whispered, half-plea, half-certainty.

"I did." The truth burned her tongue, begging to be spoken, to be told in full—the voices, the wraiths—but Papa's warning clamped her mouth shut. She only pressed Peg's hand and said, "I will ask Mrs. Abernathy to see about the flue. It must be blocked."

Peg looked at her a long moment. "But the fire's not lit, miss."

Isabella held the girl's gaze, willing her to hear all the things Isabella dared not say. "No, it isn't." She let a moment pass, just holding fast to Peg's hands, then she said, "Your mam was right. Ghosts can't hurt you. Only fear can."

Peg nodded once, fierce despite the tears that brightened her eyes. Then she slipped out, leaving Isabella alone with the echo of the wraith.

She sat long in the quiet, the ewer beading on the washstand, the shadows restless at the edge of the glow from the candle she lit. Her limbs felt hollow, as though the wraith had drunk the marrow from her bones. She did not go to the library that night. She had no strength left for locked boxes and letters that painted only sorrow. They would wait for tomorrow.

CHAPTER FIFTEEN

Tomorrow came with a sky the color of tarnished silver and a wind that poked through every crack of Harrowgate's stone. Isabella rose late, her sleep ragged with dreams of smoke and flame and a voice calling Peg's name. The taste of ash still coated her tongue when she left her chamber

She passed the long gallery with its faces in oil, turned down a dim hallway, then another until she stood with her hand on the knob of the library door, her heartbeat thudding a dull rhythm.

She opened the door to the cavernous space. Her ledger waited with its blotter; the paste pot sat capped. The brass box gleamed on the corner of the desk. When she laid her palm on it, heat came up through the metal as though fire raged on the other side. She jerked her hand away at the burn.

From deep in the walls came a whisper, angry as wasps.

The hesitation she had felt when first she opened the

box was absent now. She cared not for courtesy or Rhys's privacy. The things she had learned in the village weighed heavy on her soul.

Coincidence could not be trusted. Dr. Hargreaves's presence in Marlow could not be trusted. There were layers here she had not begun to fathom, and they frightened her, threatening to drag her down and bury her. But here in this box were answers laid down in ink, truths she could see with her own eyes, truth she would drag, hissing, into the light.

She turned Papa's key in the lock then lifted the lid.

The letters lay where she had set them the last time, creamy wove and faded ink, tidy as knives in a surgeon's roll. She ran a finger along the edges then gentled the letters free, setting aside the first two, for she had already read them. She unfolded the third.

Harrowgate, 7 April 1831

My dearest Rhys,

You must come home at once.

Our little Ned is gone. They found his cap by the willow and then—oh! my hand shakes, and I cannot be plain— Mr. Baines waded in and brought him out. The rector will speak to you when you arrive. The hour is not yet fixed. Will is distraught and will not be parted from me. Your father says he has written the schoolmaster; do not wait for a reply.

I cannot put the particulars here. They will keep until I can look at you. Only come.

Your loving Mother

. . .

Isabella set the letter down and pressed two fingers to her brow. Her vision blurred. She blinked hard and only then realized her jaw hurt from clenching. *Ned.* She recalled his name from the previous letter. She could see the willow without meaning to, its long green fronds combing the current like a woman dragging her hair. A child's cap caught. A man wading. A boy borne in his arms like a bundle of wet laundry.

She could not help but see schoolboy Rhys sitting with this letter, a single candle guttering to tallow tears. Another blow he could not set right. She imagined him shoving clothes into a bag with fingers that shook, walking too quickly down a corridor so the others could not look at his face. He had known grief and loss, this man who held himself so still, so calm.

A sound rose in the flue, a hum and tick. The whispers that clung to the edges of perception thinned, then swelled. Isabella did not look up. She reached for the next letter, a feeling of dread suffusing her.

Harrowgate, 29 September 1831

My dearest boy,

I have written and torn three letters this day because I do not know how to tell you what I must. Our Will is gone from us.

It began with a cough that would not be stilled. The apothecary sent laudanum, a soothing draught to ease his nights; a few drops in water, no more. He smiled and said he would be brave for me, and he was. By week's end, the cough gentled and the tightness left his little chest. Catrin—good child—begged to sit with him that I might close my eyes an hour. We kept the curtains drawn and the room as calm as might be. I left her with the lamp turned and the spoon set by, and kissed his temple. I settled in the chair at the foot of his bed. When I woke, the room was very quiet. His lashes lay on his cheek and his breathing grew soft as a kitten's. So soft, I bent to feel it. He slept, my dear, and he did not wake.

I could not write you before it was done. I wanted to hold him here by word if I could not by hand and you would only have run and missed his breath by a day. The rector is kind. He says the Lord gathers the little ones up and they do not fear. You and I know our Will was not little anymore, but I hope the rector is right about the fear.

I do not know how to be plain. Forgive me.

Your most affectionate Mother

The nib had bitten the paper hard in places. The downstrokes were darker than they ought to have been. Isabella touched the ink and imagined it drying, blotched by a mother's tears. Two sons in one year. The ledger of loss building, line upon line. Rhys had been away at school when sorrow had called him home and sent him out again and called him home once more. Some boys returned to school with longer legs and a new Latin primer. He had returned fewer brothers.

The horror of it crept through her.

Tap...tap...tap, the flue said, distinct, deliberate. The sound unstitched something near her heart. A fine sifting of ash lifted and fell as if the hearth breathed. Steam drifted down the chimney's throat, a thin fall that kissed the back of her hand and vanished with a hiss. She looked up then and saw the air above the grate shimmer as if heat rose from a fire though there was none. The smell, wet coal and scorched fat, curdled on the back of her tongue.

She reached for the last letter. It was written in a different hand, blunter, stronger. The paper was thicker, the fold exact.

Harrowgate, 21 January 1832

My son,

 Your mother is dead.

 You will return at once and remain for a time. There are matters here which require attention and I will not have the running of this house left to servants. I am not inclined to write more particulars by post.

 Send word of your train and the carriage shall meet you at the junction.

 Your ever affectionate Father,

 A. Caradoc

Isabella read it twice to be certain she had not mistaken the economy of words for cruelty. But she read, beneath the clipped declarations, the words of a man who would not set grief to paper because ink made it true. Aunt. Uncle. One brother, then the next. And finally, mother. All dead. The tragedy of it tore at her.

She laid the letter with the others and sat very

straight in the chair because if she bent even a little she might fold in half and not unfold again. She thought of Rhys standing in this room, grieving. She imagined him returning and returning until he had no returns left. She slid her hand into her pocket and worried the slip of ribbon between her thumb and forefinger.

The hush shifted, changing its pitch. The needles along her skin sharpened, then smoothed. Somewhere in the wall, metal dragged along stone, slow and purposeful. The same drawling scrape she had heard the first night, as if a poker were being pulled along a hearth one inch at a time, as if someone wished to make the world look up and listen.

All she had read blended with all she had learned in Marlow, stirred into a stew of confusion. Hargreaves's name worked under her ribs like a sliver. Men with a wagon at dawn. Men Rhys had hired. He had wanted something from that office, something Hargreaves had left in his bottles and ledgers and cabinets. Not the man himself, but the man's knowledge. Of what? Of whom? Her mouth tasted of metal.

She rose, certain of her destination. She could seek the kitchen, the comfort of tea and Mrs. Abernathy's good sense. She could look for Matty's solemn eyes and Peg's quick smile. She could go to her room and wash her face and lie down until the tremors passed.

Instead, she took up the lamp.

This was madness, she knew. Mrs. Abernathy would call her foolhardy. But ignorance, for her, was a greater terror than any wraith. Better to risk the house's malice than to let her mind gnaw itself hollow.

She told herself she would only look. She would stand at the foot of the north stair and breathe and listen. She would not touch any lock, any latch. She would not turn any knob. She would not go where she had been told not to go. She merely wished to know if the air was as wrong as Peg had said, if the draft came hot when the weather went cold. She wished to hear, perhaps, the chorus the workmen had heard, the howling down a cold flue, because hearing was better than imagining.

At the bottom of the stairs, she paused.

Treads pounded by centuries of feet had been worn into shallow boats. The lamps here were bracketed and cold; no one lit this place now. The dark above was heavy and thick. Isabella tested the first step with the toe of her boot, then set her weight and climbed.

The house smelled of old dust and chimney soot. And threaded through it, faint and cruel, of roses spoiled by stagnant water. Peg's whispered rhyme brushed her memory. *Iron to bind. Hearth to keep.* The words deserted her now, leaving her bare.

At the landing she stopped and turned her face toward the corridor that led to the locked doors. A current drifted along the floor growing warm, then hot, swirling around her ankles, heating her face. Her shins prickled as if she stood too close to Cook's range.

She put out her free hand to the wall to steady herself and touched sweat instead of plaster. A bead swelled and dripped down the wall like a tear. An instant later, steam filmed there, pearled, and vanished as though swallowed.

"Show yourself," she said, and hated the tremor that turned the command to a plea.

The girl obliged.

She stood three strides off, nightgown straight from narrow shoulders, pink satin at throat and cuffs, hem singed black. Not a child any longer. She had the face of a young woman now, her cheekbones high, her chin round. Her hair hung in lank ropes that might once have been glossy. A halo of shadow surrounded her.

"Who are you?" Isabella whispered, though she knew now the shape of the name from the letters. Catrin. Cousin. Kin.

The wraith's mouth softened, as if at a memory. Then her lips parted on a breath that was not air and stretched wider...wider...grotesque, inhuman.

Her lips peeled back with a wet, tearing sound, pulling away from her teeth and gums like the flesh of a rotting fruit peeling from its pit. Threads of flesh clung, then snapped. A fathomless dark seam split her face, widening, a yawning chasm, tearing a gaping strip along her forehead and down her chin with a pop of gristle that made Isabella's stomach churn.

With a brittle snap her jaw unhinged, gaping like a serpent's, as though she would swallow herself, swallow the shadows...swallow Isabella whole.

An oily, black substance oozed free and dripped over her unhinged jaw, the air heavy with a carrion-sweet stink.

With a gasp, Isabella stumbled back.

Dark streaks leaked from the girl's eyes, oozing down her cheeks in sluggish crimson-black trails. Where it dripped to the floor, the carpet hissed and smoked. Her head snapped back, the tendons of her throat bulging, her flesh moving and writhing as though something was trapped beneath her skin, trying to wriggle free.

Then, from deep in girl's chest came a piercing, keening wail that tunneled through Isabella's skull, clawing at her sanity, gouging at her emotions. Pain. Terror. Hopeless agony. She clamped her hands over her ears, her candle clattering to the floor. But the sound was inside her. Ripping. Splitting. Screaming.

Her own cry joined it before she could stop herself, ragged and raw. The corridor spun. For one terrible moment she thought she might break apart entirely, body and mind unspooling under that sound.

"Stop," she rasped, but her voice was swallowed by the relentless wail.

The girl surged forward, limbs jerking and snapping at unnatural angles, knees and elbows twisting...

Wrong. Wrong.

Isabella staggered back, stumbled. Her ankle twisted with a sharp wrench, and she fell hard to her hands and knees, the impact jolting along her limbs. Head hanging forward, stomach churning, she tried to push herself upright.

The cold hit her like a blow.

A presence closed around her, smothering, choking. The air was sharp, jagged, slicing into her chest as though she inhaled shards of glass.

Something coiled around her wrist. A ribbon, smooth as silk, strong as iron. Slick and endless, it unspooled from the wraith's unhinged mouth, holding her fast, hauling her forward. Isabella set her heels in the carpet, pulling against the inexorable drag. Another lash struck, winding her other arm, searing cold through flesh and bone.

"What do you want of me?" she cried.

And Catrin answered, not with words but with an image that flooded Isabella's thoughts, dark and terrifying. She saw herself bound in ribbons of shadow, mouth open in a silent scream, dragged down into a pit where Catrin waited. Not to kill her. To keep her.

The ribbons wove around her ankles now. She jerked

against them, frantic, but they bit deeper, looping tighter and tighter still, pulling her forward inch by inch. With each crushing coil, the whispers rose, a frantic cacophony.

The wraith wanted them. Wanted to drink from every soul that lingered within that ethereal place not quite of this world. And Isabella was the gateway between worlds.

"Stop," Isabella rasped, though there was no stopping to be had, not for either of them. She stared up at the thing that inched closer, closer, horror congealing in her veins.

"Enough," said a man's voice, Rhys's voice.

Relief reared so quickly she nearly sobbed. The air lost its frigid edge. The knife-prick chorus at the periphery of her hearing shivered and then withdrew.

The girl froze. Not stilled. Froze, as if pinned.

The ribbons slackened, shuddered, and fell away, retreating like severed arteries into the wraith's shadowed body.

Rhys stepped between Isabella and the thing. He stood as a man who understood what he faced and did not mistake it for less.

Isabella pressed her back to the wall, feeling as if the world shifted, a door she'd braced shut all her life tearing open.

He saw it. Rhys *saw* it.

"Look at me," he told the wraith.

The girl's unhinged jaw clicked back into place with a small, revolting sound. The black seep stuttered and thickened and stilled. She turned that fathomless gaze to him.

"Not her," he said. "Not in my house. Not while I draw breath."

He spoke to it as though it were a living thing, as

though one could reason with a nightmare. And it listened. The hush that fell was like a held breath, but not theirs. The house's. The wraith's.

Rhys reached a hand back toward Isabella, never taking his attention from the wraith.

Heart slamming a frantic rhythm, Isabella took one long breath and another. She put a trembling hand in his, reassured by the warmth, the strength.

He did not look back at her. In a voice that was quieter than she would have believed and steadier than she had ever heard, he said, "Catrin. I name you. I dismiss you. Go."

For an instant, one sliver of an instant, the wraith's mouth made a small shape Isabella recognized from her time at Miss Trevisham's school: The pout of a girl who wanted a sweet and had been denied. Then the shadow slid under the door and was gone.

Silence followed. Not the crushed, wrong silence. Ordinary quiet, with a draft and the strain of old timbers and the tick of a far-off pipe. Something in Isabella's chest loosened and something in her throat hurt as if she had swallowed a stone.

Rhys turned. He set the lamplight between them and looked at her.

"You—" She could not put the sentence in order. She tried again as he drew her to her feet. "You saw her."

His breath shook once on the way out. It steadied. "Yes."

"You heard—"

"Yes."

Never say it. Never show it.

She had spent a lifetime making her face a mask, every action, every glance a shield. Now, she could set it aside. Now, she could breathe. Relief surged through her, fierce and reckless.

Because she understood at last. Rhys had been condemned for the very thing she had buried in herself. He had been locked away in St. Jude's not for madness but for vision.

CHAPTER SIXTEEN

Rhys did not let go of Isabella's hand.

By unspoken agreement, they moved together through the house, her fingers cold in his, his thumb fitting the notch of her knuckles. He told himself it was for her steadiness, not his, though the lie sat poorly. Where she walked beside him, the needles of sound dulled to a tolerable prickle. He felt her shiver but did not look at her. If he looked at her now, he might gather her in his arms and the restraint that had just saved her would go to pieces.

He saw again the mouth unhinge, the black seep smoking where it struck the carpet. He had said Catrin's name and the cousin he remembered from their childhood, a shy creature in pink with jam smeared on her cheeks, had looked through him like ice. Not for the first time, he wondered how that child had become a monster, wondered if she always had been.

They reached his rooms. He pushed the door with his shoulder and guided Isabella in. The coals were banked to a low red, the air warm and quiet. He left the lamp on the sideboard and, without ceremony, drew Isabella toward the hearth.

"Sit," he managed, indicating the sofa before the fire. He set the lamp lower, as if gentler light could soften the look of confusion and dismay that drew her features taut. He poured brandy, let the glass warm in his hand for a breath, then pressed it to her hand.

She glanced at the brandy and made a face. "I have no liking for spirits. They make me cough."

"It will warm you. Small sips. Let it sit on your tongue. Don't chase it," he said, and was gratified that she trusted him enough to do as he bid and took a tiny sip.

"Are you hurt?" The question scraped his throat.

"I don't think so." She flexed her fingers then lifted her foot and moved it this way and that, testing her ankle. "No, not hurt," she said, but he heard all she did not say, all the questions she ached to ask.

"I've never seen it that strong," he said, the admission quiet and plain.

Her mouth trembled, then steadied. "All my life they've been—" She searched for the word, found one that fit. "Harmless. No weight. No hands. They cannot move a cup, let alone...me. But she—" She swallowed. "She has grown stronger since I arrived."

"She is not like the others," he said.

"Why?" Her voice did not rise. It thinned. "Why is she so strong?"

He met her eyes then, because there was no honest answer he could give that did not paint him the villain and he wanted one more moment where she looked at him as if he were the hero. The illusion, brief as a candle's flicker, was more dangerous to her than any wraith.

"Because of all she did while still living, and the

things she has done since death. The house remembers. She feeds on that remembering, and it feeds on her."

She stared at him, dark eyes wide, cheeks pale, pulse a fast flutter at her throat, beautiful even in her distress. She should have recoiled. Instead, she leaned nearer and that was his undoing. In St. Jude's he had been no one—watched, judged, locked away, an animal in a cage.

Here, with her, he was seen, understood. That thread bound tighter than any rope.

Their silence was not empty. Her quick breaths, the snap of fire, his own heart behaving badly...the room held it all. He sat beside her, close enough that the hem of her skirt brushed his boot. He did not move away. Where their knees nearly touched, the house's cacophony sank, as if their nearness tamped the sound down with a palm.

"Thank you," she said, and the words shook. "For coming."

He did not deserve her thanks. "I took too long."

Her lips tipped, not quite a smile; the expression undid him more than tears would have. She glanced toward the door, then back at him—as if choosing—and leaned a fraction nearer. The quiet between them tightened, warm now instead of cold. Gratitude brightened to something more dangerous.

"Rhys," she whispered, testing his name like sugar on her tongue.

Desire skated through him, inappropriate in this moment, but there nonetheless.

The smallest shiver went through her. He reached, slowly, so she might refuse, and brushed the backs of his fingers against her cheek. Her eyes widened, dark and deep.

Turning her face, she caught his touch against the corner of her mouth.

He forced himself to drop his hand and look away. He was not a good man; he had never claimed he was. But he was not such a ruffian as to take advantage of the moment.

Beside him, she took a slow breath and said, "I have questions. About the house. About...all of it. But one first." Her throat moved. "Catrin. What happened to her?"

He had not meant to reveal it so plainly. He had meant to measure it out, careful as medicine. But she had asked, and the truth had sat in him for years like a stone.

His gaze flashed to her, and he did not look away.

"I killed her," he said, voice steady as stone. And in the silence that followed, he waited for her to pull away, to see him for what he was. Not a savior, but a murderer.

Isabella lifted the glass to her lips and took a tiny sip, letting herself absorb Rhys's words before she spoke. The brandy burned a small sun in her throat. Then she set the glass on the small side table because her fingers had begun to shake. He sat very straight, the brights and darks cast by the fire dancing over him.

He had neither lied nor omitted. He had placed a boulder between them and named it, trusted her with it. Relief and dread braided tight inside her—relief that she was no longer alone in what she knew; dread of what truth might demand of her. And under it, a warmth she did not dare yet name for he had put the worst of himself in her keeping, and still she did not look away.

"Tell me." She did not know if she invited punishment

or absolution or simply the truth, but she would hear the tale because not knowing was making a maze of her mind. "From the beginning."

His gaze flicked to her hands, to where they knotted in her skirt, and the corners of his mouth tightened. He did not move closer but neither did he shift away. His restraint pressed on her as heavy as a touch, as if he held himself taut against the pull between them.

"Catrin was my cousin. My father's brother's daughter. She would visit when we were children, quiet, watchful. She came to live at Harrowgate after my aunt's *fall* and my uncle's *apoplexy*. I was away at school, but when I visited, I saw her careful grief and mild manners. She was ever agreeable, sometimes so precisely agreeable it felt learned, as if she fashioned herself into whatever shape the room required.

"Something about her felt wrong. I spoke with Mother. She said that Catrin had lost everything and was afraid of losing even more, that she was careful lest she be cast out, lest everyone desert her. She said only must I show her compassion."

He paused. The room sighed around them, lamp glass ticking as heat touched it. Isabella could not help noticing his hands, the long fingers, the strength of them she had felt when he pulled her from danger. She brought her gaze back to his face.

"Then my brother, Ned, drowned. Seven years old, he was, and barely that. His birthday only three days before..." He clenched his jaw and stared into the fire. "Then Will took sick. Mother did not leave his side until Catrin offered to sit with him. Even then, Mother only went as far as the chair at the foot of his bed. She dozed, and when she woke, his breathing was slow and faint and then gone altogether. You know all this from the letters." His mouth flattened. "The ordinary catastrophes of a house, one might say. But they were not ordinary."

"Catrin," Isabella said because the name sat cold on her tongue and would not be swallowed.

"Catrin," he agreed. "She was clever in the way that looks like gentleness if you want it to. And they wanted it to, Mother and Father. One believes what one must to keep the world square."

"Because believing she was a monster was more than they could bear," Isabella said, understanding what it meant to *choose* not to see, because to do anything else was inconceivable.

Rhys shook his head. "Because believing she was a monster was more than they could *imagine*. She learned to match action to expectation so the eye would see only what she wished while her hands were busy elsewhere." He paused. "Mother fell and broke her neck. Fell down the stairs she had walked for decades. Odd, isn't it, that she died the same way as my aunt?"

The fine hairs at Isabella's nape prickled and rose. In her pocket, the singed bit of pink ribbon lay, a coiled serpent.

On instinct, she reached for him, taking his hand between her own. His skin was warm, his palms rougher than her own. He did not pull away. Instead, he placed his other hand atop hers. The weight of it was a vow pressed to her skin, protective, claiming, intimate. The pulse at her wrist fluttered against his thumb.

"Father brought me home from school," he continued. "That first night, I heard them, whispers that sounded like my brothers weeping, my mother sobbing. Grief, I told myself. And then I saw him by the pond, little Ned.

And I saw the willow clear through him." He looked around. "Will came to me in this very room. Sat by my bedside, eyes dark and fathomless, face translucent gray. Mother did not come, but I heard her weeping, always weeping. I hear her still.

"I told Father what I saw, what I heard. Told him that I thought Catrin to blame. I thought, foolishly, that if I stacked my facts neat enough, he would see the truth of it. But he did not wish to see, because if I was right, if she had done all of that, then what manner of man was he that he had allowed it? What manner of man was he that he had summoned death into the midst of his family? He sent me to St. Jude's, to Hargreaves, believing grief could be taught out of a man like bad penmanship."

Isabella gasped, the name Hargreaves sending a cold finger down her spine despite the warmth of the room. She had known Rhys had been locked away in St Jude's, but knowing was not the same as hearing it stated in his voice, heavy with remembered suffering. She tasted the memory of limewash and fear, knowing that her brief encounter barely scraped the depth of what he had endured.

"Six months I was there," he said. "In the beginning, I was honest, and then I was not. Honesty would only have extended my purgatory. Instead, I told Hargreaves what he wished to hear and was sent back to Harrowgate *cured*."

The horror of six hopeless months in that place made Isabella's heart wrench. Her fingers tightened on his.

"What happened the night of the fire?" she asked. Her voice sounded even. It felt like a thread.

He drew a breath as the fire in the hearth settled with a pop and a hiss.

"I had gone to visit a friend for a fortnight, but he took sick, and I returned early. I was not expected. I found Father in his chamber, in the chair by his desk, his head cradled on his arms. The pool of blood on the desktop and the gaping wound in his skull told me he had not laid down himself. That, and the poker that lay on the carpet, bits of hair and bone stuck to it."

Isabella's stomach lurched, but she held her tongue, unwilling to make the telling any more difficult for him than it surely was. Something ticked in the wainscot, once, twice, thrice, and went still.

"As I stood there, Catrin raced in. She carried a lamp and a tin ewer of oil. She saw me but did not pause, instead flinging her arm so the oil doused the carpet, and me. She raised the lamp high."

Isabella held his gaze, horror suffusing her. "She meant to burn the proof."

"She meant to burn it all." His tone was flat, but the line of his mouth cut deep. "I reached for her, but she stepped away, brandishing the lamp like the weapon it had become. My trouser leg was soaked in oil.

"She smiled and listed every death like a catechism, her parents, my brothers, my mother. My father lay before me now, the wound in his skull dripping blood to the floor. She had murdered them all. She laughed, saying no one would believe me, a madman freshly returned from the asylum's care, a lunatic raving against a quiet, sweet girl left alive in a house of tragedies.

"A choice, I realized, my life or hers. She had killed them, all of them, everyone I loved. I would not let her go unjudged. And so I became both judge and executioner. She threw the lamp at me. As the fire caught and roared, I dove through the door and slammed it shut." He did not look away, did not flinch or retreat. "Then I barred the door, and I let her burn."

She should recoil at his admission, shrink from the man who had left his cousin to the flames. The cousin who had murdered all those he loved.

Horror tangled with empathy, all the sharper for knowing he had not set the fire. He had only barred the door. *Only*. And yet, what else was he to have done, faced with his dead father and oil on his skin, the lamp raised high? Faced with the ugly truth that, freshly returned from a lunatic asylum, his accusations would not be believed. If anything, he would be sent back, a prisoner while the murderer walked free.

Isabella pondered what she would have done if someone had taken a poker to Papa's skull, left him butchered and bleeding. The answer chilled her. She could not condemn Rhys without condemning herself.

The room held still, and the reek of scorched oil seemed to rise from the memory, singing Isabella's nostrils. Rhys's words did not look for mercy or absolution; he did not ask it. Isabella felt the truth of it settle into her like a brand. Horror…yes. And another, quieter thing: understanding of the terrible logic of a cornered act.

"When she manifests as she did tonight," he said softly, "it spends her. She draws heat, breath, memory, and fear to make the shape. Afterward she must feed."

"Feed?" Isabella asked with a shudder.

"On the house. On the dead. She cannot so easily rise like that again. It will not be tonight, or tomorrow. But it will be soon."

"Then our reprieve is counted in days," Isabella said. The thought should have broken her. Instead, the feel of their linked hands steadied the pieces. "She felt...colder than any wraith I have known. Heavier. Stronger." She paused. "Wrong."

"She *is* wrong. She has always been wrong," he said. "And you—" He hesitated, his expression softening, letting the care show. "You will feel wrung out for an hour or two. She is a thief of warmth." Her teeth clicked, a betraying chatter though the room was warm. He dipped his chin toward the glass of brandy. "Drink more."

Isabella was loath to disentangle their hands. Still, she obeyed, pulling one free to take up the glass, leaving the other resting between his, and took a small sip, the brandy a sweet-bitter throb. He took the glass from her and took a sip for himself, placing his lips exactly where she had placed her own. The simple intimacy sent a rush of heat through her that pooled low, urgent and insistent, heat that had nothing to do with the fire.

Silence rose between them again, different than it had been, vibrating with the shape of what they were to each other now. Not strangers anymore. Not friends, though there was an element of that. Something else, something dangerous and deep.

She turned her hand, lacing their fingers. He did not pull free.

"You once asked me if I would leave, go back to London... Did you want me to?"

He huffed a soft exhalation. "A part of me wanted to send you away, to see you safe, far from everything dark and rancid that leaches through these halls."

"And that part of you still wants me to go," she said, watching him carefully. "Even as another part does not want me to go at all."

"The selfish part," he said. "The part that wants your

help banishing the monstrosity that has taken residence in my home. But more than that, the part that wants you here in this house, in this room, beside me. The part that wants *you*, Isabella. All of you."

Her pulse stuttered at his bald admission. "Rhys—"

He leaned an inch nearer. She felt the brush of his breath on her cheek, and she realized she had already decided. She had lived a life pretending she did not see, did not hear, did not *want*. But here was a man who *saw* her, who wanted her. And she wanted him back.

"Isabella?"

She knew what he asked. The simplest answer rose, terrifying and bright. "Yes," she whispered.

He closed his eyes, opened them, and lifted their joined hands so his lips grazed her knuckles. He undid her with his gentleness. The ache that followed, hot and low, was not fear.

"We will finish the tale tomorrow," he said. "Tonight, you will stay where the house is quiet."

"Here," she said, because to leave him now would feel like stepping into deep water with stones tied about her waist.

"Here," he murmured. "With me."

"Yes." Her reply was little more than a breath. She did not know which of them moved that last fraction. Only that the space between them vanished and the air changed shape, desire humming through her, heady and dangerous.

For once, the house made no sound at all.

CHAPTER SEVENTEEN

Rhys caught her up, not with careful distance, no gentleman's inch between them, his mouth claiming hers like a man who had been starved for air and took breath from her lips. His kiss was not polite; it was salvation. Tangled tongues, breath stolen and given back.

Isabella clutched at his shoulders, fingers digging as if bracing against a current. He made a sound, raw, grateful, and kissed her harder. All the wanting she had hoarded and hidden and starved, every denial and silence of her life, broke loose and surged up, and she kissed him back, rising on her toes to mold her body to his.

They stumbled as one. His hip struck the edge of a chair and sent it skittering, the lamp flame jumping in its glass. She didn't care. She wanted the proof of him, the heat and weight and the litany of his name in the cradle of her mouth. He framed her face as if he feared she would vanish and then gathered her in with an arm about her waist, hauling her flush to him.

Cloth rasped, buttons pressed, the ridged line of his arousal unmistakable against her belly.

The frightened, careful part of her went quiet. This was not pretending. This was not silence. This was life.

"Isabella," he breathed into her mouth, not her name so much as a vow.

With a gasp, she chased his kiss. The urgency of it shook her, her need a fierce roar—*now, now*—her hands fumbling at his neckcloth as if all her fingers had turned to thumbs. The knot refused her.

She made a frustrated sound that would have shamed her in daylight, and he laughed, the huff of it warm against her lips, then tugged the silk loose himself, tossing it blind behind him. She pushed his coat from his shoulders, the weight of the broadcloth sliding down his arms, and smoothed her palm over his chest, claiming him by touch.

"I dreamed of you," she whispered, need tilting wildly inside her.

"No dream," he answered hoarsely. "I am here."

His mouth left hers to take her jaw, her throat. Heat flared where he licked; heat flared where he breathed. He found the spot beneath her ear and she broke, a small, shocked sound that had him swearing softly and pressing her back against the nearest wall, plaster cool on her shoulder blades through her dress. His chest to her breasts. His breathing ragged.

Hooks and eyes fought her. She cursed them in her head and then out loud, reckless and unladylike. His answering laugh was hot against her throat. His hands took over, fast now, not with the careful patience he had shown her in other moments. Eyes, hooks, ribbon. Her bodice slackened and her lungs seized sweet air.

He kissed her while he worked her clothing, and she kissed back while she unraveled, the two of them a tangle of haste and reverence. Each time a fastening gave, it felt like something in her loosened with it, something long-bound untying under his hands.

"Tell me if—" he began.

"I will," she said. "I am untried, not uninformed. Books have been my tutors." She bit his lower lip, gently, then harder. "Hurry."

He did. The back-lacing gave by swift degrees beneath his fingers. She felt the tug. The gown dropped from her shoulders and air kissed skin that pulsed with heat. She shivered and he groaned, the sound low and awed. Petticoat tapes yielded. Cloth whispered down and pooled, a soft betrayal at her ankles. Her chemise slid after, linen skimming like water, leaving her bare to the lamplight and his gaze.

She should have covered herself. She did not. She stood, reckless and red-cheeked, her heart a drum in her throat. He looked at her as a starving man looked at a banquet.

"My God," he said, reverent and rough. "Look at you."

She did not look away. She let him see her and discovered that it undid her as surely as his mouth had done. His gaze learned the curve of her shoulder, the hollow at the base of her throat, the weight of her breasts, the slope of her waist, which he traced with a palm that shook and steadied. He bent and set his mouth to her collarbone and then lower, and her knees simply... forgot how to stand.

He caught her, of course he did, arm clamped around her waist, chest caging her, his hand splayed over the base of her spine as if to say, *mine*, and also, *I have you*.

His heart thudded against her cheek, a furious

rhythm. That was what she had wanted, she realized, foolishly and exactly: to know his heart beat as hard as hers.

"Undress," she managed, and pushed at his buttons with fingers that had no dignity, only need.

"Fond of giving orders, are you?" he murmured, kissing the word into her hair, but he obeyed.

Waistcoat buttons slipped, fell. She shoved the garment away, ruthless. His shirt came next, slower, because her hands shook but at last the fine lawn parted and she put her palms on the hard planes of his naked chest. Heat. Strength. A faint dusting of hair that prickled her skin. She bent and put her mouth where his throat met his shoulder, ran her tongue along his skin, then sucked on him. He swore low and soft and pulled her closer, closer still.

Gently, she bit his chest.

"Pectoralis major," she whispered, breathless, because the lessons from those long-ago books of anatomy steadied her and teased him both.

He laughed and kissed her, desperate and tender. "Cruel girl."

"Rectus abdominis," she said, sliding her hand down the solid ridges of his abdomen, and he made a noise that did not sound like a man in possession of himself.

"Isabella." Just her name, strangled with want.

Her fingers found the fall of his trousers and fumbled there, too, until the placket gave beneath her insistence. She pushed the fabric down over his hips and her knuckles brushed the heat and silk-smooth skin of his member. He shuddered.

In the firelight, she saw his scars. His left leg was seamed and shiny, the fire's mark laddering his skin, marks of survival and pain endured. She touched one pale line with two fingers, then bent to press her lips to his marred flesh, her kiss saying what she dared not put to words: *You are not ruined. You are perfect as you are. You are mine.*

His breath broke on a rough sound.

Straightening, she kissed his lips and pressed her hand once to his member, very light, because boldness had a line and she had just stepped over it. He folded around her, forehead to hers, as if that smallest of touches had undone him.

"Come here," he said, and kissed her like he would die without it.

They reached the bed by accident, by slow retreat, by the drag of his mouth on hers and the way her bare feet sought purchase. Her calves bumped the mattress. She sat hard, breath huffing from her.

He came over her at once, braced on his arms, heat and weight and the cage of his body, careful even in his haste. She waited for terror to scissor through her. It did not come. What rose instead was a heat so fierce it was almost grief.

Deep and hungry, his kiss consumed her. And she answered, her hands mapping his shoulders, his back, his buttocks, the flex of muscle under her palms. He was so solid. She had spent a life among things that could not touch. Here was the antidote: all touch. Here was proof, undeniable and necessary, that they were alive.

His lips went to her breast, and when he drew her nipple into his mouth she cried out, shocked at the flood of sensation...pleasure, sharp as a blade and sweet as honey. He learned her quickly. He learned that a careful scrape of teeth at the edge of her nipple made her arch, that a slow pull and a soft suction made a sound leave her that she would never confess to in any other room. He lingered until she trembled and then lingered more, leaving a shining kiss where he had been, before his mouth traced lower, to the tender skin beneath her breast, to her ribs, to the soft dip of her belly.

"Rhys," she said, not to stop him but to anchor herself to something that had a name.

His hand slid between her thighs.

She went still, then not still at all, because the touch was careful, and then it wasn't careful but purposeful, and the ache at her core that had been a throb became an ache that argued for more. He learned that too, how she arched into his palm, how her breath broke in his mouth when he kissed her at the same moment his fingers stroked. She had thought herself a study in control, in denial. There was no denial here. There was only heat, and the way the world narrowed to a point of light where he touched and widened again, hungrier each time he returned.

"Tell me if I err," he said, hoarse, and the care in it made her throat hurt.

"You do not," she said, so fiercely she made him laugh again, low and amazed.

The fire settled with a sigh. The quiet held.

His fingers were a slick glide on her sex, then an intrusion, unfamiliar but wonderful as they slid inside. She wanted him in ways that felt indecent and right, half urges, half prayers. She dragged him upward by the nape and kissed him thoroughly, the kind of kiss that told a man he was wanted. It made him shake; she felt the tremor pass through him like a fever.

He reached down and guided his shaft to the opening

his fingers had teased. She felt swollen there, aching, yearning. The hard unyielding press of him now made her go rigid for a breath, not fear, exactly, but the mind's bright awareness of a threshold. He felt her stiffen and stopped, everything in him straining, held on a leash of his own making.

"Don't stop," she said, and meant that more than she had ever meant anything. "Please."

He entered her the way he had first kissed her, his thrust gentler than she expected. The stretch burned, stung. He took his time, slowly, slowly.

She gasped as he pushed fully inside her, quick, sharp, and then he went still, his mouth on her temple, his breath a broken prayer, their bodies joined, pain blossoming at her centre. For a handful of heartbeats, they didn't move at all, and in that stillness, she felt every place they touched as if it had been set alight. The burn eased.

He moved, just a little. Then more. The ache reshaped itself into something that made her toes curl.

His rhythm cautious, he thrust, slow and shallow. The feeling of being filled by him was like grief untying inside her. And as he moved faster, deeper, his thrusts filling her completely, pleasure rode her, leaving her mindless, writhing, *needing*.

There was nothing tidy in the way he pressed his forehead to hers, as if he needed her breath to remember how to take his own, nothing gentle in the way each thrust filled her and dragged her closer to an edge she could not name.

She wrapped her legs about his waist, a shameless, greedy clasp that made him groan against her throat.

"You are so beautiful, so perfect," he said, and he thrust deeper.

In that instant, she felt beautiful, perfect. He made a sound, low and rough, unlike anything she had ever heard from any man.

They found a rhythm. They gasped and missed and found again. They clutched and fumbled. They knocked the sheet to the floor and did not notice.

He spoke to her in fragments—praise, her name, a strangled curse. She whispered things, *pleases* and *yeses* and his name in a dozen registers.

Pleasure gathered at her core, a coil drawn tight. He swore softly into her hair, his hand sliding between them again, clever, unerring, finding a place that made the pleasure so keen it was almost pain.

She cried out as the world went bright and then brighter still, until she could not hold it. She broke with a yell, unguarded, grateful, and for a long moment she was nothing but sensation riding the heavens.

Then she was herself again, wrapped in him, gasping.

He held himself still, shaking, teeth clenched as if in pain. She realized with a rush of surprised tenderness that he had been holding back, waiting for her to catch him. Now it was his turn to catch her.

Cupping his face with both hands, she pulled him down to kiss her, then whispered against his lips, "Let me give you the joy you just gave me."

His control failed beautifully. He drove into her once, twice, the sounds he made rough with relief, and she felt the shudder rip through him, felt the tremor as he buried his face against her throat and found his release. She held him as if they stood on a cliff and the wind had tried to take them both. She held him as he had held her.

After, the quiet felt earned.

Rolling to his side, he brought her with him, keeping her gathered in against him. She pillowed her cheek on his shoulder and listened to his heart pound, then slow. Her own heart answered, a softened echo.

She realized she was trembling. Not from cold. From the violence of wanting, from the shattering grace of having it given, of being seen and desired. Wanted. He noticed, of course he did. He pulled the sheet up and tucked it around her shoulder with a tenderness that made her eyes sting.

"Are you—" he began and could not seem to find the rest of the sentence.

She smiled against his throat. "Yes," she said softly. "I am."

"Good," he said, and the word came out rough. "God, Isabella..."

He went quiet, his fingers tracing idle patterns along her shoulder, absurdly gentle. She pressed a kiss to the side of his throat where his pulse lived. He made a quiet sound that might have meant thank you.

In the silence, she heard the promises neither could make. Promises of forever. Even promises of tomorrow. No vows, only breath. No guarantees, only the heat of their bodies and the thud of their hearts. If dawn brought the return of the wraith's hunger, then let tonight be theirs. Tonight, they had taken something back that grief had stolen, a human thing, a tender thing.

Rhys lay on his back, Isabella's warmth pressed to his side, his breath yet uneven, his fingers tracing idle circles on her shoulder. He could not seem to stop touching her. Her hair spilled over his chest, smelling faintly of lavender.

He had not intended for it to be like this. He had intended for her to help him, to stand beside him and open the gate. He had never intended to be undone, stripped down to the quick, not by this woman's mouth and hands, not by her trust.

"Rhys," she said, her voice quiet but steady. "You have told me the worst of it. Catrin. The murders. The way you barred the door. But I have questions about Hargreaves. About Papa."

Of course she would ask. And she deserved the truth, though it painted him in poor light. That thought brought a wry twist to his lips. As if her image of him could be tarnished worse than by the truth already laid bare, that he was a murderer, marked and damned.

He brushed a kiss across her brow, selfish in the taking. "Ask, and I will answer."

"Why did you seek out Papa? Why him?"

"When I was at St. Jude's," he began, his voice rough. "Hargreaves told me he had once before encountered a case like mine. A girl who believed she heard things...saw things. He called it disappointment when her father refused treatment. I saw the truth in him. It was not disappointment. It was rage that he had been denied a specimen."

Her body went still, a knot of remembered terror drawing her taut against him. He knew that terror. The memory of iron locks and echoing corridors pressed against his ribs like a weight. Tightening his arm around her, he pressed his lips to her hair until the tremor left her shoulders. God, if he could take that memory from her and let it rot in his own bones, he would.

"I wondered about her," he went on. "The girl he spoke of. I wondered if she truly heard the noise, always buzzing at the edge of my thoughts. If she saw the wraiths. I dared not ask him about her, knowing that he would see it as more proof of the instability of my mind. So, I sopped up the dribbles he offered, not her name, not her location, only her existence.

"When my time behind those bars was done and I had convinced him that he had done a wonderful thing, that he had cured me, I left believing that somewhere out there was another soul walking masked, pretending. Not mad. Not alone."

She made a choked sound, and he suspected she understood what he had felt. The hope he had harbored.

"When I returned to Harrowgate, the house pressed in on me. My brothers begged. My mother sobbed. But only I heard them." His grief swelled, and he swallowed it back, raw and bitter. "And then my father died and I had money. I had rage. I salted Hargreaves's reputation until it rotted. When he was desperate enough, I dangled a post in Marlow. He came, and he drank himself to death. And then I took his ledgers, his notes."

He met her gaze, unflinching. "He had some notes about the girl I sought. Her name. It was a place to start. And he had listed books, tracts and treatises he considered 'germane to spectral delusion.' He believed the authors were all subject to delusion.

"I searched out sellers. Paternoster Row first. Then a secondhand man off Maiden Lane. From him to Mr. Fenwick in Holborn—"

"I know them all," Isabella said.

"It was Fenwick who told me of a gentleman, an antiquarian who collected items pertaining to 'phenomena at the edge of seeing.'"

"Papa," she said softly.

"Your father," he agreed.

"You hunted him. You hunted *me*." Her tone was flat, her eyes searching as she studied him.

"I did," he said simply. "You and..." He hesitated, then revealed the last bit of it. "You and a book I believed to be in your father's possession. To free those I love." The words came harsher than he meant. He forced himself to soften. "Even when I stood in the street, and you in the window above, you steadied me. You made the voices quieten."

"Do you think I could hate you for this? For any of it?" she asked, her dark eyes wide and searching.

Almost did he say yes. Almost did he tell her to hate him now, before it grew more difficult later.

But she whispered, "I dislike the snare. I dislike the darkness you walked in order to reach me. But I do not, I *cannot* hate you. Only... No more tricks. No more lures. No more boxes laid out to tempt me. Only ask me as I have asked you."

He buried his nose in her dark hair, soft and thick and fragrant, and he said, "No more snares. I will ask."

He had not intended for it to be like this. He had intended for her to help him, to stand beside him and open the gate. The plan had been clean, cold, brutal: Survive the house. Free his family. Keep Catrin from devouring what little remained. Nothing more. Nothing tender. Certainly not this.

He didn't deserve this.

And yet here she was, pressed against him, her breath

a soft rhythm against his skin, her hand resting on his heart. He had thought himself emptied years ago, believed that grief had burned away the part of him that dared to want. But with her quiet strength, her refusal to flinch, her defiant compassion, Isabella had slipped past to fill him again. And that fullness brought fear.

The scent of lavender threaded with the faint salt of her skin teased his senses, and he realizes he was memorizing it, hoarding it as a man does water in a drought.

Everyone he had ever loved was buried or burned. To love this woman was to gamble with ruin. If the house took her, if Catrin tore her from him, the wound she left behind would be worse than the wailing of a thousand ghosts.

Something gave way inside him, a fracture running through the stone he had carried for years. He had lost everyone he had ever loved. He could not lose her, too.

And yet, if he tried to keep her safe by sending her away, he would strip her of choice. She was not a child. Not a possession. She was a woman with a right to choose her own path. He would not take that from her.

He would let her decide to choose him—or not.

CHAPTER EIGHTEEN

Isabella woke to warmth and the unfamiliar feel of skin beneath her cheek. Rhys's chest rose under her ear, and fell, and rose, the steady pattern of his breathing.

The room was dim but not dark. Coals glowed in the grate like banked hearts. She could not hear the needles of sound that lived at the edge of every hallway here. The hush had a different character in this moment, like a blanket pulled up to the chin. She wondered if it was the two of them, connected now, the made the voices so quiet.

Rhys's arm lay heavy across her back. His hand spanned her shoulder, a weight that did not pin so much as reassure. He had fallen asleep like that, holding her as if some part of him feared the air might take her if he loosened his grip. In the close quiet, she buried her nose in his chest and breathed in the scents of citrus and mint and a man's musk.

She thought of the weight of him as he had come over

her, the shift of his muscles beneath her hand, the thrust of him between her legs, and felt her cheeks heat.

Then she thought of the corridor, the girl's unhinged jaw, the black, oozing seep, the keen that had wormed inside her skull. Catrin was not gone; this was only a reprieve.

For now, the worst of her fear had been melted by his body, by his mouth, by his name in her throat and hers on his lips. She turned her face a little against him. The small, ordinary rasp of hair on his chest abraded her cheek. Her hand had drifted in sleep. It lay now across the ridges of his belly, fingers splayed.

He stirred. "Awake?" The word was low, thick with sleep.

"Yes." Her voice surprised her. It sounded like honey poured from a jar, slow and lazy.

He tightened his arm, briefly, as if answering a question neither had spoken, then loosened it again and slid his palm to her hair, smoothing it where he had mussed it. "You're warm."

"Because of you," she said truthfully.

"Good," he said. A beat passed. Then, more quietly, "I am sorry."

"For what?" She waited for shame to come and found only tenderness, and a prickle of sorrow for the years she had taught herself not to want.

"For the fear," he said. "For the house. For—" He stopped. The hand in her hair closed, not roughly. "For what I mean to ask of you still."

"You did not make Catrin."

"Didn't I ?" he asked, his voice laced with pain. "I barred the door."

Her palm slid to his ribs. He was all hard muscle under

warm skin. "You did not teach her to kill. You did not summon her to Harrowgate, setting a viper free among those you love. You did not light that lamp."

"No," he said. "But I laid a snare for you in the library." The words entered the room without apology and without defense. "I wanted you to open that box. I bought it for the mark, Thorn & Sons, because I knew your father's key would turn there."

"I suspected," she said, because she had and because suspicion had tasted like gall until tonight. "You omit," she added, soft, "but you do not lie."

"I will not lie to you," he said, and the vow had weight. "I would rather you hate me for what I am than trust a man I invented."

"Why did you not simply tell me the whole of it from the beginning? Your family. Catrin... All of it?"

He made a soft laugh, devoid of mirth. "I told your father. Laid it bare, every damnable piece of it, save the barring of the door. I begged his help, and yours. You saw his answer. I thought it better to let you stitch together the truth for yourself, one page at a time, than to have you drive me into the street hurling insults and wrath."

She thought, with a pang that was half grief, half rue, of Papa muttering Rhys's name with scorn, of the sharp words he had used when speaking of the man now lying beside her. Only because he meant to protect her from harm. Strange how memory could cut and comfort, both. How the echo of Papa's warnings didn't lessen the warmth of the shoulder beneath her cheek.

Then she thought of the letters, of Rhys's mother's hand steady until it broke, of boys who were alive and then were not. She thought of the way Rhys had looked at her when she asked what happened to Catrin: steady, unafraid to let her see the black and the bright together. She set her mouth to his shoulder, a small press that might have been comfort or thanks.

He made a sound then, an unguarded one, and she felt it pass through him like a ripple.

As he reached for her, a knock sounded, two quick raps, then a third. Before either of them could snatch a robe or utter a reply, the latch turned, and Mrs. Abernathy swept in with a tray balanced on her forearms, steam and spice riding the air ahead of her. Two cups, two plates, two spoons, two of everything: porridge glossed with cream, buttered toast, baked apples jewelled with currants, a pot of dark tea, another of chocolate. The scents of cinnamon, nutmeg, butter, folded through the air, warm and ordinary. She set the tray on the round table by the fire as if she had placed such trays in such rooms—lovers' rooms—a thousand mornings.

Her gaze took them in. Isabella, wearing only Rhys's discarded shirt and wrapped now to her chin in the blankets she had yanked up to hide herself as the door had opened. Rhys, propped against the pillows, bare-chested and unrepentant.

If Mrs. Abernathy had an opinion on propriety, she folded it neat and tucked it away. But Isabella felt as if her face was on fire, her cheeks burning with mortification. The housekeeper had discovered her in the master's bed. *Inconvenient feelings.*

For the space of a breath, she wanted to sink into the mattress and vanish.

As though he knew her thoughts, Rhys whispered for her ears alone, "Not inconvenient."

His words made her recall whose bed she lay in, whose hand had steadied her, whose shirt she wore. She forced her chin up and met Mrs. Abernathy's gaze and found no censure there.

Rhys's lips curved. "You might knock, Mrs. Abernathy."

"I did," she returned, unruffled, and added, "sir." A faint emphasis, just shy of cheek.

She poured tea out for Isabella, chocolate for Rhys, and set the cups within easy reach. Her gaze went to Isabella and her expression softened. "How do you this morning, Miss Barrett?"

"Quite well, thank you," Isabella said, striving for composure, though embarrassment made her pulse thud like a guilty drum.

Mrs. Abernathy flicked a glance at Rhys. "I'd expect nothing less."

Isabella opened her mouth, shut it, and wished the floor might rise up and swallow her whole. Beside her, Rhys made a low sound that might have been a laugh strangled into a cough. His gray eyes gleamed with wicked amusement as he met her gaze. He shifted one hand beneath the sheet, his thumb brushing the back of her wrist in secret reassurance, and her heart leapt.

"I did not come to gawk," Mrs. Abernathy said, her expression turning serious. "Nor to intrude. But there are matters that have pressed upon me."

"Go on," Rhys said.

Mrs. Abernathy folded her hands at her waist. "Peg gave me a turn yesterday."

"Peg?" Isabella sat up, mortification forgotten. "Is she unwell?"

"She's sound but bruised. She fell on the back stair. Slipped, I gather. But..."

"Go on," Rhys said.

"She wouldn't say it if she didn't believe it. But...she says she was pushed. Felt two hands on her back and a hard shove."

Isabella gasped.

The housekeeper's mouth compressed. "Peg's not one to tell tales."

"Did she see who it was?" Rhys asked, his voice tense.

"She did not," Mrs. Abernathy said. "She only swears she smelled roses and ash. Says she heard a woman's laugh before she fell." The housekeeper paused. Beneath the sheet, Rhys lightly squeezed Isabella's hand. "But I was in the kitchen with Cook and Marry and Emma, and there are no other women in this house, except Miss Barrett."

"Are you suggesting that it was Miss Barrett who pushed her?" Rhys asked, his voice silky and dangerous.

The housekeeper looked appalled. "Absolutely not. I was only saying that every woman in this house was accounted for when Peg fell."

Mrs. Abernathy's hands smoothed the apron at her waist and Isabella sensed the woman had more to say.

"There is something else you wish to share," Rhys said.

"There is," Mrs. Abernathy said. She hesitated, then reached into her pocket and drew out a small parcel wrapped in muslin, tied with a bit of yarn. "A house grows sour if you leave doors barred too long. Yesterday, I sent Peg to the second floor of the east wing, airing, dusting, polishing."

Isabella felt Rhys tense at her side.

"The east wing," he said, his tone flat.

Mrs. Abernathy turned the packet in her hands. "Peg says the top drawer of the tall boy in the blue room"—

Isabella felt Rhys tense beside her— "would not close all the way. She took the drawer out and found this tucked in behind. She pressed it into my hands after her fall. Pale as death she was."

The housekeeper pulled the yarn, and the muslin fell away to reveal a small calfskin diary, its corners rubbed pale with use, the brass clasp broken so the strap hung loose. "I read only a page. Enough to know it wasn't accounts or linen lists. A housekeeper has no business prying into a young lady's private pages."

She offered the book and Rhys accepted it, his frame humming with tension.

"I would have you send for Dr. Linton in Marlow. Let him look Peg over and be certain she has no hidden hurt. Bruises mend, but a blow on the stair can turn itself cruel in the bones," Rhys said, his tone brooking no argument. It warmed Isabella to see his concern for those in his care. "Make sure she rests."

With a nod, Mrs. Abernathy took her leave.

Once the door was closed behind her, Isabella asked, "What is it? What has distressed you so."

He only offered her the diary, silent.

Accepting it, she hesitated. She did not need his confirmation that the blue room had been Catrin's, that this diary had belonged to her. She felt it in the tense hum that wove between them.

She opened the cover. The flyleaf bore several attempts at the same hand, ink faded with age.

Catrin Caradoc

C. Caradoc

Catrin C—

Beneath the names, in small letters, was written the

motto: *I must be what is wanted.* The words crawled across Isabella's skin.

She turned the page and read aloud the entry. It was mundane, a recitation of the courses at dinner. A mention of a new hat. The triviality scraped her. Had she not written the same in her own youthful journals? A mention of a ribbon Papa brought her. A description of a new frock. The familiarity unsettled her.

She fanned the pages and let the diary fall open where it would.

> *They see only what they wish to see. Dead sparrows in the garden, a rabbit curled stiff beneath the lilac bush. Father says it must be a fox, Mother a cat. The fire in the greenhouse? They call it an accident. They never look deeper. They never look at me.*

A chill uncurled beneath Isabella's skin. It was not only the dead sparrows or the burned greenhouse that made her stomach knot, but the truth pulsing between the lines. The words bled cruelty, but beneath them lay hunger, for recognition, for consequence. Catrin had wanted them to see, to recognize the darkness she carried.

Her parents had turned a blind eye, left Catrin alone with her secrets. Isabella swallowed, her throat tight. She had spent her life hiding her own true nature, hiding her visions, binding her lips closed with Papa's warnings. She knew the ache of hiding, of being dismissed. But Catrin had sharpened that ache into a blade.

She glanced at Rhys, but he only sat staring straight ahead, jaw set, the muscle ticking like he clenched back years of memory.

Again, she let the pages fall open where they willed and read.

I went into the woods today and found a prize wrapped in muslin, tucked in a hollow between the roots of a great oak. I fetched it home and unwrapped it to find a book, split down the spine, its halves sundered. A secret. My secret.

Isabella's breath caught. A book cleaved in two. Her pulse stuttered as guilt surged. She thought of Papa's trunk and the grimoire hidden within, her own dark inheritance. It was as if the diary had turned its dark gaze on her.

She glanced at Rhys. He sat very still, fist clenched, knuckles white. Then he reached over, flipped the pages to a new entry, and read aloud.

Washed hair this evening. A rinse with rose water because Aunt says my spirits brighten with scent and all must be cheerful for Will's sake.

His voice cracked on the last words. *Will.* The name hung in the air. Isabella's chest pinched.

Silence descended, deep and thick. Finally, Isabella moved to a new entry and read.

The roses I cut on Tuesday slid in the vase and left the water brown. I threw them and fetched fresh. Pink always looks prettiest against the nursery paper, the thorns hidden by the full blooms. Hidden in plain sight.

A shudder rippled through her. Roses, again. Scent

and bloom hiding thorns, masking rot. Pretty, polite, silent. Hide the sharp edges. Hide the truth.

She turned another page.

He coughs harder in the night. I only wish him quiet rest, untroubled and at peace. Worried for the lamp, I used more oil than is proper. Sleep, sweet cousin. Sleep.

A cold weight settled in Isabella's stomach. The words were not a confession, not quite, and yet they were. *More oil than is proper.* Her hands trembled as she slapped the diary shut.

Isabella raised her gaze to Rhys. His expression was laced with sorrow. For an instant, she saw not the man beside her but the boy he had been, powerless as sickness and shadow consumed his home.

"You could not have known the depth of her darkness," she whispered.

"I could," he replied. "I did. But I did not know how to make others see until it was too late. And even then, my word was not trustworthy, freshly home from St. Jude's as I was."

His bitterness cut like glass. Isabella squeezed his hand, fierce, as if she could anchor him back from that edge.

She fanned the pages again, a nervous flick, and froze. Inked in the margin beside a listless note about a broken gate that would not open was a small mark, no larger than a thumbnail. Two semicircles nested together. The symbol from the damaged grimoire in Papa's trunk.

Her breath caught.

"What is it?" Rhys asked, voice low and taut. His gaze

dropped to the page, then rose to hers. "You recognize that mark." He did not word it as a question.

The room tilted, shadows pressing in. In that instant, Isabella felt certain that such recognition was not hers alone. Her heart stumbled. For years she had carried her secrets, hidden behind her mask, worn her silence like armor, even with Papa. Especially with Papa. Secrecy had been her mantra, her duty.

Her fingers trembled as she lifted her hand to Rhys's face. She traced the hard line of her jaw, feeling the scrape of his morning beard against her fingers. This man had shown her his wounds, laid bare his own monstrous truth.

And he had looked into the dark with her and said, *yes, I see it too.*

Heart pounding, she held his gaze and said, "I recognize it. As do you." The words felt like chains snapping.

"Tell me," he said, not a command, a request. It struck her then that he could have forced this revelation long ago. Just as she had used the key for Papa's trunk to unlock the brass box in the library, he could have used his matching key to unlock Papa's trunk. He could have stolen her secrets, discovered the grimoire long ago. But he had waited for her to choose.

In that waiting, she saw the difference between ruin and trust, between Papa's fierce guardianship and Rhys's fraught restraint.

She smiled, rueful. "One of us knows to respect the bounds of privacy."

He laughed, low and smooth, but his hand closed around hers, thumb stroking the back as if he knew what this cost her.

Setting the diary aside, she let her fingers hover a

moment on the calfskin cover. The girlish script within spoke of roses and oil and being what others wanted. A shiver ran through her. Had she not lived the same way, in her own fashion? Smiling when she wished to scream. Swallowing words so no one would call her mad. The thought of kinship with a monster chilled her, but also sharpened her resolve. She would not be hollowed into obedience. She would not let silence be her inheritance.

She would be seen.

Her eyes lifted to Rhys's. She *was* seen.

A book, split down the spine, its halves sundered. A secret. My secret. Catrin's secret was not hers alone. It never had been.

"I will show you," Isabella said, pulse hammering.

They dressed without ceremony. When he helped her with her clothing, he did it with deft fingers, and the brief warmth of his knuckles at her hip felt like a promise kept.

"Ready?" he asked.

She touched Papa's key at her breast. "Yes."

CHAPTER NINETEEN

The corridor was quiet as they passed.

When they reached Isabella's chamber, she paused and drew a deep breath before opening the door. The room was still and silent, a strange thing, that. The quiet should have felt like a reprieve. Instead, it felt like a threat, the calm before the storm. Papa's trunk sat in the corner, the iron-banded oak scuffed at the corners. She knelt and set her palm on the lid as she had done a dozen times alone, feeling the echo of her father's hand beneath her own. Rhys remained a step back, present, but careful not to crowd.

"Once I open it," she said, surprised by how calm her voice sounded, "we won't be able to pretend we are two people who merely share a house."

"We stopped pretending last night," he said gently. "We are partners."

The word struck her harder than any vow of devotion. *Partners.* Not employee and master. Not lover and lord. Not a woman tolerated in a man's design. Partners. From his lips it was not courtesy but conviction, the scandalous belief that she stood beside him, not behind. Heat gathered beneath her ribs, so fierce her breath was stolen and returned all at once.

She pulled the key from around her neck and fitted it into the lock. The bit turned with a soft, stubborn click and the lid gave. Leather and paper breathed up: starch, dust, the faint ghost of tobacco from nights when Papa had bent long over a page. She lifted out oilcloth-wrapped books and folios. Beneath, wrapped with care, lay the book.

Even swaddled, it seemed to hum.

She set it on the rug and sat before it, peeling the cloth aside. The binding had been cleft clean down its spine, so that one board and half the gatherings remained. Brass flared dully in the hearthlight, the inlay fitting like mosaic along a broken edge, a curve that promised and a second curve missing. The design was like a broken coin, its halves once whole.

The leather was the sober brown of a gentleman's ledger, but the tooling at the border told a different story. Thorns and lilies twined, peril and beauty braided so close that to reach for one was to bleed on the other. The vellum leaves clung to their cords, notes scrawled in a small, cramped hand in the margins. Circles within circles. Words struck out and written again.

Rhys eased to the floor opposite her, a wince twisting his features as he forced his leg into submission. For a long breath he did not touch the book.

"You've been carrying a church under your arm," he said at last, voice rough.

Isabella gave a wan smile. "It has felt like a tomb."

A church. A place of ritual, of voices raised, of thresholds crossed. A tomb. A place of sealed silence and the weight of the dead. She supposed they were speaking of the same thing, only from different sides of the stone they both bore.

He lifted his eyes to hers. "You do not carry it alone, my Isabella. I have the other half." His hand hovered over the broken spine. "I found it after the fire, in Catrin's chamber, swaddled in muslin, hidden beneath her bed. Her diary makes me wonder...perhaps it chose her."

"And she welcomed that choice," Isabella murmured. "She opened her arms to the darkness like a lover."

She pressed her palm flat to the book, steadying her own pulse as much as its hum. Had it felt so alive when she had touched it before, or was it the combined presence of Rhys and herself that made it do so now?

"Tell me the truth, Rhys. Did you come to my father's house that day for me? For this half of the book? Or for something else altogether?" she asked, quiet but fierce.

His jaw tightened but he did not look away. "For all of it," he said. "For the book because I had hunted the twin to my own for years. For you. And for something else beside. For help."

She searched his face, the swell of his lips, the dark stubble along his jaw, the weight in his gray eyes. Her throat closed on Papa's old warnings. *Never say it. Never show it.* She swallowed them down. "What did you say to Papa that morning to drive him to such anger?"

"I told him my truth. All of it. The voices. The visions. St. Jude's. And for a moment, he wavered. He told me more than he meant to. About your own voices and visions, about the things he feared for you. That he had spent years gathering every volume he could, every tract and scrap, searching for a way to banish the wraiths. He wanted to free you."

The words gouged her composure. All her life she had thoughts Papa's rules meant doubt, that his silence was denial. In truth, it had been a shield. Her eyes stung.

"He wanted to save me," she whispered.

"Yes," Rhys said. "As do I. I want to save us all. You. Me. The ghosts of my family."

She swiped at her eyes with the back of her hand.

"May I?" he asked, gesturing at the book.

"Yes," she managed.

He opened the cover, the hinges complaining softly, like the creak of an old woman's joints. The first pages were half text, half diagrams: shapes that were not quite circles, not quite chains; lines that beckoned the eye and then refused to let it rest. Marginalia marched in a steady, exacting hand—Latin, Aramaic, a smattering of crabbed English. The more Isabella looked, the more she felt the press of meaning, as tangible as a palm at the base of her skull.

Rhys turned the pages, pausing on a plate where the two semicircles nestled, not married but yearning toward each other. Between them, a slim figure was sketched— no name, only a notation in the margin that made Isabella's skin prickle. *Conduit. Voluntas, duplex visus.*

"Willing," she translated, breath thin. "Two who... see."

He exhaled, the sound like something he had kept caged. "Yes. Two halves joined, two seers joined. One must be a willing conduit. Not a sacrifice, the text is clear on that point. Not blood in a bowl. Willing consent. The gate is not an instrument. It is a pact."

"The gate," she repeated, throat tight.

He met her eyes and did not look away. "To passage. To crossing. The grimoire calls it a way of easing what clings. It lets what's bound pass through, if those who stand at the threshold can bear the weight of letting go."

"The serpent eating its own tail," Isabella murmured, thinking of her conversation with Mrs. Abernathy when first she had arrived at Harrowgate.

Rhys sent her a questioning look, then his expression cleared with understanding. "The circle that devours itself eternally." He paused. "We will break the circle and free them."

"Your family," she said.

"My mother. My brothers." He was silent for an instant. "I hear them, but I have not seen them in years, not truly. Once, long ago, I saw Ned by the pond, his pinafore caught on a reed, his hair slick and dark. Will sat by my bed the first week I was home, more shadow than boy. They are caught in what was done to them, and she drinks the little strength they have. I must end their suffering.

"Every turn of the wheel in this house is a grindstone. I will not have them ground down any further. The grimoire says two willing halves, two who see, one of them a conduit who consents. It does not promise ease. It does not promise safety." He swallowed. "But it promises an end."

"For them," she whispered.

"And perhaps for me. Perhaps for you as well, my Isabella. I want to be clear on that. If you choose to do this, you are choosing danger." He squeezed her hand. "You have carried your seeing like a sin. I would be quit of making you wear it like penance."

Somewhere far away a pipe sang, one thin note. Isabella looked down at the page again. *Voluntas.* Will. Choice.

"You think I am—" She broke off, because the word that wanted to come felt too much like vanity, too much like doom.

"I think you are what the gate requires," he said. "And I will not ask it of you unless you ask it first of yourself. If the answer is no, I will find another way to break her without breaking you."

Another way. She didn't believe one existed; neither, by the flicker of pain in his eyes, did he. But he offered it because he would not coerce her, not even with desperation on his side.

Papa's words from that long ago morning rang in her thoughts. *It is not safe. You would open a gate that can never be closed. One that might well swallow her whole.*

Choice blooming like a bruise. That was what this felt like. It hurt because it was real.

She let her fingertips skim the curve of brass. The cold of the metal went through her skin, down to bone.

"If the gate opens," she said, careful with each word, "and they pass...what happens to us?"

He didn't look away. "We stand in a door between grief and what comes after. The text says it takes strength... endurance. There will be a pull. One of us must bear it while the other steadies. When it is done—" his mouth tipped, wry "—it does not promise 'happily ever after.'"

She almost laughed, the sound strangled. "But we might wake in a quiet house. Imagine."

"I do," he said, and for a breath his face was a boy's, sunlit and unscorched, before the years and fire marked him. "Every hour."

The words lingered between them, heavy as grief,

bright as hope. And beneath both lay a warning: if they failed, there would be no second chance.

For a heartbeat, she only looked at him, struck by the image of the boy he must have been and the man who had survived.

They sat together on the floor, the grimoire closed between them. Their gazes met and held, his gray eyes sparking with both hunger and reverence. Desire flared there, but so too did tenderness.

He lifted a hand, cupped her cheek, and kissed her softly, once then again, until her hands tangled in his hair, the strands silky beneath her touch. The floor beneath them was hard, unyielding, and he murmured against her lips, "Not here."

Rising, he offered his hand and drew her to her feet, guiding her back toward the bed. His hands were steady at her waist, unhurried and sure, as he freed her from her clothing. Each button undone was a truth unfastened between them until skin met skin until there was nothing left between them but heat and need.

He urged her down on her back and his gaze tracked the line of bare skin, unapologetic. A thread of want tightened low in her belly, gentler than last night, but no less sure

"This is different," she murmured, surprised at her own shyness and surprised again by the courage that rose to meet it.

"It is," he agreed. His thumb stroked the corner of her mouth, slow, deliberate. His voice lowered, rough with meaning. "Last night was storm. This is...ours."

Her breath caught. Ours. That word undid her. She answered not with speech but with her lips on his, offering herself. He took what she gave and demanded more, until all she knew was the stroke of his lips, his tongue, the soft graze of his teeth, the feel of his hands on her waist, her legs, her breasts. Heat unfurled, an unquiet tide.

When she touched the scars laddering his thigh, he caught her hand, not to stay her touch, but to join, palm over palm.

Bending over him, she let her lips brush one pale seam, and his breath shuddered as if she had kissed not only his flesh, but his pain and grief as well.

Her hand slid along his thigh, higher, until her fingers closed around the hard length of him. She had imagined, *wondered*, but reality was heat and weight and a silken smoothness over steel. He made a raw sound, and her own breath caught.

Curiosity tugged her further. She bent and laid a tentative kiss on his shaft, tasting salt, skin, him. His hand tightened in her hair. With a small, secret smile, she ran her tongue from base to tip, then closed her lips around the broad head and kissed him with lips and tongue as he had kissed her mouth. She felt his restraint trembling, his need barely held in check.

The power of it, of his strength undone by her touch, sent a bolt of heat through her.

"Isabella," he whispered, only her name, need and wonder threaded through it.

She climbed astride him, the sheet slipping away. His pupils widened, the gray iris all but swallowed, and for an instant they only looked at one another. It felt like another threshold crossed, another choice.

Then she leaned in and kissed him again, lips and tongues and teeth. A tight coil of heat twisted deep inside her.

He groaned, head falling back as his hands rose to her breasts, shaping them, pinching her nipples lightly, then harder, until she arched and moaned. Her skin flushed hot, her pulse galloping.

"Tell me if you are sore—" he began, voice raw.

"I will," she said. "But do not be careful as if I might break. Be careful as if I matter."

For a moment he stilled, as though her words had struck deep. Then something fierce and tender both crossed his face. "You matter," he said, and her vision blurred with tears, not of sorrow but of relief, of being wholly seen. She bent and kissed the words from his lips.

Sliding one hand between them, he stroked her core, teasing her until she felt hot and needy, desire building, sharp-edged and tight. She whimpered and writhed, aching for more.

A low chuckle rumbled in his chest.

He bared his teeth, a smile that was all hunger. Panting, she shifted her weight, bringing her wet folds to rest against his shaft, sliding back and forth, teasing them both.

Catching her waist, he guided her down, taking his time, his length filling her. The stretch was sharp, then pleasing, her body opening to him, taking him, their breaths breaking together as he seated himself fully. She gasped at the feel of him, at the way her body clenched around him, greedy.

Each thrust was a slick glide, both sore and sweet, pain reshaping itself into pleasure with each thrust until her toes curled and her thighs trembled. Instinct took over, and she found an angle that made her cry out, that made him groan deep in his chest.

Their rhythm changed, faster now, deeper, a little

rough. She clutched at his shoulders, nails biting, as if she could anchor herself against the current. He kissed her hard, desperate, swallowing her sounds.

When the crest came, it felt like a dam breaking wide, surprising her with the sudden peak, tearing her over the edge. She cried out, unguarded, just as he thrust hard and deep. He came undone with a strangled groan, head thrown back, body taut as he throbbed inside her.

She fell forward across his chest. He buried his face in her neck, holding her as if he would never let her go.

For a time, they stayed tangled, breaths ragged, hearts hammering. The house kept its counsel. She lay listening to the hitch and fall of their breaths, the way their heartbeats, after a time, found the same pace.

"We can make no promises," she whispered. *Not forever. Not even tomorrow.*

"We can," he said, pulling back to look at her, expression raw and fierce. "We can promise that neither will face what waits alone."

Her throat closed. She tucked herself against him, his heart steady beneath her palm, wanting to stay like this forever, knowing their time flew too fast.

A faint, wrong draft crept under the door then, cold as the inside of a well. It licked her ankles and withdrew, a serpent's tongue testing the air for prey.

CHAPTER TWENTY

The draft lingered. Isabella's skin prickled. Beside her, Rhys tensed. They both felt it, the tentative slither of Catrin's strength, returning in inches.

"Do you smell it?" Isabella whispered. "Wet ashes and ..."

"Roses, soured by rot," he finished.

Lifting her head, she met Rhys's gaze. His dark hair lay mussed against the pillow, his mouth softened by what they had just shared, but his eyes had already gone flint-hard.

"We do not have long," he said quietly.

She wanted to argue, to insist on just a moment more of stolen peace, but the words dissolved. He was right. Catrin would not leave them their reprieve.

"We must not waste it," Isabella said.

The air itself had altered...charged, insistent, impatient. Rhys swung his legs over the side of the bed, pulling on his trousers with rough, purposeful movements.

"She gathers strength," he said.

A shiver ran the length of her spine, not wholly fear. Resolve, too.

She had never thought she would know a man's touch. Always, she had believed such things belonged to other women, that attraction was relegated to the realm of poets, words she read on a page. That love would never be hers.

Yet here it was. Startling. Searing. Undeniable.

She loved Rhys Caradoc. Loved his strength and resilience, the way pain had not broken him but forged him stronger. She loved that he saw her as his equal, not expecting her to be less than she was. She loved his tender caress and his fierce kiss. She loved *him*.

She dared acknowledge the truth in her heart, in her mind. She would not say it, not now with Catrin waking and the house listening. But the beauty of her love burned bright in her chest all the same.

And if she was to step into the dark, if she was to be conduit and gate and tether, then she would carry that love with her as her anchor. Her gift.

Rhys reached for his shirt and dragged it over his head as Isabella turned away to dress. She fumbled with the laces. He crossed to her and wordlessly set them right. His touch was steady, practical, but his fingertips lingered on the tiny knobs of her spine for a moment. She smoothed his waistcoat flat, fastening the last obstinate button, and pressed her hand to his heart, brief and sure.

When at last her bodice was straight and her skirt fell smooth, she looked up to find him tying his cravat, hair still tousled, eyes hard and sharp. He looked every inch a man ready for battle, not with sword or pistol or saber, but with will and determination.

The quiet between them had no awkwardness. It was a calm stillness, a prelude to what would come.

Isabella gathered Papa's half of the grimoire while Rhys left to fetch his own. When he returned, they stepped into the corridor, carrying the two halves not as weapons but as guides, an ink and vellum record of those who had faced the darkness before them.

The air shivered and undulated, too cold at Isabella's ankles, too hot on her cheeks. Somewhere below, a stair tread flexed and settled, the house testing its weight.

"Where?" Isabella asked, lifting the lamp to cast a bowl of light.

"Not the library," Rhys said, and she felt grateful for that, for his tacit recognition of all the work she had done there and his decision not to bring this battle to a place where she found comfort.

"The nursery?" she asked, thinking of his brother, murdered there by Catrin's malice and too much laudanum, each breath coming shallower until it came not at all.

"No," he said after a moment then took her hand. He led her not up toward the nursery, but down. And then toward the north wing.

Barred doors with bolts rusted in place blocked their way. Rhys released Isabella's hand to work them free, using the poker he had brought from her chamber. Fitting it beneath the lowest bolt, he levered hard until metal screeched and rust flaked away, the bar shifting by grudging inches. The second bolt yielded only when he set his boot to the wall and wrenched with both hands.

At last, the bar clanged down, the sound echoing in the silent, ruined wing. He angled his shoulder to the panel and shoved until the warped timbers gave, the hinges making a long groan as the door swung wide.

The corridor beyond was starved of light, the air stale and fetid. The sconces held no lamps, the plaster marked by black halos of soot. Dust stirred around their ankles, a thin gray mist that made Isabella's throat itch. Their footfalls made the boards creak and bow.

They reached a door that sagged in its frame, the bolts rusted deep in their brackets. Char streaked the lintel, dark fingers reaching outward, evidence that the fire had tried to claw its way free. Rhys stood rigid, his chest rising and falling.

"Here," he said, his voice scraped raw. "My father's chamber." He drew a slow breath. "I slammed the door and threw myself against it as I tore off my coat and used it to choke the flames crawling up my leg. Then I dragged the marble console from there—" He dipped his chin, and Isabella followed his gaze to blackened hulk lying to one side, cracked down the middle, its gilt feet twisted. "—to lock her in."

She made a soft sound of dismay. In her mind's eye, she saw Rhys—not the man beside her now but the boy he had been—bleeding, shoving the weight of the marble with desperate strength, sealing himself on one side of the door, Catrin and his father's body on the other. She saw him choking on smoke, flames melting his flesh, holding the line with nothing but will. Her heart ached. And in that ache, love flared again, terrifying in its intensity. He had survived hell and stood beside her now, willing to face it again. How could she not love him?

Jaw taut, he pulled open the door. Isabella lifted the lamp higher.

The chamber beyond gaped, blackened and bare. Fire

had eaten it hollow, leaving beams split and charred. Sharp and acrid, the smells of smoke and ash layered with the damp tang of rot. The fine hairs at her nape prickled and rose. A single flame, that was all that stood between them and the devouring dark.

Rhys stepped in first, his limp pronounced on the uneven floorboards. Isabella followed, chest tight, pulse drumming too fast. Her gaze clung to the ruined hearth, the splintered beams, the scars the fire had left behind. Her mind filled with images painted by Rhys's words: a man slumped at the desk, blood pooling beneath his head. Smoke, thick and black, as Rhys dragged the marble across the door. Catrin pounding and shrieking, flames licking hungrily at her skirt.

Horror suffused her, for his suffering and the choices he had been forced to make.

The ruined chamber closed around them, charred and unyielding. The lamp flame guttered, casting frantic shadows that leaped over the wreckage.

"The hearth," Rhys said, and she followed where he led.

The stones were split and blackened, the mantel half-collapsed. Rhys crouched, one knee to the warped boards, and set his half of the grimoire on the stone. Isabella knelt beside him and did the same, the brass semicircles catching the lamp's glow. The two halves lay side by side, broken arcs curving toward each other.

Rhys hesitated only a breath, then slid the halves together. The seam met, groaned like stone on stone, and held. A hum rose from the book, low at first, then climbing until it seemed to fill the marrow of Isabella's bones.

"Give me your hands," he said.

She set her palms in his, warm skin against warm skin, a human anchor in a room where nothing else was human.

At once the hush shattered.

The walls exhaled. Soot rained in a fine sift, pattering like sand across the ruined boards. The temperature swung in lurches—heat like the breath of a furnace on her cheeks, cold so sharp it sliced her ankles. The air swarmed with voices, whispers she had always heard alone, now thickened and multiplied until she could not count them.

Shapes gathered. At first nothing but mist, pale and quivering, then forms that almost resolved: the small stoop of a boy's shoulders, a woman's bent head, another child's hand clutching at the air. Their edges rippled like candle flame in a draft, fading, returning, fading again.

"Rhys," Isabella breathed. "You see them."

His grip convulsed on hers. His eyes were wide, wet, starving. "I see them." The words were broken, reverent.

The forms wavered, reached, and then the room turned.

Ash hissed across the floorboards, pooling in unnatural drifts. The soot on the ceiling began to run in slow rivulets, black as tar, trickling upward instead of down. A low groan pulsed through the beams.

The figures faltered. The mother's bent head lifted, mouth moving in silent weeping. Her outline thinned, pulled taut, as if some unseen hook had snagged her spine. The boys shrank and wavered.

"She comes," Rhys said, his voice hard and cold.

The temperature dropped with a sickening lurch, then rose until Isabella's lips felt dry, her eyes stinging. The boards beneath them buckled with a groan, nails squealing as they tore free. The ruined walls breathed, inhaling their warmth, exhaling black.

Then the laughter came.

Childlike at first—high, sweet, delighted. Then it bent, cracked, multiplied, a dozen throats belching sound, reaching a crescendo that split the air.

Catrin.

She stepped out of the soot itself, half-formed, half-smoke. Her face flickered, perfect and monstrous in turns. The folds of her gown were slicked with oil, her pearl buttons swimming like eyes. Her jaw cracked wider than flesh would allow, splitting her face until smoke poured out in ribbons, black and slick, coiling like snakes.

Rhys's grip on Isabella's wrists tightened, anchoring her, but the force of those ribbons slammed into her chest, a hook tugging her ribs outward. Her ribs screamed. Her body arched as though she were being strung on wires. Terror clawed at her.

She gasped, head snapping back.

"Isabella!" Rhys's voice thundered, ragged, frantic.

The ribbons coiled around her waist, her throat, cold and wet as pondweed, slick as mud. They pulled. She dug her nails into Rhys's hands, not to pry free, but to hold.

Catrin's voice whispered in her ear, silk over razors. "Conduit. Pretty conduit. Be what is wanted. Be what is needed."

Be silent. Be small. Be safe. Rules she had obeyed her whole life.

The shadows swelled until the burned chamber drowned in them. Isabella's vision tunneled, narrowed to Rhys's eyes—gray gone near black, fierce, refusing.

He tried to break the pull, wrenching her back, but she shook her head, choking. "Don't... Let me—"

The black smoke filled her mouth, her lungs, her mind.

And she understood: this was the gate, and Catrin meant to claim it, claim *her*.

Rhys wrenched at her hands, trying to break the circle, to tear her free of the conduit's pull.

"No! Isabella!" His shout tore from his throat. "I won't lose you for this. I'll damn the gate, damn her, damn all of it before I lose you."

His desperation hit her harder than the smoke filling her lungs. His grip was brutal, his body bent toward hers, ready to break every vow he had made. For a heartbeat she thought he would tear her away, shatter the grimoire, consign his mother and brothers to their prison forever. For her.

Her chest burned, throat raw, but she forced the words through. "You cannot—" she coughed, black spilling between her lips, "—consign them to this for me."

"Yes, I can." His voice cracked, naked, wild. "I will. Better their torment than your death."

He meant them, those words. And it told her that he loved her.

Loved her above all else.

And her love for him would not allow her to fail.

Her vision blurred. Shapes writhed at the edges of sight, the mother, the boys, thin and stretched, Catrin gnawing at their souls. Their hands reached, trembling, pleading.

"They suffer," Isabella gasped. "You hear them—" Her head jerked as another ribbon of shadow drove itself into her mouth, gagging her. "I feel them—"

Catrin laughed, low and intimate, pressing her

phantom mouth to Isabella's ear. "He loves you not. He would unmake you for them." She dragged a finger of smoke along Isabella's throat, then licked her with a ribboned tongue. "Let go of your earthly form. Come to me. Join me, Isabella. Be free."

The voice was a sibilant hiss, laced with promise. A lure. A trap. Isabella knew it, but still—

Rhys dragged her forward, trying to haul her into his chest as though he could shield her with the meat of his body. The grimoire's hum rose to a shriek, vibrating through the scorched stones.

"Isabella," he begged. Not command. Not demand. Begging. His whole frame shook. "Come back to me. Close it. Leave it. Let her have them and I will live with the pain. I *can* live with that pain, but I cannot live without you."

Her pulse thundered in her ears. A hundred mornings with Papa's rules lashed across her memory. *Never say, never show, hide, hide, hide.*

Be what is wanted.

She had hidden so long.

But she was not a child anymore. She was not property to be shuffled, nor shadow to be smothered.

She pressed her forehead hard against Rhys's, their grips bruising. "I choose," she rasped. "Not her. Not silence. Me. I choose."

She had lived caged inside her silence, her sight smothered, her soul bound. But now she flung the doors wide. She let the voices, the visions, the dark flood through her. Unmasked. Unbarred.

The gate answered.

The air tore open.

Catrin's laughter fractured into a scream, the sound splintering glass somewhere far below. The soot bled down the walls in black torrents. Isabella's body bowed backward, every vein lit with fire. She screamed with it, a sound that felt like it would rip her throat apart.

Rhys shouted her name, his voice a lifeline. He clamped her wrists, not to hold her down, but to hold her here.

Through the blur of black and ash, she saw them, saw clearly for the first time. His mother, her eyes swollen with weeping but alight now with recognition. Will, coughing weakly, small chest fluttering, but lifting his face toward her. Ned, humming through his fear, voice thin but alive.

The sight of them filled her, but so too did the pull. It wanted her. Catrin wanted her. She felt herself being stripped into threads, pulled through the dark.

Rhys's voice broke over her. "Isabella, stay with me—please—"

She wanted to. God, she wanted to.

She wished she had told him that she loved him. She wished—

The dark swallowed her scream. Her body jerked. Pain, sharp and deep, flayed her, and she soared, floating high, her body crumpling to the floor below.

She heard the broken roar of Rhys's pain, saw him fall to his knees at her side, and then darkness closed over her, deep as the grave.

CHAPTER TWENTY-ONE

Isabella's head tipped back, eyes rolling white.

"Isabella!" Her name tore out of Rhys, raw and useless. The pull fought him, talons hooked deep, raking her toward the dark. Terror scored oozing runnels in his soul. He had thought he understood pain, fear—fire melting his flesh, nights locked away in St. Jude's, years listening to the whispers gnaw his bones, helpless to free those he loved.

But none of it touched this. To lose her was to be gutted, unmade.

Catrin rose, her form dripping black ooze that stank like rot, long hair oily and dark, her face an eyeless mass. Her laugh curdled into words. *She opened. She called. She is mine now.*

Rhys roared, the sound scraped from deep in his lungs, unholy and raw. Defiance melded with grief, hate with desperation. He hauled at the unseen tether until every muscle burned, and it did not matter. He could not wrench Isabella free.

But he would not let go.

"Take me," he shouted. "If you want blood, take mine. Take me, Catrin. Leave her."

You? she crooned. *I'll have you as well. But not before I hollow her out. She is the key. She is the door. She is the willing one.*

Isabella's lips moved, faint and soundless.

His heart lurched, savage and stunned. He had thought her gone, her soul already stripped away, her body but an empty shell. But she was still here, still fighting.

He bent close, caught the ghost of her breath against his jaw. The terror and grief that had hollowed him a heartbeat ago surged into wild, aching hope. He clasped her hands in his, bowing his head, willing his own strength into her veins.

And around them, the smell of rotting roses and smoke and ash grew stronger until it was more than just a stink in his nostrils but a taste burning his tongue, a burn eking through his pores.

"I...choose..." Isabella whispered.

Her eyes opened, black threaded with fire. Her fingers twitched in his grasp and then tightened, hard, answering his hold.

Catrin screamed, sharp and high. Soot bled down the walls in black ropes that writhed and twisted. Isabella arched in his arms, spine rigid, neck extended, the gate tearing through her as if she were hinge and threshold.

"Together," he said, hoarse. "Always." An oath. A prayer.

The dark recoiled as if seared.

Plaster split with a crack, long seams crawling jagged

across the walls. Catrin ballooned and unraveled, her shape bleeding into every corner. One moment, she loomed vast, ceiling to floor, her gown dripping black ichor like blood, her face flickering through child, maiden, crone.

The next, she flattened thin, a smear of teeth and eyes that slithered toward them, the chamber itself her skin.

Door. Door. She is the door. Open, and all is mine. Her voice pricked his skin like shards of glass, tearing at his ears, gouging his thoughts.

He curled his body over Isabella like a shield as he felt the pull wrench through his arms. Her wrists burned beneath his palms. He braced her with both arms and still she slipped.

"Isabella, no—" Panic split him raw and he glanced at the hearth. He would wreck the book. He would fire the wing again. He would damn every name he had begged as a boy if it kept her breathing under his hand.

She turned her head the smallest fraction, her mouth brushing his ear. The voice that threaded out was thin but steadier than his. "Rhys...let me."

"No." The word broke in him. "Not you."

Her eyes shone with tears and with courage, steady and true.

Love. She did not speak the word for it; neither did he. She gave it in the pressure of her hand. He gave it back. He would follow her into the fire, into ruin, into death itself.

"If I let go," he said, his voice rough, "she takes you. If I hold, she drains you."

"Don't let go," she whispered with all the trust in the world.

Light woke along the grimoire's brass seam, unfurling

from glow to blaze, searing through the dark like a brand holding heat. The split arc found its mate and the newly formed whole sang a note that struck him deep, shivering through his teeth, his bones.

And then he saw them.

For years he had heard only fragments of coughs deep in the walls, sobs woven through floorboards, a lullaby splintered by the wind. Now, he saw them in truth. His mother, her hair braided down her back, eyes alive with recognition as she lifted her face to him. Ned, hand outstretched, lips curved in that sweet grin, two front teeth missing. Will, still a boy just starting to go gangly. They were not shadows, not stretched and hollowed by Catrin's hunger. They were his. For the first time in over a decade, they were his.

Catrin's laugh shattered on stone. *You see them because of her. Without her, you are nothing. And when I have drunk her dry, you will be nothing again.*

Isabella convulsed. Her hand slipped for one beat of his heart. In that beat he saw the life that would remain to him if he lost her: the endless silence of her absence. He would be a husk, a shell, his ribs empty, his breath an echo.

He shouted, a sound that rattled the scorched rafters. He crushed their hands together until bone ground on bone.

"You will not have her," he said.

Catrin reached. Shadow-hands plunged into Isabella's breast. Heat ran up his forearms as if those claws held his pulse, too. He shoved his arm between them, useless meat between hunger and the thing that wanted.

"Take me," he said through his teeth. "Take me."

You are already mine, cousin. You always were.

Isabella's fingers crushed his. She found his eyes through smoke and light. "Rhys...do not listen to her lies. Hold fast. Only...hold...."

Truth hit like a post driven clean. He tightened until their joined hands went bloodless, set his brow to hers and felt the shaking and under it, the steadiness that did not break.

The room convulsed. Fire bent inward as if the hearth had a mouth. Catrin went to pieces, shadow tearing from bone, teeth to dust. She clawed and wailed; the pull did not heed her. It heeded the circle they made, and the hinge of Isabella's will.

"Let them pass," Isabella whispered, and the air rang as if a bell had answered.

They came. They brushed him like cool breath, his mother's sleeve, Ned's small fingers catching his, Will's thin shoulder resting, a remembered weight against his chest.

Then they were gone.

Catrin's shriek broke and dropped away. The blaze sank to coal, then ash. The pull slackened. His arms found he was holding a woman again, warm, breathing, living.

He sank with her to the blackened boards. "Isabella— God—"

Her cheek turned into his shirt. He felt her mouth shape the words against him. "I am here," she whispered, fragile and defiant at once.

Silence fell, heavy and whole.

Not a pause before the next harm. Not the breath the house took before the whisper began again. Silence like a shore after storm the air clean.

He had forgotten its shape.

He set his face in her hair, lavender and salt and smoke.

"It's done," she said at last, as if the words might wake something. Her voice was dry and parched. "Rhys, it's done."

He listened for any small tap. Heard only their breathing. A laugh came up in him. "It's done."

She tipped back. Even streaked with soot and blood she was the most living thing he had ever seen. "You did not let her take me," she said.

"I would have burned the world," he said. "I would have damned them all if it kept your breath."

Her palm found his cheek. "I could not have left you with that."

Relief and grief tangled until he could not tell one from the other. He let himself see what he had not let himself hold... his mother's mouth shaping thanks, Will's cough softening into nothing, Ned's hum fading.

"They're gone," he said, and the word did not mean loss. "Free."

"And Catrin," she murmured, her gaze on the ash where a monster had stood. "She will never harm another soul."

He had lived so long with Catrin that the absence of her felt hollow. He would fill it with light and joy and love.

He bent and kissed Isabella's brow. His mouth shook. "I have nothing left to ask of you."

"Then ask me for myself," she said, quiet. "No snares. No tricks. Only ask."

He would. But not here. Not in this place, not in this moment. She deserved better than a vow made in the aftermath of terror. But perhaps she heard them in the way his hands held her face, the way his lips traced her brow, the way his heart beat for her.

They stood together, unsteady. His leg flared and he did not care. The ruined chamber stayed behind them as they walked away, arms wrapped around each other, bringing the quiet with them. They walked corridors that no longer listened, down a stair that remembered its work and not its malice, through a hall without eyes in the corners.

The silence held as they climbed the stairs, not fragile but whole, filling the house like balm poured over an old wound.

In Rhys's chamber, the fire had been stoked high, flames casting a steady, unblinking light. A steaming bath waited, summoned by his command. Isabella stood at the threshold, trembling, unsure if her knees would hold. Rhys's hand steadied her.

Her gown sagged, streaked with soot, stinking of smoke. Her hair hung in stiff tangles.

"Sit," he said quietly, his voice ragged from shouting her name.

"I'll ruin it." She made a helpless gesture to encompass first the state of her gown and then the chair.

"Then I'll burn it," he said. "Sit."

She obeyed, lowering herself to the chair, holding his gaze as he knelt before her. His fingers worked at the fastenings of her gown, loosening ties, unhooking stays. His hands were cut and burned, marked by their ordeal, his touch careful, almost reverent, as he slid the ruined fabric from her shoulders. Piece by piece, he stripped away the wreckage of the night until only her shift remained, blackened and frayed.

Then he lifted her despite her protests and carried her to the bath. The steam curled around them, fragrant with rosemary and lavender. He eased her down into the water, his big hands steady beneath her arms until she was settled. The heat lapped at her skin, pulling the ache from her bones, the soot from her pores.

Rhys dipped a cloth, wrung it slow, and passed it across her throat, down her arms, over her hands. Soot melted away. Isabella let her head fall back against the rim of the tub as he soaped her skin, her hair, then rinsed her clean.

"Rhys," she whispered, her throat raw.

He paused, the cloth dripping into the water. His jaw flexed. "I almost lost you."

Her heart twisted at the vulnerability in his voice. "But you didn't."

He exhaled, ragged, and returned to his task. Each stroke was steady, deliberate.

When her skin shone clean, he set the cloth aside. He stared at her as if she were both miracle and torment. Then, with no word, he stripped off his coat, his waistcoat, his shirt. The rest followed—boots, trousers—until he stood bare in the firelight, unflinching beneath her gaze. Scars ridged his leg, pale seams carved by fire. He did not hide them. He let her see.

Then he stepped into the tub, the water rising as his body sank. She shifted, making space. He gathered her into his lap, her back against his chest, the crown of her head beneath his chin and she knew pure joy in this moment, the two of them, flesh to flesh, breath to breath, their hearts beating in the same rhythm.

Isabella let her head fall to his shoulder. The strong line of his arm curled around her waist, the heat of him steady against her spine. The water lapped soft and warm, sluicing away the last remnants of ash.

She thought of Papa, who had shielded her with rules and silence. She thought of Rhys, who had trusted her enough to stand at his side, who had seen her without her mask and not asked her to hide. This man was her world.

The words rose in her chest, impossible to contain. "I love you."

He went still at her back, no breath, no sound.

Then his mouth pressed to her wet hair, his voice breaking open against her crown. "I love you, my Isabella," he said. Fierce. Certain. Unashamed. "God help me, I love you."

She closed her eyes, the words sinking into her like light into stone. "Say it again."

He turned her in his arms, water sloshing over the rim of the tub. His too-pretty gray eyes shone raw in the firelight, his mouth claiming hers.

And then he whispered it again, "I love you, my brave, beautiful, brilliant girl. My Isabella."

She answered with her lips on his, sealing truth with truth.

They clung in the warm water, steam rising around them. The house was quiet. For the first time, truly quiet. No whispers. No shadows leaning to overhear.

Only them.

Later, when the water had cooled and their limbs were heavy, he lifted her from the bath and wrapped her in blankets, his own body damp and bare against hers. They lay tangled in his bed, skin to skin, and though sleep tugged at her, she stayed awake long enough to feel his heart steady beneath her palm.

Later still, when Rhys slept, Isabella rose. She donned his shirt and wrapped the blanket around her shoulders, then padded barefoot through the hush of the corridors, the two halves of the grimoire cradled in her arms. The house did not whisper, did not stir. Its silence pressed gentle as a hand on her back.

In the library, she set the grimoire on the desk, brass seam glimmering. Once it had been weight and threat, inked with grief and fear. She laid her fingers on the cover, braced for a tremor, a tap, the bite of some unseen hook.

Nothing.

Only stillness.

She gathered the volume and carried it to a shelf. The leather was cool against her palms, the brass no hotter than any hinge. She slid it between two sober treatises and stepped back. There, it looked almost ordinary.

She sighed, not in sadness or despair, but relief. All her life, she had feared that she was nothing but a vessel for other people's rules, condemned to wear a mask, to let no one know her true soul.

But she had tossed her mask aside, and Rhys loved her for who she was.

The blanket shifted on her shoulders. She turned and found Rhys leaning against the doorframe, hair damp and rumpled, eyes heavy with sleep. He said nothing, only watched her with a look that made her heart beat a little faster.

He crossed to her and took her hand, rough palm warm against her fingers as he twined them with his own. She leaned into him, their joined hands resting against her breast, the steady thud of her heart beneath.

She opened his fingers and pressed his palm to her heart. He bent and kissed the inside of her wrist, a vow spoken without words.

And when they left the library, it was not as haunted souls clinging to survival. It was as equals, two who had walked through fire, chosen each other in the dark, and stepped together into what lay beyond. Together.

EPILOGUE

The carriage jolted to a halt before Harrowgate's front steps. Isabella descended and smoothed her skirts, still smiling from the Burns sisters' chatter in Marlow. The house rose before her, quiet and watchful, but no longer menacing. Its windows caught the late sun, glass flashing gold. In recent weeks, Rhys had hired additional staff to set the house to rights.

Peg hurried down to meet her, cheeks flushed, curls escaping her cap.

"Mrs. Caradoc," she said, breathless, offering Isabella's new title with all the weight of delight. It still felt strange to hear it. Only days had passed since she had stood with Rhys in the church and spoken vows. Strange, and wondrous.

"You must come quick. There's—" Peg lifted her hands, at a loss. "Well, you'll see."

Inside, the hush was punctuated by the scrape and shuffle of unfamiliar footsteps. The air smelled not of soot but of polish and fresh timber. Hammers rang from the north wing. Rhys had hired men from London to come and restore the damage.

She glanced at Peg, but the girl only beamed and led her up the stairs.

Her chamber door stood ajar and inside, boxes, dozens of them, tied with twine and stamped with London merchants' crests, were stacked high along the walls. On the bed lay a gown of cornflower blue, its skirt spilling over the counterpane like water.

Isabella stilled in the doorway. "What is all this?" she whispered.

Rhys stepped from the shadowed corner, cravat loose, hair untidy from travel. His smile was a private thing, crooked and soft.

"Hello, Mrs. Caradoc," he murmured, taking her in his arms and pressing a kiss to her lips.

"Hello, Mr. Caradoc," she whispered, and kissed him back.

With his arm looped at her waist, he gestured at the boxes. "This," he said, "is your wardrobe for Paris. And Italy. And wherever else you choose to walk."

She laughed, the sound astonished out of her. "Paris?"

"You told me once," he said, "in the library. That you dreamed of Paris. A dress the color of cornflowers. A book under your arm. Sunlight on the Seine. I listened." He touched the gown, then her hand. "I mean for you to have it all, my love."

Her throat tightened with joy, with disbelief, with the sweet truth of it. She set her palm against his chest, felt the steady thud of his heart. "And you, Mr. Caradoc? What is it you mean for yourself?"

His hand covered hers. His eyes, once bleak as a winter sky, warmed. "To walk beside you. Always."

Mrs. Abernathy bustled in then, carrying yet another box, pretending not to see the moment she had interrupted. "I've ordered the footmen to move the boxes to the dressing room," she declared. "And Peg...mind you begin untying those parcels. Mrs. Caradoc can't go to Paris without shoes."

Peg bobbed a curtsy, grinning wide, already tugging at the first knot. Isabella laughed again, freer this time, and let Rhys draw her closer.

And as they turned toward the door, a faint shimmer stirred, no menace now, but a wisp of ghost-light brushing past. Isabella felt its chill slip along her skin and knew she could open herself wider if she wished. She chose not to. Rhys's hand on her back was steady and sure, and she sensed the same quiet restraint in him. The sight was theirs to command now, a gift that answered only when they called.

They stood amid lace and linen and silk, the light scent of lavender curling into the air. The future waited, not with shadows and whispers, but with light woven of love, bright as the dress on the bed, sure as the man who stood at her side, wide as the world they would walk together.

The End

Thank you so much for reading Darkest at Dusk. I hope you love Rhys and Isabella as much as I do! Please consider leaving a review. Word of mouth is an author's best friend!

What should you read next?

1. If you love historical gothic mystery romance, check out my Dark Gothic series. Book 1 is Dark Desires.

2. If you're a fan of dark urban fantasy/paranormal romance, start the Sins Series with Sins of the Heart.

3. And if you like dark Mafia romance, check out the books I write with a partner under the name Becca Kane.

EXCERPT FROM DARK
DESIRES

CHAPTER ONE

London, 1828

A thick gray wall of fog hovered over the damp stones of Hanbury Street, carrying the stink of old blood and rotting entrails. Darcie Finch shivered as chilled wisps curled like talons about her slim frame, and she hastened her steps, her feet sliding precariously on the wet cobblestones. Clutching her battered leather folio against her side, she tried in vain to close her senses to the stench.

The frightened lowing of cattle drifted on the rank air, carried from the nearby abattoir. Come morning, the stones on the next block would glisten wetly; not from mist and rain as they did tonight, but from a river of blood flowing over them. Despite her attempts to block the sound, the piteous noise intruded.

Darcie dragged in a shaky breath, fighting the panic that threatened to claw free of her breast. Did she feel the same dull fear as those poor beasts being herded to their doom, the same sense of the inevitable horror to be meted out by unfeeling hands? She could not help but compare their fate to hers, to the sorry lot she had chosen. But therein lay the distinction. The animals had been condemned without benefit of trial, born to the ending that awaited them—the slaughterhouse one block over. Those poor dumb beasts had no choice.

Her breath whistled through her teeth. As if she did.

Darcie gave herself a mental shake. There were always choices, and she had made hers. Better to accept responsibility than to brandish her fist at the fates, crying and wailing against the burdens that were hers to bear.

She moved her feet mechanically, her worn boots scraping along the cobbled road as she rubbed her fingertips across the raised, puckered scar that marred the skin of her left hand. *Destiny.* Steppy had talked of destiny as though it were an old friend, or perhaps a mortal enemy with an ancient grudge. He always said that destiny brought all men to the same fate, a shroud and a bed in the cold hard ground.

Darcie clutched her flat leather case tighter against her chest. She knew now that Steppy had been wrong. A person might not find their end in the ground. A person might be dug up from a fresh grave and find their final end on an anatomist's table. Whitechapel was a favorite haunt of the resurectionists—unscrupulous men who plundered fresh graves and were whispered to hasten the dying on their way.

Shrugging off the morbid thought, she willed her exhausted body onward. Tragic and pitiable was the life that lay ahead, but no worse than so many young girls had faced before her. She sighed softly. Once she had believed in dreams and fairy tales, had relied on a gossamer web woven of privilege and fantasy. Now, she believed only in the harsh reality of life, relied only on her own ingenuity.

A sound. A shadow. Something made her stop, every fiber in her body alert. Icy tendrils twisted around her heart. Her gaze darted this way and that, searching the darkest corners of the narrow thoroughfare. The certainty that she was no longer alone slithered across her mind. She could feel something—no, *someone*—and sense an evil intent. Peering into the shadows that loomed dark and frightful along the deserted street, she tried to place the cause of her unease.

Nothing materialized from the mist. Walking on, she shook her head at her own foolishness, at the fear that was a remnant of a time when she had lived a better life, a time when she would never have even considered roaming the back alleys of the worst part of the city. Those days were dusty memories. For so long now she had lived on these streets, existing from moment to moment, from meal to meal.

Again Darcie rubbed the length of the raised scar that crossed her hand, a memento of a poor choice, a reminder of Steppy. For a moment she thought of him as he had been, before storms and foolish decisions had taken his merchant's fortune to the black bottom of a pitiless ocean. Her stepfather had once been a man of means and a man of morals.

Just a few more steps and she'd be at Spitalfields Market. She knew the way, knew the safest route, and the most dangerous one as well. The scar began to throb and ache. It seemed to swell beneath her touch as she trudged onward, her folio of drawings tucked under one arm, her mind rooted in the past. She ought to have run in the opposite direction that day, ought to have chosen the safe road. Ought to—

Well, it didn't matter now.

Her footsteps faltered as the hair at the nape of her neck prickled and rose. Her earlier feeling of unease grew stronger, more insistent as it clamored for her attention. There *was* someone on the street with her. Slowly she turned to face the way she had come. The mist was thick as pottage. She could see nothing. No one. But though she could not see him, she could sense him, and she'd learned by trial and error that some senses didn't lie. Intuition was often the only safeguard between life and the oblivion of death.

Added to her own instinct was the weight of rumors that hovered over the streets of Whitechapel. Rumors of murder, of vile and painful death. Darcie knew the value of gossip. There was the probability of a frightening kernel of truth hidden beneath the layers of speculation and exaggeration.

Pulling back into the shadowed niche of a doorway, she used the night and the fog to her advantage. The thought that she had imagined the whole of it, that the sound was only the footfall of some poor soul on his way home from a hard night's labor, was one she wanted to consider. Still, instinct argued against the possibility.

Hide in the shadows. Run, girl. Run! Steppy's voice calling her from beyond the grave.

Darcie wedged herself into the dimmest corner of the doorway, praying that the mad pounding of her heart was audible only to her own ears. She sensed that whoever, whatever, shared the street with her was on a quest, a search for the surest path to misery—her misery.

As if conjured from her most terrible imaginings, the shape of a man emerged from the mist. No sound heralded his arrival, just a ripple, a current that moved the air. Darcie dared not breathe, though an odor, foul and frightful, came uninvited into her nostrils. The smell of evil.

She could hear the sound of his breathing, low and rough. He was close enough now that she could lean out and touch his cape if she were of a mind to summon his notice. The garment was long, nearly to the ground, black in color, and of a fine material. She could see the smooth surface of his highly polished Hessians, splattered by the mud of the road. A man of money, she surmised. A man of money who had come to the East End, to Whitechapel, to prey on the poorest of the poor.

Seconds ticked by with agonizing slowness. Abruptly, he turned and began to walk away, the hollow sound of his footfall ringing on the stones. A sense of relief so acute as to be almost painful washed over her.

As the echo of the man's footsteps faded, Darcie slunk from the shadows, cautious, ever watchful. But the street was deserted.

She continued on her way, meeting no one as she walked, and when her stomach gave an ugly rumble, she ignored it. There was no choice given that she possessed not a crumb of food. The hour was close to dawn. The prostitutes and the men who searched them out had left the street for the night, and honest folk had yet to stir.

A rat scurried across her path. Watching it blend into the shadows, she remembered another life, when such a sight would have drawn her revulsion, even her fear, a time when she had lived in a small house in Shrewsbury, with Mama and Abigail and Steppy. And later, with

Steppy alone. Wispy memories teased her thoughts. Warm cocoa and soft hugs, the smell of Christmas morning, the childhood innocence that allowed her to feel safe.... Ruthlessly she shoved the thoughts of a better time to the back of her mind. No sense pining for the past when the present was what she must face. She was so close to the end of her desperate journey.

Tears filled her eyes, not of relief, but of despair. The end of her journey would bring only grief. The irony was a bitter tonic.

"So, you have come, Darcie Finch. I wondered how long it would take you."

A woman with garish face paint and cold eyes stood in the doorway of 10 Hadley Street, summoned there by the scantily clad girl who had answered Darcie's tentative knock. Her lips were pulled in a tight sneer and her brows rose mockingly as she looked down at Darcie, who stood rain-damp and bedraggled on the single timeworn stone step that led to the open door. Darcie swallowed and hesitated, though the woman swept her hand across the portal in a clear invitation to enter.

"Are you in, or out? I haven't all night. Not unless you've got a stiff rod and a bagful of coin." She barked a harsh laugh at her own joke.

Darcie tried to answer, to tell the woman why she had come. Her throat moved and she meant to speak but, despite her intentions, no sound issued forth.

"Lost your wits, girl?" With an impatient click of her tongue the woman closed her fingers around Darcie's wrist.

A sharp tug, and Darcie stumbled into the house. Grabbing the edge of the marble entry table to steady herself, she stopped just short of landing in an ignominious heap at the other woman's feet.

The place smelled of smoke and strong perfume. And some other smell that was heavy and cloyingly sweet.

"Is he dead and buried, then?"

Darcie swallowed convulsively and nodded. *Dead, dead, dead.* Steppy was dead. Buried? She had no idea.

"You'll call me Mrs. Feather, like the other girls. No special treatment for you."

"Of course, Mrs. Feather." Darcie found her voice at last. She had heard of Mrs. Feather's house—there were few in Whitechapel who had not. But when she had realized that the address she sought, taken from the faded and ratty old letter that was her final link to the past, was actually Mrs. Feather's house, she had been shocked beyond words.

Darcie stared at the woman before her. Hard and bitter, she bore the marks of a sad and savage life. Could this cold creature really be Abigail? Pretty Abigail who used to sing Darcie to sleep and hold her in the night when the bad dreams came? A heaviness burdened Darcie's heart as she realized that this shell was all that remained of her sister.

Mrs. Feather caught Darcie's chin between her thumb and forefinger, regarding her shrewdly through eyes that glittered like chips of ice. She stared without speaking for a long moment.

Darcie returned the perusal with a sidelong glance, noticing that Mrs. Feather looked old and worn, when in truth she was barely thirty. The bright color painted on her lips could not disguise the furrows that bracketed her mouth. The powder and rouge that colored her skin did little to hide the deep grooves that marked her brow, the brittle cast to her features, or the sallow complexion.

Saddened, Darcie lowered her gaze, unwilling to acknowledge this woman who was but a caricature of the sister she remembered. She immediately realized her mistake. In looking away she had changed nothing, for she was yet confronted by the reality of her sister's life. Her gown was tight and low, her full breasts pushed up to the point that they nearly spilled over the top of her bodice, and the scent of her perfume swirled around Darcie in a sickening cloud.

Suddenly, Mrs. Feather snatched at the battered folio that Darcie clutched under one arm. "What's this, then? You're not still scratching out pictures?"

Darcie's fingers curled protectively around the edges of the tattered leather case, resisting Mrs. Feather's attempts to take it from her.

"Yes. I still sketch, though it has been some time since I could buy any supplies to draw with. These pictures are old. Treasures. Memories." Darcie couldn't suppress a sad smile. "I have one of you."

"Not one of me," Mrs. Feather said in a flat voice. "What you have is a picture of a girl who died a long time ago."

Darcie made no reply. There was nothing to say to that.

"How old are you now?" The question was sharp, impatient.

"Twenty, come June."

"Well, you look younger," Mrs. Feather said, her eyes narrowing as she peered at Darcie's face. "I remember you being younger." With an impatient click of her tongue, she turned Darcie toward the large gilt-framed mirror that hung on the wall. "Look at yourself and tell me if you think I have much to work with. Eyes as sorrowful as a whipped puppy. And that hair. I don't know what to make of it. And you're as skinny as a post. Men like a woman who's soft and curved."

Darcie stared at her reflection. She did look a sight. Her brown eyes were huge in her face, made all the more so by her hollow cheeks and pale skin. The ill weather had done a thorough job of drenching her, and the mahogany hair that had once been soft and pretty was plastered to her skull, hanging in uneven clumps over her shoulders. The severe, uninterrupted black of her apparel did little to enhance her appearance. In all, she looked like a walking corpse, though a corpse likely boasted more color in its cheeks.

"It doesn't matter how I look," she said. "I don't care. I only want—" She broke off as a man stepped into the entry hall, his passage followed by raucous laughter that belched from the front parlor as he departed. From the corner of her eye, Darcie caught the swirl of garishly colored gowns, the images of rouged lips and kohl-rimmed eyes. Women of the night, she thought as the door closed, cutting off the scene.

Her attention returned to the man as he moved behind Mrs. Feather, one hand curving around her waist and the other sliding over the bare skin of her shoulder until his fingers rested just inside her gown, lying casually on the plump fullness of her breast. Darcie swallowed, staring at this violation of her sister's person, unable to look away. *This* was how men would treat her.

He was of medium height, sharp featured and dark, the cut of his superfine coat accentuating his stocky build.

Some might think him handsome, but the way he touched Mrs. Feather made Darcie's stomach roll with nerves. She took a step back, wishing she were anywhere but here.

Mrs. Feather cast Darcie a hard glance, then turned from her, her lips curving in a practiced smile as she moved.

"Lord Albright, how lovely to have you grace us with your presence this night. All is arranged exactly as you desire. The red room, as you requested."

"Is this the girl?" he asked, his voice cold. Darcie shifted her gaze to the floor. "Looks like Haymarket ware. She's not as pretty as I wanted, or as young. And she looks completely lacking in spirit. You know I like a bit of excitement."

"This girl, my lord? She's just a maid. I have a lovely treat waiting for you upstairs."

He grunted, pulling his hand from Mrs. Feather's breast. Abruptly, he stepped toward Darcie, brushing his fingertips over her bodice. With a cry she shrank from his touch, banging her arm sharply against the marble-topped table at her side. Lord Albright's eyes lit with a glow that made Darcie cringe from him.

Mrs. Feather moved smoothly between them, linking one arm with practiced ease through Lord Albright's and reaching behind at the same time to deliver a sharp pinch to Darcie's forearm with the other.

"Come, my lord," she purred. "We wouldn't want the tempting dish I've arranged to get cold, would we?"

Lord Albright bared his teeth. "I shall enjoy sampling her, warm or cold."

Revulsion rose in Darcie's throat.

As she guided Lord Albright toward the staircase, Mrs. Feather glanced back over her shoulder.

"Stay there." She mouthed the words soundlessly at Darcie, her lips moving with exaggeration.

Sagging against the wall, Darcie tried to force her racing heart to slow. She felt sick. Lord, it wouldn't do for her to toss up here on the shiny polished floor of the front hall. No danger of that, really. There was nothing inside of her to throw up.

The dull ache in her abdomen turned momentarily sharp, doubling her over with the sheer intensity of the pain. She was reminded of exactly how desperate her straits were. The subtle torment was always there of late, gnawing relentlessly at her empty insides, reminding her that a full belly was a dream of the past. The minutes and hours would creep by, and just when she thought she could bear it, the agony of ever present hunger tore at her with a pain that gnashed its evil teeth, lacerating her stomach, taunting her with her own desperation.

The sound of boisterous laughter filtered from the front parlor. Raising her head, Darcie forced herself to look about, to take in the reality of the choice she had made. *Mrs. Feather's House.* The name was so innocuous, so unassuming, but Darcie was hard pressed to imagine anything worse than this place. No mere house, it was a den of debauchery. Mrs. Feather catered to the best of society, providing them with the means to indulge in their darkest, vilest desires.

A high-pitched scream echoed from above, and then another. The hallway spun before Darcie's eyes. She couldn't remember when she'd eaten last. Last night. No, the night before that. She'd snatched a potato that fell from a bushel at Spitalfields and devoured it raw. Nowhere to sleep. Nothing to eat. For weeks she'd banged on every door, pleaded for gainful employment at any job. Laundry maid. Step girl. There was nothing to be had. She was faced with a terrible choice. Sell herself on the street—what had Lord Albright called her? Haymarket ware—the lowest girl who sold herself in a doorway, a back alley, the darkened corner of a pub. Or she could sell herself to her sister.

Or she could die.

She'd thought of the poorhouse, but she had no illusions there. It was simply a longer and slower death.

Darcie pressed her balled fist into her belly. Her gaze strayed past the black-and-gold-papered walls of the front hallway, to the staircase that led to the upper floor, then flicked rapidly to the doorway that led to the parlor that Lord Albright had exited earlier.

Slowly, she began to back away. Her hip bumped against something, and she glanced down to find the knob of the front door pressing against her. The smooth cold surface of it beckoned.

Her fist closed around the brass knob, and she whirled, twisting the handle and flinging the door open. The darkness and the fresh smell of rain greeted her. Coming here had been a dreadful mistake. She couldn't do this. Whatever had made her think she could?

She took a deep breath, preparing to flee, when a hand clamped over her arm, the fingers biting into the sore place where she had banged it earlier. With a gasp Darcie turned and faced Mrs. Feather. Her heart plummeted. Too late to run.

"Here, take this." Mrs. Feather pressed something into Darcie's palm. "But don't come back. You have no place here, and there's no more for you where this came from."

Looking down in amazement, Darcie stared at her sister's gift. A shilling. A fortune to a girl who was starving.

Her gaze collided with the madam's, and for a single beautiful shimmering moment, she saw her sister, Abigail, looking at her from behind Mrs. Feather's hard, cold mask.

"Thank you," she whispered, closing her fingers around the money.

"Go," Mrs. Feather said brusquely. "Go to Curzon Street, to Doctor Damien Cole. Tell him I sent you and that I'll thank him to do this one favor for his old friend, Mrs. Feather."

"To Curzon Street," Darcie echoed, barely able to believe in her good fortune or her reprieve. Impulsively, she cast her arms about her sister. "Thank you... Abigail."

Mrs. Feather squeezed her tight then pushed her out into the street.

"Don't come back," she said, her voice strangely hoarse. "And mind, have a care of him. Dr. Cole. He is a hard man, a man to fear. Stay out of his way. Stay clear of his work. And keep your nose out of his secrets."

Darcie gave a quick nod then hurried away, the shilling clutched in one hand pressed against her heart, her leather case tucked beneath her arm. She had escaped the horror that awaited her, had been granted a reprieve from the fate that was her sister's. Tears of relief stung her eyes. She would gladly scrub floors from dusk to dawn, scrub the steps, empty slops, anything, if she was but given the chance.

Armed with a name, Dr. Damien Cole, and the reference of her sister, the notorious madam, Mrs. Feather,

Darcie forged onward. Her sister's warning swirled through her thoughts. *A man to fear.*

The words became a litany, spinning over and over in her mind as she pressed on. Soon she was beyond exhaustion, her mind numb to all but the need to reach Mayfair.

So blunted were her senses that she did not hear the rolling turmoil of horses' hooves on the cobblestone street, did not see the dark bulk of the carriage as it bore down on her. At the last second a shout penetrated the fog that shrouded her awareness, and she turned to see four great beasts pawing the air above her head, their hooves slashing dangerously close to her face. She threw herself to the side, landing with jarring impact on her right shoulder. Stunned, she lay on the wet ground, staring at the horses as their driver brought them under control.

When they quieted, he climbed down from the seat and approached her where she lay.

"What's wrong with you, girl? Have you not eyes in your head? Or ears? Did you not hear me coming? If I'd been moving any faster—here...." The man crouched at her side and offered his hand. His words were bitten off in harsh tones, but focusing on his eyes, Darcie found only concern mirrored there.

"Is she hurt?" A second voice, mellifluous in both texture and pitch, washed over Darcie's shattered nerves like a soothing balm.

"I don't think so, sir. Maybe shaken up a bit," the driver replied.

Turning her head, Darcie studied the second man, his confident stride bringing him into her line of vision. Her heart gave a hard, sharp kick against her ribs as she took in his long black cloak and polished boots, splattered with the mud of the road.

The fears she had entertained earlier that night on the mist-shrouded street echoed through her mind. Was this the same man who had followed her, the ominous presence that had caused her to hide in the shadowed doorway?

Panicking, she scuttled backwards, the memory of the threatening stranger on Hanbury Street fresh in her thoughts. She stared at the man who approached her now, his long cloak and boots too similar for comfort. Her pulse raced as she struggled for reason. On Hanbury Street she had sensed evil buffeting her in great crashing waves that rolled violently from the stranger on the street, yet she sensed no such threat now, sensed no evil emanating from the man approaching her.

Her gaze shifted to his face, and what she saw made her eyes widen and her fear fade away, replaced by a surreal sense of resignation.

She had died, then. And here was the angel who'd been sent to guide her.

He moved closer, his stride graceful and sure, until he loomed over her. With a negligent flick of his wrist, he set the wings of his long coat aside and hunkered down, close enough that Darcie could see the stormy gray of his eyes. The hint of a frown shadowed his brow as he studied her with a long, slow perusal.

In the watery gray light of dawn, Darcie stared at him, her common sense telling her that he was just a man, surely no celestial being, despite her initial impression and despite the strange fascination that suffused her.

"Are you hurt?" he asked.

She shook her head, afraid to trust the sound of her

voice. Her body seemed to tingle in each place his gaze rested.

"Have we a blanket, John?" He glanced at the coachman, and as he turned his head, his burnished gold hair caressed his shoulder. Darcie had the strangest urge to touch it, to see if the honeyed strands were as thick and soft as they looked.

"I don't think so, sir."

"I do not require a blanket. I'm fine," Darcie managed, her heart drumming loudly in her ears.

"Are you?" The man turned a dispassionate gaze on her. Slowly, he raised one hand, reaching out to rest his fingers on the side of her throat. She jumped at the sensation of his warm hand against her chilled skin, at the feel of her pulse fluttering wildly against his touch.

"Y-yes," she replied.

His brows rose. "How fortunate," he finished dryly, and she felt bereft as he drew his hand away.

Rubbing her sore shoulder, Darcie lowered her eyes and pressed her lips together, uncertain of what to say. The stranger remained crouched at her side, his weight resting on the balls of his feet, arms folded casually across his bent knees. With a careless gesture, he motioned the coachman off.

"What day is it?" he asked, his gaze fixed on her.

Darcie stared into his eyes, caught by the intensity of his expression. "T-T-Tuesday," she stammered. "At least, it was Tuesday last night. So I suppose it is now Wednesday."

He offered a short nod, and the frown lines between his brows vanished.

"Well, you seem to be quite rational," he observed. "No dizziness?"

Darcie shook her head.

He almost smiled, the barest curve of his lips. "This position is extremely uncomfortable and my leg is beginning to lose circulation. Would you mind terribly if we regained our footing?"

That said, he rose gracefully to his feet and offered his hand. Darcie stared at it for a moment, her thoughts fuzzy and vague. With a soft sound of impatience he twined his warm fingers through her icy ones and pulled her to her feet. She stood before him looking straight ahead at the elegantly simple buttons of his waistcoat. He was tall, she realized, more than a head taller than she was. Tipping her head back, she found him watching her. She had the strangest urge to smooth her bedraggled skirt and pat her hair into some semblance of order.

Suddenly, she realized that her hand remained linked with his, a warm bond in the chilly air of the breaking dawn. Embarrassed, she tugged her fingers from his grasp.

He glanced down, but made no comment.

Darcie bent forward and retrieved her leather folio from the ground, her movements slow and careful. Her fingers moved over the battered surface, quick, assessing little touches meant to determine the damage to her one worldly treasure. She released a tiny sigh when she found the case undamaged.

She looked up once more. He was watching her, cool gray eyes glinting like polished metal, his features reflecting only polite interest.

"I shall not ask what you are doing hurrying about on the outskirts of Whitechapel at this hour of the day. But I should like to offer the use of my carriage to take you to your destination."

"Oh," Darcie said, astonished by the offer. She closed her arms tighter around her folio, rocking it slightly like a baby. "Oh. I am looking for Curzon Street."

"A somewhat distant but worthy place." The man's brow furrowed questioningly. "Did you intend to walk there? Clear to the other side of town?"

At her single brief nod, his brows rose in surprise.

"Indeed. And whom do you seek on Curzon Street?"

Darcie glanced at the ground. How much to tell a stranger? And why was he even asking? She was clearly a woman beneath his touch.

As if reading her doubts and concerns, he spoke, "I ask only because I myself am for Curzon Street. It would be a matter of little difficulty to see you safely there." His glance flicked over her, impersonal, assessing. "I suspect you will not make it if left to your own devices."

The driver had returned to the coach. Darcie watched from the corner of her eye as he climbed up and took the reins. The horses shifted restlessly.

The man gestured at the fidgety beasts. "Come. My horses won't tolerate the delay."

Without waiting for her reply, he strode to the waiting carriage, and Darcie found herself trailing behind him. In her exhausted state it would be sheer stupidity to refuse the ride. Hiking up her skirt, she paused, startled, as he offered his hand to help her into the carriage as though she were the finest lady out for a morning ride. Such courtesy for a common girl whom he'd nearly run down in the roadway. She was amazed.

She had barely settled on the seat when he climbed in and lowered his body down beside her, his shoulder pressing against hers in the confined space. He smelled clean and fresh, and Darcie was ashamed of her own state of disrepair. Likely he bathed every day, while she felt certain *she* smelled like the docks. Each morning she performed her ablutions as best she could, searching out a rain barrel, or any clean water that was handy. In her small, black cloth bag she carried a sliver of scented soap, a luxury she had splurged on in a moment of supreme foolishness. The soap was nearly gone now, melted by her attempts at personal hygiene. The money would have been better spent on food.

Dragging in a shaky breath, Darcie looked down at her hands, clasping the tips of her left fingers with her right. She pressed her lips together and cast a sidelong glance in the man's direction.

He had let his head fall back against the seat, baring the strong column of his throat. His golden hair fanned across the dark velvet upholstery. His eyes were closed and the curled sweep of his lashes formed dark crescent shadows against his skin. Everything about this man was beautiful. The sculpted angle of his cheek. The straight length of his nose, accented by the tiny bump at the bridge. Forcing her gaze away from him, Darcie turned to look out the side window, uncertain what to do, what to say.

The coach lurched and began to move, picking up speed as the seconds passed. Darcie stared out the window, watching the buildings move by in a blur. Tears pooled in her eyes. She was exhausted, hungry, and disgusted by the horror she had nearly been driven to. But the dormant flame of hope ignited in her breast because she had a name—Dr. Damien Cole—and a reference. So much more than she had started out with.

Unwanted, her sister's warning crept to the fore and echoed hollowly in her mind. *He is a man to fear. Stay out of his way. Stay clear of his work. And keep your nose out of his secrets.*

Shifting on the seat, Darcie looked straight ahead into the dim confines of the coach. With a start, she realized that there was a third person in the vehicle. A man was sprawled on the velvet upholstery of the seat across from her, his clothing coarse, his boots scuffed and worn. In the burgeoning light of morning he seemed unnaturally pale. Watching him for some minutes, Darcie frowned. There was something strange about the man, something odd about his posture.

Darcie ducked her head and looked through the rain-dampened tendrils of hair that had escaped her pins, toward the man at her side. Her rescuer.

"Y-your friend is sleeping very deeply, sir." The words jumped from her lips before she could restrain herself.

He opened his eyes, but kept the base of his skull resting against the seat back. When he spoke, he did not look at her, merely stared at the roof of the coach.

"He is not my friend."

"Oh." Darcie looked again at the sleeping man across from her. He half sat, half lay across the cushions of the opposite bench. He had not moved, had not made a sound. "That man...Is he ill? Or drunk?"

Her companion made a harsh sound. Darcie thought it might have been a laugh. She turned to face him and found that he was regarding her intently, the strangest expression in his eyes.

"No, he is neither ill nor drunk." The words were low and soft. "He's well past the possibility of either."

Darcie's stomach clenched, not with hunger, but with an irrefutable certainty. A chill crawled across her skin, raising goose flesh. She drew a deep, shuddering breath.

Unable to tear her gaze from the stormy depths of her rescuer's eyes, she whispered the question to which she already knew the answer.

"Is he dead, then?"

His expression did not change, betraying neither emotion nor concern. Darcie watched his lips form the words, though the rushing in her ears nearly obscured the sound of his reply.

"Oh, yes. He is dead. Has been for several hours. Anything more than that and the stench would chase us from the carriage."

And he smiled most amiably as he said it.

Darcie swallowed against a rising nausea as she stared at her companion in dismay. She shared the coach with two men, one dead, and the other quite possibly mad.

ALSO BY EVE SILVER

BOOKS FOR ADULTS:

HISTORICAL GOTHIC MYSTERY ROMANCE:

REVENANT ROSES SERIES

(Books in this series can be read in any order)

Darkest at Dusk

DARK GOTHIC SERIES

(Books in this series can be read in any order)

Dark Desires

His Dark Kiss

Dark Prince

His Wicked Sins

Seduced by a Stranger

Dark Embrace

URBAN FANTASY, PARANORMAL, AND SCI-FI ROMANCE:

THE SINS SERIES

Sins of the Heart (Book 1)

Sins of the Soul (Book 2)

Sins of the Flesh (Book 3)

Body of Sin (Book 4)

Sin's Daughter (Novella, can be read at any point in the series)

❀

NORTHERN WASTE SERIES

(Eve Silver writing as Eve Kenin)

Driven (Book 1)

Frozen (Book 1.5)

Hidden (Book 2)

❀

COMPACT OF SORCERERS SERIES

Demon's Kiss (Book 1)

Demon's Hunger (Book 2)

Trinity Blue (short story)

❀

DARK MAFIA ROMANCE:

BOOKS WRITTEN AS BECCA KANE

The Vegas Vicious Series

Twisted Fate

Ruthless Vow

Dark Promise

BOOKS FOR TEENS:

THE GAME SERIES

RUSH

PUSH

CRASH

Join Eve's VIP Reader Group for the latest info about contests, new releases and more! www.EveSilver.net

Follow Eve on Bookbub!

ABOUT THE AUTHOR

National bestselling author Eve Silver has been praised for her "edgy, steamy, action-packed" books, darkly sexy heroes and take-charge heroines. Her work won the OLA Forest of Reading White Pine Award 2015, was shortlisted for the Monica Hughes Award for Science Fiction and Fantasy 2014, was listed as a 2013 American Bookseller's Association Best Book for Children and a Canadian Children's Book Centre Best Books for Kids and Teens. She has garnered starred reviews from Publishers Weekly, Library Journal, and Quill and Quire, two RT Book Reviews Reviewers' Choice Awards, Library Journal's Best Genre Fiction Award, and she was nominated for the Romance Writers of America® RITA® Award. Eve lives with her husband and two exuberant border collie/Australian shepherds.